DARRAN MCCANN was born in Co. Armagh in 1979. He graduated from Trinity College Dublin and Dublin City University before becoming a journalist with Belfast's *Irish News*. He went on to write, teach and study at Queen's University Belfast. His play, *Confession*, was produced at the Brian Friel Theatre in Belfast in 2008. He lives in Ireland with his wife and son.

# DARRAN McCANN

# *After the Lockout*

FOURTH ESTATE · *London*

First published in Great Britain in 2012 by
Fourth Estate
An imprint of HarperCollins*Publishers*
77–85 Fulham Palace Road
London W6 8JB
www.4thestate.co.uk

1

The lines from 'Epic' by Patrick Kavanagh are reprinted from
*Collected Poems*, edited by Antoinette Quinn (Allen Lane, 2004),
by kind permission of the Trustees of the Estate of the late
Katherine B. Kavanagh, through the Jonathan
Williams Literary Agency.

A catalogue record for this book is
available from the British Library

ISBN 978-0-00-742947-9

Typeset in Minion by G&M Designs Limited,
Raunds, Northamptonshire

Printed in Great Britain by Clays Ltd, St Ives plc

MIX
Paper from
responsible sources
FSC® C007454

FSC is a non-profit international organisation established to promote the
responsible management of the world's forests. Products carrying the FSC
label are independently certified to assure consumers that they come
from forests that are managed to meet the social, economic and
ecological needs of present or future generations.

Find out more about HarperCollins and the environment at
www.harpercollins.co.uk/green

*For my parents, whose love, support and example made possible the writing of this book, and so much else.*

*… I inclined*
*To lose my faith in Ballyrush and Gortin*
*Till Homer's ghost came whispering to my mind.*
*He said: I made the* Iliad *from such*
*A local row. Gods make their own importance.*

– Patrick Kavanagh, from 'Epic'

# ONE

Two steps before me in the procession, the Countess swings her hips like she knows I'm watching, her arse bobbing like a Halloween apple begging me to take a bite out of it. She and I are the only ones here in the full uniform of the Irish Citizen Army, and we look splendid. Most of our lads make do with a scrawny red sash because they're too dirt poor to afford a uniform, or because there are men with guns in this town who'd shoot them for wearing one, but we can afford it and we're safe here, now, in this admiring crowd. Up ahead the Volunteers are singing God Save Ireland said the heroooooooes, God Save Ireland said they all, and beside me Bob Sweeney roars out our own version about God doing the same for Big Jim Larkin.

'There must be quarter of a million here,' says Bob between choruses. They're saying the back of the funeral was still at O'Connell Bridge while we were at Glasnevin for the burial, three miles away.

'Half a million. Or a million. Always revise numbers up. Be sure the peelers will revise them down,' I say.

He rolls his eyes, but who knows how many people are here? There are flags everywhere. Golden harps on emerald green. Green, white and orange tricolours. Eamonn Carr with our

Starry Plough. One stalwart fellow with a banner of deepest red in his clenched fist. All the unions are here. The Gaelic Leaguers. Sinn Féin. The women's leagues. Jesus, the Boy Scouts. The Dublin Fire Brigade: engines and carriages and blue-coated firemen. The bloody Lord Mayor of Dublin. How many of them had even heard of Tom Ashe eighteen months ago? They all want a piece of his martyr's bones now. Look at them all, snaking piously along the streets behind the mournful musicians and a hundred fucking priests. I spit.

'We're going up to Monto later, all the unmarried boys. You coming?' says Bob. Eamonn Carr nods enthusiastically.

Pair of jackeens, all bluff and bluster. The Countess glances over her shoulder and catches me looking at her arse again. Her so-called husband away in Bohemia or wherever the hell these past five years while she's slumming it with the socialists. She must be nearly fifty but I definitely still would. The Monto whores have nothing to teach posh girls, honest to God they don't. 'What sort of a socialist colludes in the exploitation of working-class women?' I say.

'All right, misery guts, just trying to be friendly.'

I see a flash and I'm blind. 'Mr Lennon, Edgar Andrews, *Irish Times*. Does your presence here today indicate the Irish Citizen Army and the labour movement generally supports the prisoners' campaign for political status?' asks some beanpole. 'What do you make of reports from Dublin Castle this afternoon that the Executive is to concede the demands of the Sinn Féin prisoners?' I'm just trying to get my vision back. I see his starched white shirt, boater hat, bright white rose on a tailored lapel. Another fellow, with him, more throughother-looking, shouldering a portable camera. Smoke rises from the light bulb.

'You nearly blinded me with that thing, pal.'

But he's all persistence. 'What do you make of the force-feeding of the hunger strikers, Mr Lennon?'

'You've got the wrong man.'

He retreats looking sceptical, but we're at Amiens Street, within staggering distance of the pubs the journos live in, the lazy toadies, so they're coming like locusts now. There's a fellow talking to the Countess. Indo, probably – not as well turned-out as the fellow from *The Times*. No white rose. Another fellow confers with the photographer who almost blinded me. That suit was probably decent in its day. A *Freeman's Journal* suit, I'd say.

'What's your name, sir?' asks another fellow in a soft felt hat with a press card in the ribbon. Looks like he slept last night in a pub or a brothel or the street. Or all three. *Herald*, no question.

'You can fuck off and tell your boss he can fuck away off too.'

I don't suppose he'll pass the message on to Mr William Martin 'Murder' Murphy but it feels good to say it.

As we pass Amiens Street station I feel a hand squeeze my shoulder and turn to see Dick Mulcahy, the wiry bastard. An hour ago he was in uniform firing the graveside salute but he's back in his civvies now.

'Come with me, there's a man wants to talk to you.'

Just as perfunctory as that. I haven't seen him in ten months, since they released us from Fron Goch, and not even a hello. I haven't missed those dead eyes.

We slip out of the procession, unnoticed in the clamour, and climb the steps into the station, beneath the great clock on the wall showing five bells. Up the platform, Dick exchanges nods with a porter who doesn't ask for tickets, and another uniformed railwayman turns away and pretends to see nothing as we slip into the first-class carriage. Someone in the distance shouts my name but Dick pushes me aboard the train before I can look around. There's a man in the hallway with his hand inside his coat. He sees Dick and nods. He opens the door behind him. Leather upholstered seats, silk curtains, deep-pile carpet, mahogany and brass everywhere, every man with his own ashtray. The train starts its click-clacking way. Arthur Fox and Mick Collins and Bat McClatchey look up.

'First Class? Some revolutionaries you are.'

Mick smiles. 'We meet wherever we can. There aren't many safe places to meet these days, Victor.'

Bat McClatchey I'm not surprised at. We're from the same county, he and I, and I have to say I like him, mainly for that reason, but politically, well: I expect to be fighting against him in the real revolution to come after this one. Big nationalist, big Catholic and every bit as reactionary as all that sounds. But Arthur Fox I am surprised at. Arthur's one of us. He's one of the Gardiner Street silk weavers, one of the men who helped organise the Citizen Army. Arthur saw real action in South Africa and he flattened more peelers during the lockout. Thank God for him during the Rising, telling Mike Mallin to retreat to the College of Surgeons away from the turkey-shoot on the Green. Thank God our army had a few actual soldiers as well as bad poets.

'I saw you got your photograph taken there. That was careless, boy,' says Mick in that sing-song accent of his.

'That fellow from the press? He said he was a reporter from *The Times*.'

'It just so happens he was telling the truth, but you didn't know that. The one with the camera was a G-man, down from the Castle. Fuckers stand out like blood in the snow. You shouldn't be letting anyone take your picture.'

I've better things to do than stand here being lectured by some lilting sleveen from West Cork. He's younger than me for Christ's sake. I always pegged him for an eejit to be honest. But he cleaned up at cards in Fron Goch. Maybe that was his secret. Six foot plus and you never saw him coming.

'We need you to go on a trip for a few days. But we need to be sure you're committed,' he says.

'I'm committed to a Marxian republic, not some Fenian gombeen version of what we have already.'

'Victor, you've been letting that mouth of yours run away with you too much lately. You've been drawing attention to yourself. It has to stop,' says Dick Mulcahy.

'Don't give me orders, Dick, I'm Citizen Army, not a Volunteer.'

'I'm Citizen Army and I say that's no longer a meaningful distinction,' says Arthur.

'Arthur, these altar boys want to change the flag and nothing else and you know it.'

'Jesus, but youse socialists are a barrel of laughs,' says Mick, with all the usual aggressive collegiality, but Dick Mulcahy grabs me roughly.

'Damnit, Lennon, if we want freedom we need a revolution and for revolution we need bloody fierce-minded men who don't care a scrap for death or bloodshed. A real revolution is not a job for children or for saints or scholars.' He lets go of me. 'Like I keep saying, in a revolution any man, woman or child who is not with you is against you. Shoot them and damned to them,' he says to Mick. 'This fellow is too soft for our purposes.'

'You're being too hard on him, Dick,' says Mick. He's watching me closely, reading me. I keep looking at Arthur. Yes, it's him I'm surprised at.

'Connolly himself said there's no more Irish Volunteers, no more Irish Citizen Army, only the Irish Republican Army. I'm sick of losing. These lads have a plan that might work,' Arthur says.

'Can you be trusted to follow orders?' says Mick. He knows Bat has already approached me. He knows I've already wriggled out of taking the secret oath of the Irish Republican Brotherhood. They only want political revolution, but I've been shouting from the rooftops that without social and economic revolution, it's a waste of time. I don't suppose they like it. Besides, virtually every IRB man I know is a fucking prick. But I can't really say that to these lads.

The train is slowing, I'm guessing we're approaching Harcourt Street. Mick peeks out under the bottom of the drawn blind, and seems suddenly impatient. 'You were at the GPO and Fron Goch, fair enough, but that isn't enough any more. Go to Phil Shanahan's and wait, there'll be someone to meet you there later. Go straight there now, no detours.'

'I'll need to go home and change out of the uniform.'

Bat pulls down a suitcase from the overhead compartment. It's my suitcase. He tells me he stopped by my room earlier and picked up some things. 'Sorry about your door.'

'You'll be at Shanahan's,' says Dick, wearing a look that makes clear it's not a question. For now, it's easier just to agree with them. I nod.

'Good man,' says Mick.

Dick Mulcahy shows me out onto the marbled platform of Harcourt Street station. I'm on the plush, loyalist south-side now. Not such a smart place to be wearing this damn uniform. I straighten my sloped green hat, keep an eye out for peelers, and make for the nearest public toilets to get changed. Back in the civvies, I'm stepping out of the jacks when I hear someone shout my name. I turn and I see a face from another lifetime.

Charlie Quinn.

He's older. Skinnier. His hair used to be an auburn thatch but it's thinner and greyer now. He's still handsome in a country sort of way. He sports a Kitchener moustache and he's walking with a hell of a limp. He lurches forward and throws his arms around me. 'I've been in Dublin for days looking for you,' he says. 'I knew you'd be at the funeral.'

He feels slight and bony. Charlie comes from shopkeepers, he should be pink and fat and boyish like his da, but he looks older than a docker of his age, and dockers age the quickest. 'Was that you shouting my name back in Amiens Street?'

'I followed you onto the train. I didn't think you'd heard me.'

'I wasn't sure I did.'

He smells of ointment but beneath that there's something else, something like you'd smell in a butcher's specialising in offal on the turn. It's like the smell of Connolly in those last hours at our little Alamo on Moore Street, when there was nothing left to do but ensure the surrender was worded properly before the ceiling came in around us. Two days after a ricochet ripped into his ankle. Two full days of agony and morphine, and he was laughing and crying at the same time, like only someone hopped-up to the eyeballs can. Charlie is holding a thin wooden cane against his left leg; he lifts the cane and gives it a little tap against his left shin. The sound of wood on wood. He smiles bravely.

'The doctors tell me I should wear this prosthetic all the time, but to tell you the truth, I hardly ever do. It chafes something terrible. Could have been worse. At least I kept the knee.'

'What happened?' I say, but I see his greatcoat and the little patches of wool darker than the rest, where regimental insignia have been stripped off.

'Shell fell right on top of us. I was lucky, really.'

'King and fucken country, Charlie? How could you be so stupid?'

He waits till I exhale, so he knows I'm finished. Not the best way to start a conversation with an old friend, I confess. 'I've come to bring you home,' he says. 'It's your da, Victor, he needs you.' Charlie lifts his hand in a drinking gesture. 'Worst I ever seen.'

'My da isn't the sort of man would be taking advice from me,' I say. It's the most unexpected thing, and I'm trying not to show it, but I feel like I've been waiting a long time for this invitation.

'Och, Victor, don't be like that. Everything is forgot about now.'

'I haven't forgot nothing.'

⋆　⋆　⋆

Stanislaus let himself in the front door and found Mrs Geraghty waiting in the hall, clutching a telegram in her fist. 'Jeremiah just delivered it. It's from Dublin, Father,' she said, half breathless.

'Thank you, Mrs Geraghty,' he said, and started up to his study, leaving her disappointed at the bottom of the stairs. He stopped halfway up. 'I'm sorry to keep repeating myself, but the correct form of address for a bishop is Your Grace.'

'I thought that was only for proper bishops?'

'An auxiliary bishop is a proper bishop.'

In his study Stanislaus set the little post-office envelope on his desk beside the newspaper he hadn't yet read and sat down. He picked up the telegram, sliced it open, then set it down again. Unready. He looked around the bulging bookshelves that lined three walls of the room. They made the place claustrophobic. He turned the chair around, as he always did, to the window, which commanded a view straight down the middle of Madden village. The chapel, the graveyard, National School, Parochial Hall, post office and Poor Ground; all the comings and goings were under his gaze. He could almost see into the terraced homes of his parishioners. The women were indoors, the men were in the fields, the children were at school. Red flags fluttered from homes and telegraph posts, and bunting crisscrossed the street, but aside from that, things were mostly right with Madden. He looked again at the telegram. Whatever it contained, it was bound to vex him. He picked up the newspaper instead.

## ULYANOV 'LENIN' DECLARES RUSSIA 'WORKERS' STATE'

He threw it down again. Once, this had been his favourite time of day. Morning mass finished, pastoral visits done, he'd have an hour to look out the window and read the paper. The symmetry of keeping one eye on his parish and the other on the events of

11

the world pleased him. But since the war, there had been nothing but bad news, and it was all Russia these days. There was no pleasure left in his ritual. He was no monarchist and did not miss the tsar – a king who couldn't feed his people didn't deserve to be a king – but these Bolshevists … Ulyanov had said the events last Easter gave an example to be followed and it seemed Dublin last year had its sequel in Petrograd this year.

The clock chimed four. Father Daly, the curate, came in the door like an unbroken colt and said Mrs Geraghty had told him of the telegram. Stanislaus nodded and the curate picked it up, his fringe flopping over his forehead as he opened it. He set it back on the desk, text facing up. Stanislaus couldn't help but see it now.

```
VL arrive 10 o'clock train STOP
Need transport from station CQ STOP
```

'So he's coming then,' said Father Daly. 'Do you think he'll be able to get his father back on the straight and narrow?'

'We must hope so.'

They had given up any hope that Pius Lennon might sort himself out. Stanislaus called often but the door was never answered. Pius's life seemed to revolve entirely around poteen; a lamentable state for a man formerly so substantial. He had taken to wandering the parish at all hours of day and night, flaming drunk, with a bottle in one hand and a loaded shotgun in the other. Not long ago he wandered up the street while the school-children were on their break, scattering them in terror. The postman Jeremiah McGrath said he remembered when Pius Lennon first came to the parish to marry his Deirdre, before he became the respected pillar that Stanislaus knew. Jeremiah said people were right to be terrified of Pius.

'His method is different but I fear Pius is going the same way as his wife,' said Stanislaus.

Pius owned several hundred acres in the east of the parish and Madden's economy had long depended on the Lennon land. Pius had started his drinking after his Deirdre's death. They said Deirdre had been the belle of the county in her day, but when Stanislaus knew her, that had been hard to credit. He'd had no choice in refusing her a funeral or burial. Church teaching was clear and unequivocal. The drinking accelerated as each of Pius's children left, one by one, till they were all gone. Now he lived reclusively, letting his land go to ruin, and no longer offered work to anyone. So Stanislaus had compiled a list of the Lennon children and all the places to which they had emigrated, and wrote to the Cardinal's office for church contacts in each place. The reply came quickly. It seemed he still drew some water in Armagh. He wrote to parishes and dioceses around the world and, over several months, the replies came. Stanislaus was flattered that some of his colleagues in far-flung places had heard of him and were familiar with his work. They were keen to assist. He got addresses for all but one of the fifteen Lennon children. Of the fourteen, he knew the Sarah girl was only thirty miles away at the Monastery of St Catherine of Siena, but he would not interfere with her vocation. The fifteenth name he circled in red ink. He had no address for that one. It would be a last resort even if he did have one. He sent out thirteen letters.

*Dear Mr/Miss Lennon,*

*I write out of concern for your father, Pius, who I must inform you, has succumbed to the evil of drink. His maintenance of the land and his spiritual and physical wellbeing are of concern to all in the parish, and though we have attempted to divert the self-destructive course on which he is set, it is my pastoral experience that only family can save a man in times of moral despond.*

*I beg that you return home and care for your father, or failing this, that you ensure another of your siblings can do so.*

*Yours in Christ,*

*Most Rev S. Benedict, Bishop Emeritus*

Six, seven, eight months passed. Jeremiah McGrath assured him nothing was wrong with the long-distance mail, even with the war, and slowly Stanislaus came to accept that there would be no replies. The name circled in red ink rebuked him. The Victor fellow had left Madden boasting of Brooklyn or Botany Bay, but everyone knew he was in Dublin since his name had appeared in the margins of the press during the industrial unrest. He had been a minor figure, not a Larkin or a Countess Markievicz, and Stanislaus had denounced Larkin's union from the pulpit, as per the Cardinal's policy, but he knew the parishioners had a sneaking regard for 'their' Victor. When their Victor joined the insane adventure of Easter week, sneaking regard flowered into strident pride. No-one from Madden had ever been famous before.

Victor's best friend Charlie Quinn had volunteered to go to Dublin to find him. Stanislaus asked Charlie whether he thought Victor would agree to come home. Charlie said he didn't know.

What he was willing to predict, though, was that Victor would still be every bit as angry as he was the day he left Madden. Stanislaus was discomfited to think of the rage-filled boy coming back into his life a full-grown man. He pushed the newspaper across the desk under Father Daly's nose and pointed to the Ulyanov headline.

'This is the kind of man we're talking about. A bolshevist, you know,' he snapped.

'He can't be that bad if he was with Connolly, God rest him,' said Father Daly.

'Connolly was a communist.'

'Only in life. No-one will remember that whole communist thing in the long run.'

Stanislaus got up from his desk. He had no intention of debating with a guileless liberal not five minutes out of the seminary. 'I'm going for a walk,' he said. He went downstairs, opened the door and pulled on his coat as he strode out the gate into the street. He grimaced at the red bunting and flags as he passed under them. Otherwise good parishioners openly disobeying his injunction – and the Cardinal's – against Gaelic games. They'll all be thrilled when they hear of their Victor Lennon's return, he thought. He whispered a prayer for the peace of the parish.

*　*　*

*It's your stick. You found it. It's the best stick you've ever seen: three feet long, thick but pliable enough to bend double without cracking. Your brothers are jealous of it. Charlie's jealous of it. Even Maggie's jealous of it, and she's a girl. You use it to hunt, to fish and a hundred other things. It's yours, and the bastard thinks he can just take it. Phelim Cullen. You know the name. Everyone does. He's three years older than you, looks like he's nearly six foot, fifteen and out of school with the cigarette to prove it. He tells you to go away, stop pestering him. You are far from home, five or six miles at least, in his parish to watch the Madden footballers take another hammering. It's his parish and he says he's keeping your stick. He's laughing but he's threatening to lose his good humour any second. But it's your stick and he can't have it, no matter what.*

*'You rotten thieving bastard.'*

*His expression darkens and he swings the stick at you with a terrifying whoosh. Last warning. Christ but he's a vicious bastard. Charlie and Maggie are looking at you with pleading, terrified eyes.*

*'If you don't hand over the stick I won't be responsible for what happens to you.'*

*The crowd gathered around winces as his open palm cracks loudly against your cheek. A slap in the face. Wouldn't even dignify you with a closed fist.*

*Well, you'll dignify him with one.*

*He doesn't see it coming. Not in a million years did he think you'd do it. He's stunned, and he's not the only one. Your fist opens his nose like a knife through a feed sack. You swing again and again and the blows land again and again, till he drops your stick and flees like a beaten dog. You pick up your stick, gingerly, since your knuckles are bruised and bloodied. But it's not your blood.*

*Charlie and Maggie look at you differently now. It's like they're scared. You're a little scared yourself.*

\*   \*   \*

Charlie follows me onto the Number 14 tram. My old route. Once upon a time I knew every tram driver in Dublin but I don't recognise this young, ignorant-looking fellow with the shirt collar too small on him. He yanks the handbrake too sharply and rings the bells like he's Quasimodo. Everything about him screams non-union. A bastard scab. We sit down among the well-heeled, law-abiding south-siders and trundle past Carson's house, the Stephen's Green and the College of Surgeons, still pocked and scorched by bullet and fire. Ladies in expensive fabrics promenade prettily beneath the awnings of Grafton Street. They're carrying parasols. In Ireland. In November. Businessmen, bankers, professionals in starched collars walk stiffly around College Green, Trinity College, Westmoreland Street. Little boys and girls strut after their parents in collars and jackets and short pants, and there's a fat Metropolitan peeler on every corner watching protectively over the oppressing class. We cross the Liffey to the north side, where the oppressed live. The Kapp and Peterson building stands on the corner of Bachelor's Walk and the street they call Sackville and we call O'Connell, unscathed and alone like a cigar stump in an ashtray. Further up, the shell of the General Post Office stands at the centre of a square half-mile of rubble. I look at Charlie. At where his leg used to be. I shake my head. 'What possessed you? Home Rule? Rights of Small Nations?'

'Can't say it was. Can't say I even understand what any of that stuff means.'

'Little Catholic Belgium then, being raped by the Protestant Hun?'

'I didn't give a damn about Belgium nor about the Hun either. I just wanted to see what this Great War was like. I wanted to get a gun, see a bit of the world, and feel like a grown man.'

The bastard scab announces the Nelson Pillar and we hop off, electric cables crackling overhead. We reach Montgomery Street. Canvas awnings promising Meats, Drugs, Tobacco or News shade the broad pavements of Monto and gentlemen in fine suits walk quickly with their heads down, hoping not to be seen. A gang of malnourished, barefooted gurriers, none more than ten or eleven, idle by the corner and eye us suspiciously. There's an army of gurriers in this city, I see them all the time, trying to huckster a living either side of the tram line. Some beg, some pick pockets, some shine shoes or hawk early editions of *The Herald*. These lads are typical: bony and dirt-caked with narrow, cynical slits for eyes and cigarettes clamped between black teeth. 'Have you a penny to give these lads?' I say, and Charlie stops to rummage in his tunic. I take a couple of pence from my pocket.

'Ah, keep your money, mister. You're Citizen Army, aren't ye?' says one of the gurriers. I nod. 'We'll not take an'ting off you, but we'll take it off your man.' He points to Charlie, 'John fucken Bull, wha?'

Further up the street two women lean out of a ground-floor window of a tenement. One of the women is big and brassy and could be anywhere between thirty and sixty. Her face is painted white, her lips are scarlet and her head is covered by a raven-black wig, stacked high and precarious. The other one is only a young thing. She's painted and dressed up the same but that only makes the contrast all the more obvious. The usual combination: an old whore for the young lads fresh up from the country with dreams and virginities intact, and a young floozy for the older men. Working girls festoon most of the windows around here.

'Come on in till I wet yer willy mister,' jeers the old whore, cupping her hands around her chest. We walk on. The young floozy catcalls after us, are we men at all at all. Peggy O'Hara is leaning out the bottom window of the tenement I live in. Peggy is our tenement's old whore. Charlie's appalled that I live here, he can't hide it.

'Howya, Victor. Who's your friend?' says Peggy, pushing forward her young floozy, a pretty wee thing, perhaps fifteen with big, bewildered brown eyes and cheeks plastered preposterously in rouge. 'Dolores here's a real patriot. If he's a friend of yours, she might do him a discount.'

'Only a discount, not a free go, for a national hero?'

'Look around you, Victor. Youse heroes have damn near put us out of business.'

She's right. This place used to be black with soldiers, all loose change and aggression, looking for a good time in the red-lit windows of the Second City of the Empire. But the soldiers are confined to barracks now. Of course the high-end houses for the rich are still here, and go out the back of any pub on a Friday night, you'll see the bottom end of the market relieving careless working men of their pay packets; but the servicemen were always Monto's bread and butter. The Monto girls have cut down more British soldiers with knob rot than all the generations of rebels ever managed with muskets and pikes.

'Better to die on your feet than live on your knees,' I say.

'I *make* my living on my knees.'

I have to laugh. Whores are my favourite capitalists. They're the most honest, and often among the smartest. Every smart whore I've ever met has the same dream: to own her own place and run her own girls. Peggy O'Hara's only complaint about the grinding boot of capital is that she's not wearing it.

We don't go inside. No detours, Mick said. 'It's an eye-opener around here, isn't it?' I say.

'I've been here before,' Charlie replies. 'I was billeted at Beggar's Bush before they sent us to France. We spent a lot of time up here. They were giving free ones to boys in British uniforms that time.'

'Whores and armies are well met,' I say.

I wonder what I'd have said if we'd met then, as he was getting ready to go and fight for the king. I don't think I'd have been able to look past the uniform. Soldiers are fucken pigs. I think I'd have spat in his face. 'That coat of yours sticks out like a sore fucken thumb so it does.'

'I took off the epaulettes,' Charlie protests.

'You don't think people know what it is?'

There's a time and a place, Victor, let it go. Life is in the letting go.

The doors of P. Shanahan Wines Spirits Ales Licensed Imbibing Emporium are locked and a large billboard announces the premises are Closed By Order Of The Lord Lieutenant Until Further Notice. Beige blinds bearing the legend Select Bar are pulled down over the windows. I knock till a voice from inside asks who it is.

'Fron Goch prisoner 19531977.'

The door opens a few inches and Phil Shanahan ushers us in fussily. 'Who's this with you?' he asks.

'Friend of mine. He's all right. Is it all right if I wait here? There's supposed to be somebody coming to meet me here later on. I was told to wait.'

Phil waves around the empty room in agreement. The room is long and narrow and the bar runs its full length. It's all dark corners. It used to be full of people like me talking politics, or naïve country lads newly arrived in the big smoke; desperate for anything familiar, they'd make straight for the premises of Phil Shanahan, the famous hurler. There's someone in the snug down at the bottom, I can just about see movement through a gap in the snug door. I pull up a high stool so Charlie can sit down, plant my elbows on the bar and duck my head under the window. Phil stands squarely across the bar from me with his thumbs looped in his waistcoat pockets. 'What'll it be, men?'

'Bushmills.'

'Oul Protestant whiskey.'

'Good Ulster whiskey.'

Phil smiles and sets up the bottle and three glasses. He leaves me to pour while he reaches under the bar and produces a dog-eared newspaper page that looks like it has passed through many hands. He sets it down in front of me and smirks. 'Did you see this? I've been showing it to all you socialist lads.' I finish pouring the whiskey and take the paper from him. It's from the *Freeman's Journal*, couple of months back. Yes, of course I fucken saw it. Down in the bottom left corner. Our glorious leader.

## LARKIN MAROONED

The Sydney New South Wales Correspondent of the 'Daily Mail' cables: – Jim Larkin, the Irish Labour leader, left the United States for Australia in a steamer which was to make its first call at Auckland, New Zealand, but the captain, according to instructions, landed Larkin at

Pago-Pago in American Samoa. Larkin indignantly
protested to the American Administrator, who replied
that he had no power in the matter. Larkin is virtually
marooned in the middle of the Pacific.

Phil roars laughing as he lifts his glass. 'Up the Republic!'

'God save Ireland,' says Charlie.

'All power to the soviets,' I say.

The first drink of the day rasps against my throat. I light a
cigarette and pour another drink. Phil excuses himself and goes
back to the snug.

'How come the place is empty?' says Charlie.

'They took Phil's licence after the Rising.'

'He doesn't seem the sort to be mixed up in that sort of thing.'

True, Phil's idea of a political opinion is to moan about how
hard it is for an honest publican like himself to make a living. If
I've heard his joke about his membership of the Irish Publican
Brotherhood once, I've heard it a thousand times. Yet there he
was on Easter Monday morning, walking across the deserted
street toward the barricade outside the GPO where I stood
guard, a rifle strapped across his back and a toolbox full of
ammunition in his hand.

'Is it yourself, Victor? Is it the socialists are rising out? I heard
ye were having a crack at the English.'

'Go on home, Phil. We haven't a chance of winning.'

'I'm not in the least bit concerned whether we do or not.'

I remember thinking for a moment that if a man like Phil
Shanahan was with us, maybe we had a chance after all. Charlie
asks for a cigarette. He inhales and splutters. 'You should smoke
more,' I tell him.

'I know. Did you keep the card?'

I hand it over. Cigarette cards don't interest me, but people are religious about them. 'What are they, Navy Cut?'

'Gallaher's.'

He's disappointed. 'I've nearly got the full Player's collection: the Large Trench Mortar, the Stokes Trench Mortar, the Vickers Field Artillery Piece. I only need the Lewis Automatic Gun.' The card read *Plants Of Commercial Value*. Charlie's face squirrelled up with distaste. 'Flowers, like. *Papaver rhoeas is a variable annual wild flower of agricultural cultivation. The four petals are vivid red, most commonly with a black spot at their base.* Blah blah blah. Who gives a damn?'

I down the whiskey and pour another. Through the gap in the door of the snug I see one of the fellows with Phil take out a shiny gold pocket watch and fidget with the chain. I recognise that fidget. Alfie Byrne, the Shaking Hand of Dublin himself. Such a nervous fellow, if he didn't have someone's palm to pump, he would take out that bloody watch chain and fidget with it. Couldn't sit still for a moment. He had shaken hands all the way to the House of Commons. I down the whiskey.

'You have to come home, Victor. Your da isn't the man he was. The drink has him.'

'A man with fifteen children can afford to lose one son.'

'He has nobody.'

Nobody? The Lord said Go Forth and Multiply, and by God Pius Lennon took him up on it. He made my ma into a production line.

'They've all left. Everybody's gone. Pius is alone.'

Most of my brothers would knife the old man in the guts if they thought it'd get them their inheritance a day sooner. The

Lennon land is worth a lot, at least in the conception of Madden people. 'What d'you mean gone? Gone where?'

'The four winds. We've tried everyone else. You're our last hope.'

I get up and knock on the door of the snug. I ask Phil to lend me pencil and paper. He goes behind the bar to see if he can find anything, and as he rummages, I wave to Alfie Byrne. Alfie looks well, with his crisp moustache and stiff collar and expensive shoes. He waves back. Is he starting to lose the hair? He won't like that, the vain bastard. I can only see the knees of the third man, who stays seated in the snug. Phil hands me a pencil and a copy of the *Picturegoer* magazine.

'It's all the paper I can find.'

'Do rightly.'

According to the *Picturegoer* there's a new five-reeler coming soon starring Kitty Gordon. Don't think much of her to be honest, but apparently she's the Most Magnificently Gowned Woman On The Screen. I thumb through the pages quickly to see if there's a picture anywhere of Mildred Harris. I like Mildred Harris. Don't see one. I throw the magazine down in front of Charlie. 'Fifteen is a lot to keep track of. Write on this.'

Charlie opens the *Picturegoer* at a random page and glances at the picture. 'There's a new picture palace only after opening in Armagh,' he says.

'Is that a fact?' I say as I take it back from him. If you want something doing, honest to God. 'I'll write. Let's start with Seamus. Where'd he go?'

'Boston.'

I scribble it down. 'Emily?'

'Manchester.'

'England or New England?'

'England. Mary's in Cape Town. Anthony's in Wellington, Thomas is in Sydney.'

'Fucken empire-builders.' I down my whiskey and pour another.

'Oliver is in Buenos Aires. Maybe you should slow down, Victor.'

'Bonus what?'

'Buenos Aires. In the Argentine.'

'Jesus. What about Patsy?'

'Melbourne. Theresa, eh …' Charlie thinks about it for a second: 'Glasgow. Johnny is in Chicago. Agnes is in New York.'

'Wee Aggie? She's only a child.'

'She's twenty-two. She's married over there, I think. Rosemary's in Toronto. Who am I forgetting?'

I tot up the numbers quickly. 'We're missing four.'

'Including yourself.'

'Three then. Brigid?'

'Philadelphia. Peter went to London. He got conscripted. He's in France now.'

I pour another whiskey. 'Fucken eejit.'

'I met him out there. In Paris. Small world, eh? Two Madden boys meeting away on the other side of the world. Him and a few of his cockney pals were paralytic. They were asking me did I know where was the Moulin Rouge.'

I smile. Peter's the youngest, he was eight the last time I saw him. 'Dirty wee bastard. I'm sure you told him off.'

'Sure I was on my way there myself.'

I laugh loudly and take a long slurp. There's a name missing from the list. 'What about Sarah?'

'Sister Concepta. She's been with the Dominicans in Drogheda these last five or six years.'

'You must be fucking joking me?' I'm off again, laughing like I haven't laughed in years. Fifteen Lennons and not one single city big enough for two of them. Pius has scattered the family like I said he would. My sides hurt.

'Keep it civil down there,' Phil shouts across the room.

'Is she married?' I ask Charlie. 'You know damn well who I mean.'

'No, she's not. She's the schoolteacher.'

'Did she send you to come and get me?'

'Jesus but you're full of yourself.'

'Then who's we? You said *we* wrote to all our ones.'

'Bishop Benedict.'

The name is like a nail on a blackboard to my ears. I presumed he'd be dead by now.

'Pius needs help, Victor, he'll die if he doesn't get it. The property is gone to hell. There's cows dying of old age, Victor.'

I pour another drink hoping it'll settle my head but it does no good. The room is spinning on me. I hear a voice – not Phil's, not Alfie's – pronounce in a stentorian Cork accent: 'Alfred, the Irish Party is finished, Mr Shanahan and his friends have made sure of that. My little party is certainly a spent force. We must all now make our peace with Sinn Féin.' I know the voice but can't quite place it. I open the door of the snug to return Phil's pencil. Phil looks up watchfully.

'Just leave it on the bar there, Victor.'

Alfie looks up and fidgets.

'Ask him, Phil. Ask Alfie where was he when he heard they'd shot Connolly.'

'Take it easy now, Victor,' says Phil.

'He was in the House of Commons cheering and singing God Save the fucking King when he heard, weren't you, Alfie?'

'I was on me holyers at the time,' Alfie protests.

Phil stands up. 'Right, Victor, that's enough. Alfie and Mr Healy are here to try and help me get my licence back, so sit down and calm yourself. You're drinking too fast.'

The third man sticks his fat head out from behind the door, his face all whiskey and sirloin and silver service and gout. Timothy Michael Healy, Member of Parliament, King's Counsel. As Murder Murphy's thug in the Four Courts, he was one of the bosses' bluntest instruments during the lockout. Healy looks like dead king Edward, with his full white beard and his big, fat, balding head. 'Healy. I'm sure you cheered the loudest when you heard.'

'I wasn't even in the House that day. Victor, whatever our differences, Connolly's execution offended every drop of Catholic blood in me.'

'Every one of your boss's newspapers was baying for blood. Well, by God your boss got what he wanted.'

'Mr Murphy isn't my boss. I'm just a lawyer.'

'Mr Healy's trying to help me get back my licence,' says Phil. 'He's representing Tom Ashe's family at the inquest too. Leave him alone.'

Charlie is beside me now, trying to coax me away. 'Where did that happen?' Healy asks him.

'Messines.'

Healy gets up and shakes Charlie's hand. 'My boy was in the Dardanelles. People say Irishmen shouldn't be fighting for England, and maybe they're right, but there are many good and patriotic Irishmen in the trenches.'

Charlie directs me halfway back across the room but I'm still looking at Healy, standing at the door of the snug with smugness splayed across his big, blotchy face.

'You were his right-hand during the lockout. I haven't forgot what you did, you and the rest of them. I haven't forgot the lockout,' I cry.

'Oh, for goodness sake, nobody gives a damn about the lockout any more,' he says.

I shrug Charlie off and fling a whiskey tumbler as forcefully as I can towards Healy, but I stumble and my aim is off. The tumbler crashes into the window above the bar. Shards of smoked glass fly everywhere. I move towards Healy with every intention of ramming his head into the wall but before my third step Phil is standing before me with hurl in hand. He pulls hard and I feel the warm smack of the ash against my shoulder. I topple sideways and collapse in a corner, but in a flash Phil wrenches me powerfully to my feet and pushes me towards the exit. He's still the right side of forty and built like the athlete he is. He holds me with one arm and opens the door with the other before propelling me onto the pavement outside with a mighty push. There's a good reason why Phil's pub is the cleanest and safest in Monto. I crawl to the gutter and empty my guts of all the spuds and bacon and whiskey in me. Behind me, far away, a voice barks bitterly and a door slams. Lying on my back, I look up and see Charlie hovering.

'All right, I'm ready to go home now,' I say.

*　*　*

*It's been so long since she last even left the house you doubt your own sight. She's standing at the edge of the lake like a will o' the wisp, looking like she might blow away. You reach the spot, your spot, where you and Maggie meet, and look up at her in her billowing white robes. She doesn't seem to see you. The sun is melting like it does in autumn, and the wind gusts. You shout out and she turns to face you, an old woman at forty-five. She smiles beatifically, and you glimpse your mother, not the banshee she has become.*

*'Victor, son: life is in the letting go,' she says.*

*She turns away and steps off the high edge of the lake. You watch her fall, serene as a snowflake.*

\*   \*   \*

Stanislaus felt not a day over sixty-five as he reached the crossroads, a mile and a half's walk from Madden, mostly uphill. Not bad for a man passed over on health grounds ten years before. He turned back and kept a good, even pace, his footsteps ticking like a metronome. Walking was always good for clearing the head. He thought about full bishops promoted since his retirement, all of whom Cardinal Logue, in his vast wisdom, had recommended. He knew of four who were not well and three more who frankly were incapacitated. Soon Madden was in sight, nestling in the gentle hollow. The street lamps flickered against the failing light. From up ahead, just outside the village, came bad singing and laughter, and Stanislaus saw two lads of perhaps eighteen horsing around. Stanislaus's knuckles whitened on his stick. 'John McGrath and Aidan Cavanagh,' he cried. They stopped dead and straightened up in exaggerated protestations of sobriety. Eyes red like diseased rabbits. The stench of

29

cheap spirit damned them. 'It's not even six o'clock and you boys are drunk as lords. Have you no work to be at today?'

'Everybody quit early the day, Father,' said McGrath, the postmaster's son.

'Where did you get the drink?' Stanislaus demanded.

'I don't know, Fa'er,' said young Cavanagh, the schoolteacher's brother. Stanislaus slapped the blackthorn stick against the boy's thigh. 'Pius, we got it off Pius!'

'Is this. How you. Behave. When your families. At home. Haven't even. A spare penny. To waste?' Stanislaus uttered bitterly, punctuating his speech with slaps to their legs. They yelped like puppies. 'You should be ashamed of yourselves.'

This business of Pius Lennon and the poteen was getting out of hand. He was making the stuff in such prodigious quantities and selling it so cheaply that he was bringing many others to ruin with him. Nevertheless Stanislaus was troubled by the thought of the Victor fellow as the correcting influence, to Pius and to the wider problems connected to Pius's dissolution. That such a person would be anyone's idea of salvation! Obedience and discipline were the answers to vice, indolence and dissolution. People needed leadership from the cloth, not from radical politicals. Stanislaus had read many of the socialistic texts. Mostly screeds written by palpably troubled souls. He found most striking the universal rage and the rejection of authority – the former a consequence of the latter, he believed. Marxians said the meaning of life was struggle, but Stanislaus knew that grace required acceptance. True freedom came through surrender. Only rage was possible where grace was not. In lands where grace was banished, no depravity was unthinkable. The Russian experiment, for example, was sure to end in horror. He hung up his overcoat in the kitchen and opened the range door. As he poked at the fire and watched the flames rise higher, he wondered if he might work up his ruminations into a paper.

'It's after a quarter past six. I wish you would tell me where you're going out and didn't keep me late, Father,' said Mrs Geraghty, standing behind him with her cloth coat pulled tight around her.

'Your Grace,' Stanislaus muttered, but knew it was pointless to keep correcting her. She'd never learn to address him correctly. At her age and station, she was disinclined to take in anything new. 'Dinner smells wonderful,' he said.

'It's been in the oven so long it'll be dry as communion,' she said with a bitterness he knew was affected. 'Oh, and Father,' she went on, softer now.

She gently removed a letter from her coat pocket and held it up. 'There's a letter for you, Jeremiah McGrath brought it special delivery. It looks very official, Father.'

Stanislaus reached for it but Mrs Geraghty seemed reluctant to let it go. She recognised the seal as well as he did.

'Thank you, Mrs Geraghty, I'll be fine from here on,' he said.

'If you're sure there's nothing else you need,' she said, at length letting go.

'Quite sure, thank you,' said Stanislaus, nodding to the clock.

'I'll say good evening then,' she snorted. She raised her chin and eventually took herself out the door. Stanislaus sliced the envelope open, relishing the crisp rasp of the water-marked paper coming apart. The handwriting was unmistakable. Only close friends and colleagues got handwritten letters.

*My old friend Stanislaus,*

    *I have this morning returned from Rome where the Holy Father has briefed the Conclave on a crisis of the gravest urgency. In accordance with the Holy Father's instructions I am gathering together the most senior principals of the Church in Ireland to discuss the emerging crisis. I expect to see you at the Synod Hall in Armagh this coming Sunday at three o'clock.*

    *I pray this letter finds you well and fully restored from your illness.*

    *Your Brother in Christ,*

    *Michael Cardinal Logue + +*

Stanislaus read and reread the letter. The most senior principals of the Church in Ireland. Ten years had passed since Stanislaus had risen from his sickbed to be told he wasn't getting the Bishopric of Derry. It was no reflection on his abilities of course, everyone thought the world of him of course, his counsel would still be invaluable of course. But His Eminence the Cardinal, the Archbishop, the Primate, had never sought the counsel of the parish priest of Madden. Not till now. In time of crisis though, the Cardinal wanted his old friend at his side. Poor old, sick old, pensioned-off old Stanislaus Benedict. The old enforcer. The man who made enemies so Mick Logue, the Northern Star himself, didn't have to. Father Daly came bounding down the stairs and into the kitchen. He opened the oven door and reached for the plates, then withdrew his hand quickly and waved around chastened fingers. He bit his lip so as not to swear, then made a glove of a dish cloth and lifted the hot plates from the oven.

'You're ready for your tea, Your Grace?'

Stanislaus nodded and sat at the head of the table. The curate set out forks, knives, a jug of water and two glasses on the table and when he sat down, they bowed their heads. In nomine Patris et Filii et Spiritus Sancti. Benedic, Domine, nos et haec tua dona quae de tua largitate sumus sumpturi per Christum Dominum nostrum, Amen. Stanislaus chewed slowly. It wasn't quite as dry as communion wafer but it was overdone. He put some of his food onto Father Daly's plate – it seemed that, no matter how often she was told, Mrs Geraghty would not accept that a man's appetite shrivels with the years – and the curate nodded appreciatively. Stanislaus set the Cardinal's letter on the table. Father Daly stopped chewing. He swallowed and picked up the letter. He read it quickly, then seemed to read it again. 'It sounds serious, Your Grace. I can drive you to Armagh in my motorcar if you wish?' he said.

'Yes, I'd appreciate that. After the last mass.' Stanislaus paused. 'Have you any thoughts on what it might be about?'

'Well, the fact that the Holy Father called together the Conclave … it's not a local matter. And this talk of urgency … probably a temporal issue. The war, maybe? Perhaps there's a peace treaty in the offing.'

'Or perhaps things are about to get worse.'

Father Daly finished his dinner and Stanislaus permitted him to smoke. 'There was something I meant to say to you,' the curate said as he exhaled. 'Some of the parishioners want to use the Parochial Hall tonight.'

'What for?'

'They're holding a homecoming dance for Victor Lennon.'

Aidan Cavanagh and John McGrath had said everyone in Madden finished work early today. Stanislaus hadn't thought to ask anything further, but now here was the explanation.

'I thought it was an innocent enough request,' Father Daly began falteringly, as though realising he might have overstepped his authority. 'Everyone seems so excited about this fellow coming home.'

'Who gave you the right to make that decision?'

'Your Grace, I …'

'What sort of man do you think this Victor Lennon is?'

'Your Grace, I hardly think …'

'He's a communist and a bolshevist and he has been up to his eyes in every kind of radicalism. Tim, people idolise this Lennon fellow, and we don't know what he's planning.'

'Will we cancel the dance?' said Father Daly.

Stanislaus sighed. Father Daly and young priests like him would be responsible for the future of the Faith. Stanislaus feared they lacked the necessary toughness for dealing with the threats arrayed against it. 'It's too late for that if you've already said yes. The dance may go ahead. But it must be strictly teetotal. I met youngsters on the road and they were full drunk. And I want everyone out by eleven.'

'Victor and Charlie probably won't have arrived by eleven.'

'Those are the conditions. And Father: this is not to happen again. The use of parish property is in my authority and mine alone. Is that understood?'

\* \* \*

*Pius is still apologising extravagantly as he closes the door on Benedict. You hadn't planned it, it was an unconscious reflex. You look to your big brother Seamus but he turns his eyes to the floor. You look to Anthony, second eldest, your favourite. To Mary. To Sarah. To little Agnes. They all turn their faces away. Perhaps spitting at the bishop was too much, but at least it was unequivocal. The spit will wash away but the act won't. You look at your mother, shrouded in white on a table in the corner, unmoved. The gesture means nothing to her. Pius unbuckles his belt.*

*'Da, please ...'*

*'Don't you Da me,' he hisses, pulling the belt from his waist, loop by loop. 'You do that to a priest? You do that to a bishop?' He wraps the belt round his knuckles, doubling the leather. Nausea rises in your nostrils, hot and horrible. The room is dark, with only the hearth's dying embers giving light; Pius's face is half red, half shadow, the margin flickering down the middle. You can smell his hot breath. He never drinks, but there's poteen there, the wildness in his eyes confirms it. The belt lashes across your face. You don't feel anything yet.*

*'He comes over here and tells us Ma is going to hell? The bishop can go to hell and so can you,' you cry. Defiance is all that is left to you. His fist connects with your jaw and the pain is such that for the briefest of seconds it feels like you have departed this life. You're crumpled on the floor absorbing the blows as Pius swings and swipes and the belt leather cuts deep into your arms and back and head.*

*'I'm going to kill you,' Pius cries, and it sounds like the most absolutely truthful statement he's ever made in his life. You hear women scream and they're all telling him to stop but they're all too spineless to make him. You peek from your foetal position*

*and, seeing a lull, launch yourself at him. You clatter into his midriff and crash over the table. Tea and wake sandwiches go flying. Back on your feet, you see your mother through eyes bathed in blood and tears. A slice of ham has landed on her cheek. Pius puffs desperately for air, his face is purple. Your mother is dead and this yellow-belly runs away into a bottle just when you need him most.*

*'You're nothing but a drunken coward,' you say as you run out the door.*

\*   \*   \*

We have the compartment to ourselves. Not many heading north at this time of night. I pull down the blinds and scrape the flecks of bacon and carrot off the lapels of my suit. Charlie's too civilised and conscientious to put his feet up on the empty chairs beside him but I'm not. I pull the trilby hat down over my face and make myself comfortable. It's a rickety old bone shaker but I'm soon nodding off. One minute we're between Clontarf and Sutton and Charlie is saying something about how the Madden footballers have reached the county final; the next he's poking me with his cane and telling me to wake up, we're near Armagh. The train is stopped. I see lights further up the line, but outside it's darkness.

'This isn't a scheduled stop,' Charlie says.

The train starts moving again, chugging its last mile or two, and I hear compartment doors being slid open up the hallway. I peek out. Two soldiers stand in the hallway a few compartments down smoking cigarettes and pointing their rifles to the ground. A third soldier, tall and slender and wearing an eye-patch, comes out of the compartment, and they move on to the next one. They'll be in on top of us in a moment.

'I'm not even home yet and already the harassment starts.'

'I'm sure they're not looking for you, Victor.'

'When you've been lifted as many times as I have, Charlie, you know fucken tyranny when you see it.'

'Don't start now.'

'I bet you the officer puts on an English accent. Wait till you see.'

'Victor, please.'

There's no way the train will get to the station before they get to us, snailing along like this. I lie back on the seat and pull the hat down over my face and a moment later, I hear the compartment door slide open.

'Right, wake up, we need to take a look at your …' the officer begins – he *is* putting on a sort-of English accent – 'Charlie Quinn! Get up and let me shake your hand,' he cries, sounding fit to burst.

'I'd like to, Hugh, but' – Charlie makes a tap, tap, tap – 'I'm not as good on my feet as I used to be.'

'Oh. Of course, I'm sorry.' Hugh slumps down into a seat and sighs. I'd love to get a look at this fellow, but I stay hidden beneath the hat.

'How's the eye?'

'Doesn't bother me at all. I got away very lightly compared to some.'

'True enough. Poor old Frank Jennings lost half his face. And you heard about Bob Morrow?'

'No justice, is there?' Hugh rises and stands over me, close enough that I can smell the tobacco off him. I fidget. 'This fellow with you?'

'Cousin of mine. Name of John Swift. Why, who are you looking for?'

'Just keeping our eyes open.'

'I'll wake him up and check him,' says another voice, a Scottish accent this time.

'Let him be, Hugh,' Charlie says calmly, 'he had a lot to drink earlier.'

'Shut it, you,' the Scottish accent snaps.

'Stand down, Campbell,' Hugh barks. 'This man deserves your respect and with God as my witness, he will have it.' The train hits the buffers with a jolt of sufficient violence to wake any man except John Swift. I tense up, waiting to be unmasked. But instead I hear first Campbell, then Hugh, apologise to Charlie. They leave.

'Jesus Christ, Charlie,' I say when I come out from under my hat.

We disembark the train. Not more than a handful of people are in the station, so there would be nowhere for us to hide, but the soldiers aren't on the platform yet. We move as quickly as we can out of the station and into the refuge of the shadows. The night is still and calm and the full moon lights up the empty street. It's late. In a few hours the mills around here will be thronged. Up ahead, lights flash and an automobile splutters beneath a street light. A military vehicle. Behind us Hugh and his men exit the station. I drag Charlie into the shadow of the arches at the front of the station and we watch the soldiers pass by, no more than a few yards from us. Hugh talks to the driver of the truck, and they climb into the back. The truck retreats into the distance and I breathe again.

It's quiet now. I see a horse and buggy idling outside a large red-brick house at the top of the street, and as we move cautiously in that direction I pull the hat down across my face and try to make out the features of the man sitting on the trap. When we get close, the faceless horseman says: 'Is it him?'

Alarmed, I look to Charlie. He nods. 'You got my telegram.'

The horseman claps his hands together and cries gleefully: 'Welcome home, Victor. Erin go fucken bragh!'

'Ssssshhh! Keep it down, will you? The Baptist minister lives in there,' says Charlie, pointing to the red-bricked house. Curtains twitch in the upstairs window. The horseman giggles and tells me to throw my suitcase on board. I hesitate. He's late thirties, tall and strong-looking, with the floury face of a man too fond of the drink. He's familiar. A Madden man presumably. Damned if I can place him. Charlie senses my confusion.

'I sent a telegram ahead asking for Turlough to come and pick us up,' he says.

Of course. Turlough Moriarty. I was in school with his younger brother Sean. Big, strong fellow too, Sean was, if a bit soft in the head. Turlough was the smarter of the two, relatively speaking. All dead-on people, the Moriartys. I climb onto the buggy and thank Turlough for coming. He gives the horse a light lick of the whip and we're on our way. We go up over Banbrook hill past the pubs at the Shambles, up English Street with its proud, polished shop fronts, the gleaming terraces of Market Square and Thomas Street, the huckster shops of Ogle Street and onto poor Irish Street. Not a sinner to be seen. We cut through the slums of Culdee and pass the long sail-less windmill of Windmill Hill, and soon reach Droim Gabhla at the edge of the town. I tell the lads about something a great, wise and knowledgeable man once told me: how the official name for this little hamlet is not Drumgola, as would have been the logical

Anglicisation, but Umgola, because some careless clerk some-where made a balls of it and left out the 'Dr'. This little Irish townland has a name straight out of deepest, darkest Africa because of the tin-eared ignorance of the foreigners who took it upon themselves to rename our country. We share a bitter laugh. I look back to the little town, the tiny city of Armagh, lit by a moon bright as a cool blue sun. 'Crazy place to build a town, the whole place is hills,' I say.

'Built on seven hills,' Turlough sings, beginning the chorus to the old Armagh song.

'Like a little Rome.'

After a few miles we turn left and the lights of Madden village glow softly, down below us in a hollow. The horse snorts tiredly. Somewhere in the distance is a fast, throbbing hum, faint but growing louder, like it's coming from under the ground. Madden looms. I make out the chapel spire first. Then the Parochial Hall. A handsome if not beautiful façade of plain rose window above double doors. At the top of the town, the Parochial House, proud and immoveable as a Papal Bull. The three Church buildings all sit on slightly higher ground than the rest of the village, which is why they're the only buildings in Madden that have never flooded. The National School is the only other building in town worth a damn, and it too is controlled, if not owned, by the dog-collars. Same story in every town in Ireland. But I see in the gaslight that flags, yes, *red flags*, are draped from every window, and bunting stretches across the street. Everything red, red is the colour. My God, Charlie said I was a hero, but the place looks like Paris in '48! The subterranean throbbing is identifiable now. It's a drum. There's fiddles and accordions too, coming from the Parochial Hall. We move towards the music.

'They're holding a dance in your honour,' Charlie says.

'People's awful proud of you, Victor,' says Turlough. We stop outside the Parochial Hall, its grey façade is broken by splashes of frenetic colour behind the steamed-up windows. The noise is cacophonous. 'Come on, we're very late.'

A young priest with a mop of blond hair emerges from the Hall. He nods and hails me with a toothy smile. 'You must be Victor?' I nod. He takes his watch from his pocket and fidgets with it in a way that reminds me of Alfie Byrne, then looks distractedly up the street towards the Parochial House. 'Thank goodness you're here, we're supposed to finish up at eleven and it's past that now.'

'Gone half past, I make it,' I say, glancing at my watch. The others look at theirs, then back at me confusedly.

Of course, they're all twenty-five minutes behind me, I keep forgetting. They didn't bother to tell us in Fron Goch about the so-called Daylight Saving Hours. Apparently we're in line with Greenwich now. After being released I walked around for weeks not knowing about it.

'I seem to be ahead of everyone. My watch still gives Dublin Mean Time,' I say.

When we get the Republic we'll fix the clocks, and no more of this Greenwich nonsense. How supine are people who allow the government to overrule the clock – the *clock*? It's frustrating, though, that everyone else's watch is slow. Being right is cold comfort when the whole world is wrong. 'I'll be in directly,' I tell the priest.

He nods and turns but as he opens the door he is almost knocked over by a boy of maybe seventeen, who staggers out and around the side of the building. Out of sight, he retches violently.

The priest shakes his head and goes inside. I take my suitcase around to the other side of the building, looking for a shadow so I can change back into my uniform. When I'm changed, I spit on my hands and pat down my hair. A shave would be good, a bit of soap could do wonders, but perching the sloped hat on my head, I suppose I probably look all right.

'Come on, you're gorgeous,' Charlie calls, and I step into the light just as a tall figure all in black strides past Charlie and Turlough, ignoring them as they call out their salutes. He walks with an impressive sprightliness, gripping his cane like Phil Shanahan grips a hurl, and throws open the door of the Parochial Hall without breaking his stride. The old bastard looks like he hasn't aged a day.

*　　*　　*

*Maggie answers the door with a grimace of condolence but her expression gives way to horror when she sees the battering you have taken. She rushes you inside the house, scattering her younger brothers and sisters with matriarchal authority, and lies you down on the sofa by the range. It's warm and smells of baking bread. Maggie's father is perched in his usual armchair. God knows what he makes of you; one eye lolling madly is the only sign he's alive at all. Maggie goes out into the scullery and comes back with her father's old leather medical bag, towels and two bowls of water. She puts one bowl on the range and heats it.*

*'Look up at the ceiling, we have to keep the wound elevated. If we can't stop the bleeding you'll have to go and see a proper doctor.' She immerses a towel in hot water, wrings it out and sets it against your eyebrow. 'Help me apply pressure to the wound.'*

*From your good eye you look at the graceful curve of her neck and want to take a bite out of it. She's wearing a red and brown dress with little lace frills at the edges. She's close enough that you can smell her distinctive smell.*

*'I told you to look at the ceiling,' she says. Her father's daughter.*

*When the bleeding stops she washes the wound with a soft wash-cloth. You grip the sofa tightly and grit your teeth while she pours liquid from the spirit bottle over the cut – 'Isopropyl. It'll prevent infection,' she says – and uses tweezers to remove what she calls debris. She makes up a dressing with surgical adhesive tape and gauze. 'But it won't be enough,' she says. 'The broken skin won't knit together on its own. You need stitches.'*

*You nod quiescently. You're so tired. You ask if you can sleep in her shed. You are grateful she doesn't ask for an explanation.*

*'What will you do tomorrow?' she asks.*

*'I'll bury my mother.'*

*'Afterwards?'*

*You're too tired to think. 'I know if I stay here I'll kill him.'*

\*    \*    \*

From his window Stanislaus watched everyone arrive. He had a dusty volume of theology in his lap, lit by a single candle, but it was a mere prop. It took two hundred people to fill the Parochial Hall and from early on, the place was full. The cheering and clapping from the Parochial Hall grew louder and rougher as the night got later, and Stanislaus was relieved as eleven o'clock approached and the guest of honour hadn't appeared. The moon, full and large in the cloudless sky, shone across all but the darkest corners of the parish, so Stanislaus would have seen him. But eleven o'clock came and went and there was still no sign of things winding up. Eventually Stanislaus rose and readied himself to intervene, but he wobbled and sat back down. He gripped the arms of the chair. His vision swirled before him. He held his face in his hands and felt the cold sweat on his brow. But this was not a stroke and it soon passed. He looked at the bottle. It didn't seem like he'd had all that much to drink. He had gone for years of his life without a drink, it wasn't something he was a slave to, but it was true that he had acquired a taste for brandy in his old age.

Outside in the distance the light of a lantern appeared and as it grew bigger Stanislaus made out three figures atop a buggy, drawing closer. Charlie Quinn's leg stuck out in silhouette. Hulking Turlough Moriarty drove the buggy. Typical. The Moriarty boys were perennial foot-soldiers, from their grandfather, a locally famous Fenian of the sixties, on down. It was no surprise that they would regard Victor Lennon as a great fellow altogether. The third man sat between Charlie and Turlough with the brim of his hat pulled low over his face. It had to be him. He watched Father Daly emerge from the Parochial Hall and speak to the men on the buggy. They spent a moment looking at their watches. Obviously Father Daly was explaining the time, and that the dance was over. The third man got down from the buggy. Father Daly made to go back inside but as he opened the door he was almost knocked aside by Aidan Cavanagh, who dashed round the corner and heaved up his guts on the wall of the Parochial Hall. Stanislaus gripped his stick in his fist and bounded furiously down the stairs. By the time he reached the

Parochial Hall Aidan was gone and only Charlie and Turlough sat on the buggy. They called their greetings but he didn't stop to acknowledge them.

Inside, smoke, sweat, music and colour blasted Stanislaus's senses. Musicians clattered ever faster, all aggression and artless volume, and the wood floor vibrated like the skin of a drum under thudding feet and bodies crashing to and fro. It barely passed as dancing, this hauling and mauling. Overhead was a banner fashioned from an old green tablecloth that read Erin Go Bragh Welcome Home Victor. Stanislaus felt suddenly vertiginous. Standing near the door, tapping his foot and observing passively, was Father Daly. He turned white when he saw Stanislaus.

'Is this how you supervise an event? I said teetotal,' Stanislaus seethed.

'I haven't seen anyone taking drink.'

'Open your eyes, man.' People would always come up with schemes for concealing liquor but a good priest would be wise to them. Stanislaus tutted disgustedly at the curate's failure. 'It's well past eleven.'

'Victor has just arrived. I thought another few minutes wouldn't be any harm.'

Stanislaus stalked away. Further discussion would only aggravate him. He moved towards the stage at the top of the hall, and word of his arrival spread perceptibly as he moved through the crowd. The dancers became less frenetic, then stopped altogether. It was like water dousing a flame. As Stanislaus ascended the stage, the musicians stopped playing and held their silent fiddles and banjos and bodhrans guiltily. Standing centre stage, he didn't have to wait long for silence.

'It's very late. The dance is over. Don't anyone make any noise on your way home,' he said. The crowd looked back dumbly. 'I said this dance is over. Good night to you all.'

'Victor is here!' cried a voice from the back of the hall.

Everyone turned. The hall seemed suddenly bigger with two hundred people facing away rather than towards him. Men wrestled past each other, women too, to converge on the doorway, where Victor Lennon now stood. He wore a tattered military uniform, bandolier and big sloped hat. Had he changed his clothes? Shrewd. He was a striking sight in the uniform.

'I'm sure the bishop won't object to another few reels, since I've just arrived,' Victor called out, crisp and clear, the voice of a man who knew how to project. A musician ran a bow across fiddle strings and waited to see what would happen. Stanislaus and Victor locked eyes on one another over the heads of the people. 'Sure you wouldn't, Your Grace?' said Victor, jabbing the words mercilessly precisely. The dizziness was returning to Stanislaus. The fiddler scratched the opening notes of some fast reel, and the other musicians joined in. People clapped the rhythm and quickly the floor filled with dancers. It was as though Stanislaus wasn't there. People queued up to shake Victor's hand and shower him with kisses.

'Are you all right, Your Grace?' whispered Father Daly, climbing onto the stage.

'For all you care, seminarian,' said Stanislaus, mustering his strength to walk off the stage, beating a path through the people with his stick. Father Daly took hold of his elbow, and though he tried to shrug him off, there was little force in his protest.

'You don't look well, Your Grace.'

As they passed him in the doorway Victor Lennon nodded, smiled and gulped heartily from a huge bottle. He laughed as he looked at the bishop. Stanislaus wanted to stop him, to insist that the event was teetotal, but his knees buckled beneath him. Had Father Daly not held him up, he'd have crumpled.

'Are you all right, Father?' said Charlie Quinn, smoking a cigarette with Turlough Moriarty by the door.

'I'm surprised at you, Charlie Quinn, I'd have expected better,' Stanislaus wheezed as Father Daly helped him into the street. 'There would've been no problem if you'd ended proceedings when you were supposed to. If you only …' Stanislaus said to Father Daly, but hadn't the breath to finish.

'You just need rest, Your Grace, you've been overdoing it lately,' said the curate.

'If you'd made sure it was over by eleven like you were supposed to,' Stanislaus said again as they arrived at the Parochial House, suddenly more weary than angry now that he was inside his own front door. Almost immediately, his eyelids started to droop. 'Victor Lennon may be the only layman in the parish who knows how to address me correctly. Isn't that funny? Isn't that awful?' he said.

Stanislaus's last thought before he fell asleep that night was the look on Charlie Quinn's face as he'd chastised him. The young man had seemed genuinely distraught.

\* \* \*

People are cheering for me and shaking my hand. Benedict looked so strong and unyielding up there on stage, laying down the law, but I knew the people were with me. There's a huge banner draped from the ceiling, and yes, it's green when it should be red, but it is a tribute to *me*. He looked around the packed hall, five hundred people here at least, and saw sheep in need of a shepherd. I saw comrades in need of example. The young priest with the blond hair has to drag the old bastard off the stage and out the door after the musicians and the dancing start up again. Some ruddy-faced fellow thrusts a bottle into my hand just as Benedict is passing me at the door, and I take a drink, assuming the clear liquid inside is water. Come to think of it, a stupid assumption. It tastes of nothing but pain, and my face screws up as the poteen goes down. The young priest steers Benedict to the door and he's gone before I get my breath back. I feel like I've been punched in the windpipe at the very moment I should be enjoying my victory, Benedict's defeat. He was so very white-looking! So beaten-looking. Like a prize-fighter being helped from the ring after being knocked out. I remember a couple of years ago how the audience in the Volta Picture Palace tore the place apart with excitement after the newsreel showed Jack Johnson getting his comeuppance. As they all line up to talk to me, to shake my hand, to pay tribute, I feel how Jess Willard must have felt after he knocked the big nigger out. Champion of the bloody world.

I know a lot of faces but I'm struggling with names. 'Stay close to me and drop people's names into conversation in case I forget,' I say quietly into Charlie's ear. 'Try and not make it too obvious.'

'Hello, Colm, how are all the McDermotts this evening?' says Charlie to a man of fifty who comes up to me, and a matronly woman beside him.

'Welcome home, lad, welcome home,' says Colm McDermott, shaking my hand like he's trying to wring something out of it.

I tell him it's great to see him again, and take a punt on the woman beside him. 'And how are you, Mrs McDermott?'

'Ah, Victor, I see you didn't lose your manners away in Dublin. But sure you know to call me Kate.' She pushes grey wisps of hair behind her ears, grabs me and kisses me on the lips. 'God bless you, Victor Lennon, and God bless Ireland.' She's drunk, like most of the men who shake my hand and the women who slobber my cheeks and lips. Charlie keeps me right with the names. The Kellys, the McCabes, the Gambles, the Murphys, the Sweeneys, the O'Kanes, the other Murphys, the Vallelys, the Campbells. The music is loud, the dancing raucous. The place stinks of sweat and smoke and hooch with a thin sliver of Lifebuoy in the mix. Youngsters who should be in bed are still running around. Old-timers are falling asleep in corners. All in tribute to me.

'Did they do anything like this for you when you came back from France?' I ask Charlie. He makes an effort to smile. Barely perceptibly, he shakes his head. Sean Moriarty, Turlough's brother, comes over and lifts me off my feet in a bear hug. He nearly squeezes the puff out of me. Strong as an ox, he is. They all have questions, crowding around me like I'm a famous tenor or something. What's it like being a national hero? Did they really shoot Connolly, and him strapped to a chair? Who was the best fighter? How do you say that name, Dee Valeera? And what's a Spaniard doing fighting for Ireland anyway? Sean, though, is only interested in the football.

'I heard Dick Fitzgerald was at Fron Goch, and all the prisoners played football every day. Dick Fitzgerald! The man has three All Ireland medals,' says Sean, as if anyone didn't know who Dick Fitzgerald was.

'Ah well now, there was a lot of hours to fill and we wanted to stay fit.'

'So you did play?'

'Every day.'

'And was Fitzgerald there or was he not?'

'You couldn't throw a stone in Fron Goch without hitting a county man. Frank Burke. Paddy Cahill. Brian Joyce, boys like that. Frank Shouldice, he was in the Four Courts garrison. And you had Phil Shanahan, Seamus Dobbyn. Hurlers, like, but they wouldn't let us have hurls in the camp. Good footballers all the same. And aye, if I recall, Dick was there too,' I say coyly.

'If you were playing with Fitzgerald and them boys every day for a year, you must have got good enough yourself. Maybe you'll turn out for Madden in the county final?'

I am fit, I will say that. That was one good thing about Fron Goch – it was ten months off work. Circuit training beats shovelling coal or digging ditches. Of course, I'm nowhere near the class of Fitzgerald and the rest, but as time went on, my presence on the same field as those lads became less and less absurd. 'Och, I'm all right I suppose,' I shrug. They're rapt, watching me. There's children here weren't born when I was last home. Young fellows who were wearing short trousers when I left. They've heard of me like they've heard of Redmond O'Hanlon, the bould Robert Emmett and the gallant Henry Joy. I feel like Robin Hood. They crowd me, press up against me, everyone wants to touch me. I feel like the Pope. 'Tell us a story, Victor,' they say.

'I'll tell you one about the lockout.'

'Tell us one about the Rising.'

'I said I'll tell you one about the lockout.'

I'm about to start when I see her across the room. I don't suppose she wants to approach me first. Fair enough, I'll approach her. Let them wait for my story. She's wearing a pretty white dress. Shows that seeing me is important to her. Her brown curls are all tied up save for a few that refuse to be bridled, that cascade across caramel skin into hazel eyes. Her mouth is fixed in a polite smile. She's trying to look like she's surprised or something, though like everyone else, she's come here to see me. I know it and she knows it and she knows I know it and she knows I know she knows it. Her lips are pink and full and oh my sweet God she's more gorgeous even than I remembered. To think I might've been master of this. 'Are you dancing?' I say, as if not a day has passed, and I can't read her expression, I don't know whether she wants to kiss me or box me, but she takes the offer of my arm and follows me into the body of the hall. People cheer and slap me on the back as we set ourselves to dance but in this moment they're not important. The musicians start a slow ballad, thank God. I take Maggie's hands and hold her up close to me, and look from her eyes down to her neck, graceful as a swan, and down to the triangle between her throat and the undone top button of her blouse. She takes quick, short breaths. I tingle. We shuffle together slowly and the smell of the sweet perfume on her skin comes drifting into my senses, gentle and lemony. I inhale her.

'You never got that wound looked at,' she says at last, her voice warm and melodious. I put my hand up to the weak skin above my eye and feel a piquant twinge. Maggie looks like Mildred Harris. I love Mildred Harris. Although Mildred's only a skinny wee girl. Maggie is a proper woman. Like Florence La Badie. I love Florence La Badie. Maggie's lips. Let me choose, in this very moment, and I'll choose those lips over revolution.

51

'It's good to see you,' I say. She smiles and glances down to where I'm sticking into her. I blush as the dance takes us away from each other and into a quick spin with other partners. Maggie pairs up with a gangly young lad with boils on his neck who looks totally smashed. I'm with a toothy girl with dark hair and dark eyes and I'm trying to be polite and distant but the toothy girl doesn't seem to want to let me go. When eventually I get Maggie back in my arms, I say: 'So Charlie tells me you never married.'

I shouldn't have said that. Jesus Christ, Victor, you haven't seen the girl in ten years. Stupid bastard. Always the young bull, never the old. Her shoulders shoot up. She pushes away my hands and gives me a look that says I have a bloody nerve, and she's at the door by the time I catch up with her. I put my hand on her shoulder out on the steps of the Parochial Hall, and I try to look as plaintive as I can. The cool night air is a relief. She waits, her patience dwindling.

'I had to leave my mark on the world,' I say.

She blinks and her lips curve softly. 'I know, Victor.'

She turns and walks away and I watch, thrilled by the swing of her hips. She's halfway down the street before I think to ask if I can walk her home. She pauses a second and without turning, says over her shoulder: 'No.'

I keep staring up the street long after she has disappeared out of sight. When at last I turn back to the Parochial Hall Charlie is waiting in the doorway. He's giving me a look. I ignore him and go back inside. I approach the ruddy-faced fellow with the poteen and ask him has he any more. Surreptitiously he takes the bottle out from his inside pocket – no mean feat to conceal such a large bottle there. Charlie's in a huff about something and stays silent instead of helping me identify the fellow. I smile and nod like a simpleton as I drink the man's poteen and tell him what good stuff it is. It definitely goes down easier second time around.

'From your own da's own still,' he says.

He's tall and rangy with teeth like an old graveyard and eyes that shift here and there. I have him now: TP McGahan. We were in school together. I take another sip. It *is* good stuff. Should've walked Maggie home regardless. She was glad to see me, no matter what she said, she was glad to see me. Who knows, might've even marked my first night back home. It's been a while and a man has needs.

'Take it handy with the drink, Victor,' says Charlie.

'I'm all right, Charlie, sure I used to be in the Pioneers,' I say. He laughs, but I'm serious. 'It was the Pioneers that drove me to drink in the first place.' It was true, I had been secretary of the Monto branch. I fell out with the rest of them the time Findlater's gave us a donation of ten pounds. It was ridiculous for a temperance movement to take money from a wine merchant, but the rest of them said I was right *in theory* but I had to be *realistic.* 'There was a priest on the committee said I was being *dogmatic.* Can you believe the neck on him? A bloody priest!'

'So what did you do?' says Charlie.

'I flung my Pioneer pin at the chairman, the fat, red-faced bollix, and went straight to the nearest pub away from the fucken hypocrite gombeen bastards.'

I take another drink. Charlie's right, I'd better slow down. It takes a lot less poteen than whiskey to reduce a man to his hands and knees. There's a bit of a spin to the room. TP McGahan has a notebook and pencil in his hands. 'How about a few quotes for next week's paper? I work for the *Armagh Guardian*.'

'You don't have a camera? I don't want no photographs.'

'Go away and leave him alone, he's giving me a dance,' says the toothy girl with the dark hair and dark eyes I danced with before. She grabs my hand and leads me through the crowd before I can protest. We line up alongside three other couples and start into a lively reel, and though I'm supposed to dance with everyone in turn, my partner, whoever she is, keeps seizing me back. Her arms are surprisingly strong. Eyes dark and wild. Thick, black, *black* hair. White skin. Red lips curled in a pout like a spoonful of jam in a glass of milk. She's probably about twenty-one and looks like Theda Bara. She could be gorgeous or she could be hideous. She smacks against me violently and I notice the other dancers stand back and give us plenty of room. I'm not sure if I want to hop on her or run for my life. 'What's my name?' she says.

I grope around for the faintest memory of this primal, kinetic creature, but there's nothing. 'Of course, I know you surely.'

She laughs and throws her head about, sending her hair flailing, but her eyes, spread wide, never seem to waver from me. 'Have I changed a lot?'

'Not a bit.'

She's strange. The dance ends and I'm glad to retreat from her. Charlie, Turlough, Sean and TP are standing by the door sipping poteen and watching me. Charlie shakes his head. TP still has his notebook out. He asks again if I have any quotes for him.

'I don't think Victor wants his name going in the paper,' says Charlie.

'Fire away, TP,' I say.

'Why are you home?'

'To see my family. And I'm delighted to be back among my own people.'

'Is it true that you want Ireland to become communistic?'

His eyes shift in his beak-nosed face. I shouldn't indulge him, I really shouldn't. Journalists are all the same. Weasels. Sometimes they can be harnessed and directed towards some useful work, but they're no less verminous for that. 'Are you going to stitch me up, TP?'

'Och, Victor, I'm just an old friend writing a puff piece for the local paper. I'm just wondering if you think people in County Armagh are ready for communism? Cardinal Logue in particular has taken a very strong line against it.'

The girl, the one looks like Theda Bara, reappears and thrusts a bottle into my hand. Her eyes sparkle like the Liffey under gaslight, all treacherous depth. I sense, vaguely, that the lads around me are uncomfortable. I screw the cork from the neck and take a glug. I see Theda's luxurious lips make an open-mouthed smile and I want them. The room sways. There was something I wanted to say.

'Victor? Cardinal Logue has taken a very strong line against communism,' says TP, face expectant, pencil poised. There's a bit of a crowd around us now.

'Let me tell you something about Cardinal fucken Logue,' I begin.

# TWO

Stanislaus sorted through the great ring of keys to the parish properties as he walked, coming to the correct key just as he reached the Parochial Hall. Someone had cleaned up around the side where Aidan Cavanagh had been sick. There were no windows smashed. In fact they looked clean – but if there was one thing broken or one item not put back where it was supposed to be … He opened the door of the hall and walked into the middle of the floor. The place smelled of bleach and soap powder. The chairs were stacked neatly to the side. The floor was mopped and clean, except for the muddy footprints he himself had just left on the not-yet-dry floor. He removed his shoes and went to the store cupboard to look for a mop. After he had cleaned up his mess, he locked the front door of the hall after him and sat on the steps to pull on his shoes. Hearing someone coming, he looked up the street and froze when he saw it was Victor Lennon.

'Morning, Your Grace,' the Victor fellow said.

For the first time since he was a child, Stanislaus seemed unable to tie his laces. He abandoned the knot and started again. Lennon did not stop as he passed, and Stanislaus left off warring with his laces to watch him disappear up the road. Where was he going, so early in the morning? Or coming from? He wore the same ragged uniform and still had his suitcase. He hadn't been home yet; where had he been? Stanislaus looked back to his laces, tangled stupidly, and methodically set about undoing the tangle.

When he got home Mrs Geraghty was cleaning up at the sink. Father Daly was at the table, using a slice of bread to mop up the fatty juices and gristle that remained of his breakfast, while looking at the newspaper laid flat beside his plate.

'I started without you, Your Grace, I wasn't sure how long you'd be.'

Mrs Geraghty set a plate of liver and kidneys down for Stanislaus and he tore hungrily into it, cutting through the liver and releasing a dark, pungent trickle of blood onto the plate. He still wondered about Victor Lennon, to be slinking home at this hour. Mrs Geraghty might be able to shed some light. She was usually able to. 'What time did the festivities finish at last night, Mrs Geraghty?' Stanislaus asked.

'There's no need to shout.'

Father Daly did not look up from his paper. Stanislaus forked his food and took a gulp of his tea. He wanted to know everything and by God they would tell him everything. He began again, louder this time. 'Tell me all, Mrs Geraghty. What happened after we left? Did Mr Lennon enjoy himself?'

'Oh, he enjoyed himself all right, talking out of turn,' she said vexedly. She paused and closed her eyes a moment, as if struck by a sudden pain. On opening them Stanislaus met her with a look that demanded she go on. 'Well, he was talking to TP McGahan and they were doing an interview and everybody was listening to them.' She took a scouring pad from the sink and started scrubbing roughly at the work surface, as if she could ever scrub roughly enough to make Stanislaus stop asking her questions. Stanislaus let his knife and fork drop loudly.

'What did he say?'

'I can't remember exactly.'

'Give me the gist.'

'Father, I have too much work to be gossiping,' she said, throwing the scouring pad into the sink.

If Mrs Geraghty was offended, surely others would be too. It hadn't taken long for their Victor, their boy of Easter Week, to reveal his feet of clay.

'I just saw Victor this morning. He looked a little the worse for wear,' Stanislaus said coyly. Mrs Geraghty stopped and turned slowly. Now she was interested. 'Yes, it was the strangest thing,' Stanislaus went on. 'He was coming up from the far end of the street, and he was wearing the same clothes – that silly uniform – and carrying his suitcase. It was as though he hadn't been home.' Stanislaus picked up his cutlery and ate a large forkful of kidney. Mrs Geraghty's expression turned distracted and grave.

'It was terrible, the things he was saying last night,' she said. 'He was full drunk as well, honestly, he was a disgrace. I suppose that's what happens you when you go away to the big city with all its loose morals and …'

'What did he say?'

'Terrible things. About the Church. About Cardinal Logue.' She paused. 'God forgive me, Father, but he said terrible things about you yourself. I couldn't even repeat it. And politics as well. He thinks these communists are great fellows altogether.'

'What exactly were his words, Mrs Geraghty?' Father Daly put in. 'The detail could be important.'

'The tenor is fairly clear, Tim,' Stanislaus said impatiently.

'Sometimes people get called socialists but they only want to help the poor. Sometimes they're not as opposed to the Church as they seem. Or even think themselves to be.'

'The objective of the Church is to save souls for Christ,' Stanislaus snapped.

'Of course, but a lot of souls will be lost if we refuse to adapt to the realities of the modern world,' said the young man.

Stanislaus sighed. He felt like beating the liberal fool around the head with his Rerum Novarum. He turned back to Mrs Geraghty. 'How did the people react?' he asked darkly.

'I'd say maybe half the people walked out.'

'And the other half?'

'God forgive them, they cheered.'

Mrs Geraghty returned to the sink. Stanislaus dabbed his napkin against his lips. Father Daly, seemingly unsure whether to speak or return to his newspaper, sat silently like an idiot. What on earth was the matter with the young man, that he didn't grasp the scale of the challenge before them? Half the parish had cheered on a radical who had denounced the Church. Half the parish, and on the Church's very own property! 'Where do you suppose the young hero stayed last night?' Stanislaus said.

'Charlie Quinn's perhaps? Or Moriarty's? It would be understandable if Victor wanted to wait till morning before going to see Pius.'

'Yes, that's surely what happened,' said Mrs Geraghty.

It was plausible. The Moriartys lived at the other end of the village, and if the people were split, the Moriartys were sure to be on the wrong side. Charlie Quinn was more difficult to judge. He and the Victor fellow were close friends, but, on the other hand, Charlie was a good, solid boy.

'Who was he dancing with?'

'Pardon me, Father?' said Mrs Geraghty.

'With whom did Victor Lennon dance?'

'I only saw him dancing with two girls. Margaret Cavanagh was one. And when I left he was dancing with Ida Harte. They were both drunk at that stage. Now, Margaret Cavanagh is a respectable girl but as for that other one, well …'

Stanislaus raised a hand to silence Mrs Geraghty. 'You must not be so uncharitable to the Harte family,' he said.

But Mrs Geraghty was not finished. 'Who are these Harte people anyway? Why have they moved here, where nobody knows them?' she said. The Hartes had taken over Dan McCusker's land a couple of years previously, after Dan had finally met a bottle that finished him before he finished it. They were the first family without local connections to have arrived in Madden in living memory, and people didn't like it.

'They're from County Monaghan. I'm from County Monaghan. It's not even ten miles to the county border,' said Father Daly.

'It's thirty mile or more to where they're from. And you're here to do the blessed work of the Church, Father. Why would they move thirty mile from their home place? They must be running away from something, that's why. You look at that Ida one. She's the sort that would get into trouble all right.'

'Mrs Geraghty, that's enough!' Stanislaus cried, with a vehemence that fairly blasted the housekeeper from her rhythm. Visibly chastened, she fled the kitchen.

Stanislaus was not interested in the fact that Victor had been dancing with Ida Harte. She had neither friends nor significant family connections. In fact, Stanislaus was offended by the naked prejudice with which so many of his parishioners treated the

Harte family; the dark, swirling rumours that they were gypsies, travellers, tinkers, just generally *not long off the road, themmuns*. On the rare occasions when the wicked assumption was challenged, *just look at them* would be the answer. They did look wild, it was true: Ted Harte was a hairy, ruddy fellow with broad shoulders and hands like cudgels; his wife Martha had straggly hair all down her back. They were old and though they had many grown-up children scattered around, only their youngest daughter had come with them when they moved to Madden. The reasons why the family might have split up this way were much-speculated. But it was poor Ida that suffered the worst slanders of the poisoned tongues. Many of the matronly ladies who backboned his parish believed, absurdly, that she had designs on their husbands, and Stanislaus knew they would have been scandalised at the sight of Victor dancing with her. Yet Stanislaus found himself oddly fond of Ida. She was as he imagined women had been back in the thirties: without reticence or propriety, certainly, but neither charmless nor irredeemable. In one of the few memories he had of his mother, he saw her laughing lustily as some nameless hag affectionately told her she was *as a meabhar*, clean off her head.

Margaret Cavanagh was another matter. He would have to keep an eye on her. The late Dr Cavanagh had given his eldest daughter extensive home-schooling, quite separate from the curriculum of needlework, singing, reading and arithmetic offered at the National School, and since his stroke ten years before, and later his death, Margaret had been the nearest thing to a doctor in Madden. Dr Cavanagh had been a man possessed of the most independent intellect, the Lord alone knew what he had introduced her to. She had continued her self-education after her father's incapacitation, something Stanislaus viewed as akin to swimming out to sea without hope of safe return. Recklessly cultivated intellects were often resistant to the higher truths of which the Church was guardian. She and Victor were around the same age and must have known each other growing up. They were, in the narrow context of the parish, of roughly equivalent social standing. The doctor's daughter, the rich man's son. Perhaps there had been an attraction. Perhaps there had been more than an attraction. Hadn't she, after all, spurned several perfectly presentable suitors? Previously Stanislaus had seen this as dedication to her younger siblings – any husband would be within his rights to send them away, even if it meant the orphanage or the workhouse – but now he wondered whether Miss Cavanagh had remained needlessly unmarried for other reasons. Miss Cavanagh was the schoolteacher, and education was a dangerous thing if not applied correctly. Perhaps behind a blameless exterior there lurked independent notions, dangerous to the parish's most impressionable minds. Yes, he would have to keep an eye on Miss Cavanagh.

\* \* \*

*You're comfortable on the straw, considering your bruises. You lie looking out the open window of the shed at the clear sky. The heavy rain earlier has purged the atmosphere, and the stars are a hundred thousand pinholes in the cloudless curtain of night. The metaphor of the stars representing the departed is too commonplace for you not to think of Mam. You pick a faint, light-blue glimmer beside the North Star. Not the North Star itself, the one next to it, twinkling from some unfathomable distance. That's her.*

*A lantern approaches. You sit up in the straw. It's not cold but Maggie shivers in her shawl. Without a word she kneels beside you and you reach for her. Your lips lock savagely, directly, violently. You move her onto her back, into your little straw bed, ignoring your aching ribs, and you grope stupidly at the cords attaching her stockings to her girdle. 'Let me,' she says as she helps you undo the knot. She lifts her hips from the straw and slips off the garment. You undo the buttons on your union suit, and as you make love, she holds you in her arms. Protecting you. Cherishing you. You hold each other all night.*

*'You have my heart, Victor. Take care with it,' she says as she slips away with the dawn.*

*   *   *

A cock wakes me. Inside my head a demon drummer thumps a painful rhythm. I'm in a large shed. God knows which. My back and legs itch against the hay that has been my bed and a thick old blanket is draped across me, keeping my naked body warm. My naked body, and the other one with which I'm entwined. I don't dare breathe let alone move. My suitcase is lying upside-down near the door. My uniform and my boots and my pants are strewn around the place. So too are the clothes of a woman. My first thought is of Maggie. But this isn't Maggie.

I think back. What time did the céilí end? Late anyway. I'd had a lot of poteen, but I do seem to remember talking to someone. TP McGahan, that's who, about politics. People were gathered around to listen. It was coming back to me. An interview for the paper. Not the best idea I ever had. Should be keeping a low profile. We talked about capital and labour and the exploitation of the working class. And religion. Oh yes, and religion. Cardinal Logue came up. Benedict might've got a touch too. People clapped. Some of them anyway. Sean Moriarty said I should be the first President of the Irish Republic because I had the sand to come out and say what needed to be said.

The woman's face is buried in my chest and thick hair is spread across it like black ivy. Damned if I can remember her name. Her body is a hot coal against mine. The wild one with the poteen. Dead ringer for Theda Bara. After the céilí Charlie tried to drag me to his house but I wanted more poteen and this girl had it. I remember Charlie and Turlough telling me I shouldn't be anywhere near her. They weren't at all diplomatic about it. Maggie must never ever know about this. Slowly, gingerly, I slip out from under the blanket. She stirs and sits up, her hair splayed in all directions. She smiles and I freeze. My clothes are just out of reach and I stand naked in the chilly morning air.

'Hello, soldier,' she says, a laugh woven into her odious voice. 'Looks like you're ready to go once more unto the breach.' I'm standing stiff as a beefeater. Mortified. Her opal eyes gleam. I pull on my trousers clumsily. I should say something.

'Once more unto the breach. You know Shakespeare?'

'I knew a man one time used to come out with all that shite.'

I button my shirt and summon the courage to look straight at her. There's a little roll in her eyes, as if they're not quite fixed properly in her head. She reaches out from under the blanket to her frock, rumpled and discarded on the ground, and takes out a packet of Gallaher's. She lights one and offers it to me. My head is thumping and my mouth is like a sewer, so I'm grateful for it. The first drag makes me feel a little better. 'I had a fine old time last night, Victor. A fine old time. You don't have to rush away so soon, do you? Pius won't even be awake yet. You know how he likes to sleep in.'

I keep dressing in silence.

'It's Ida, by the way.'

'I knew that. Of course I knew that.'

'Of course you did.'

I do up my top button and lift my suitcase. I suppose I have to say something before I can walk out. 'Ida, I don't remember much about what happened but I suppose something ... something of a physical nature has taken place between us. I'd just like to apologise for letting things get out of hand.'

She knows what I'm saying and I'm grateful she doesn't make me say it. They usually do, women. They push you all the way. As if they actually want to hear you say I wanted you last night but I don't want you now. And then you're the devil for saying such a thing. Why is that so terrible anyway? There was a snooty south-side girl I knew one time who said I was only after one thing, and it was true, but so was she. She wanted a husband. I only wanted her for one night, she wanted me for a lifetime; but I was the selfish one? Ida drags long and deep from her cigarette, exhales down her nostrils, runs her tongue along her lips. They're red as rosebuds. 'You love the schoolteacher,' she says.

'Ida, promise me you won't tell anyone about this.'

She gets up, lets the blanket fall to the ground, and she stands naked, shockingly, offensively naked in the morning chill, the shape of a cello, brazen as sin. Colour comes to her milky skin for the first time: murderous purple. She spits but it falls short at my feet. She lifts one of my boots and flings it at me. 'Victor fucking Lennon, the big fucken socialist hero, is too much of a snob to be seen with me, isn't that right?' she shrieks. 'Get out of here, you miserable bastard.' Happy to comply. I run out the door and out of earshot quick as I can.

Back outside again, I discover that Ida lives in the last house in the row at the top of the town; the end houses have bigger yards than the others and large sheds beside them. I have to walk past nearly every door in Madden, and I hope to God nobody sees me. Beside Ida's is Quinn's General Stores, Charlie's business and home. Directly across the street from Ida's is Moriarty's. Next to Moriarty's is the National School but it's not open yet. It's still very early, few people will be up, thank God. There won't have been anyone there late last night either. Nausea rises up in me at the thought of meeting Maggie now. Is there anything incriminating about my appearance? The suitcase and uniform show I haven't been home, but that doesn't prove anything.

As I walk down the muddy street between the houses, breathing deep, with each step I feel better. Nobody knows how I marked my first night home. The only ones who might are the lads, and I don't mind them knowing. Turlough and Sean are men of the world. So is Charlie. He's been in the war, for God's sake. Even if they do know anything, they'll keep their mouths shut. Deep breaths. I'd forgotten what the air without smog tastes like. I know I should be ashamed but I'm not. As long as no-one finds out, I've no regrets. My hurried clip slows to a stroll and I take the old place in. It hasn't changed. Only the red flags and bunting hung out in my honour tell me it isn't nineteen-ought-seven any more. But it feels different all the same. That's perspective, I suppose. I try and remember the names of the families who live behind each door as I pass by. Sweeney. The Fenian Roche. Kelly the gambler. Vallely. McCabe. Campbell. O'Kane. The other Murphys. McCann the baker. McKenna.

Gamble. Johnny Morrissey the drunk. Murphy. McDonagh the tinker. McGrath's post office. My mother used to remark on how the paint had been flaking off that door for years ('You'd think Sheila McGrath would get him to do something about it, it's showing up the whole street') and it seemed Jerry had finally gotten around to painting it a nice, bright red. Gallagher's, with the window that was always slightly open because Mrs Gallagher was forever complaining of being too warm, whether rain or shine, summer or winter, night or day. TP McGahan. Kate and John McDermott. I'm pleased with myself that I still know them all. I'm near the chapel, with its neatly tended graveyard and its limestone steeple spiralling skywards. Directly across is the Parochial Hall. Its doors are shut now: three inches of mahogany with straps and hinges of wrought iron. You have to respect doors like that. And sitting in front of them, staring at me from the Parochial Hall steps, is Benedict.

He's pretending to tie his shoelaces but I'm not fooled. I say hello as sweetly as I can and walk quickly past him. He'll wonder what I'm doing up and about at this hour, still in last night's clothes. None of his damn business. I feel his eyes on my back as I pass the barren, stony Poor Ground, and follow the road as it swings left at the top of the village, past the Parochial House, which stands at the bend. That high-ceilinged palace, with the front door, black and expensive like a Merrion Square door, with a big brass knocker that can be heard from down the street. Above the door is the high window of the priests' study where they sit, watching. When I was a child I believed the priest could see everything that happened in the parish from that window. Even secret things behind closed doors. Even as I got older and started to know better, when I would touch myself or sneak a drink or read a book I wasn't supposed to, it was hard to shake the thought that somehow, the priest knew.

I continue up the road a quarter mile till I reach the laneway from the road up to our house. It is overgrown so I pull out a long hazel wand from the bushes to start to hack my way through. It's an overreaction, the lane is not nearly so bad that it's actually impassable, but it has been neglected to the point where a dramatic gesture seems necessary. And the hazel wand makes a pleasing whooshing sound as I whip it through the air. A country boy knows the value of a good stick, and I haven't been a country boy in a long time.

I reach the yard at the top of the lane and see that the old place is worse than I'd feared. Nettles and thistles stand waist-high through the concrete. The house and outbuildings look like they're crumbling, with huge clumps of whitewash fallen from the walls and strewn around like debris. The paint on the doors and eaves is flaked away to nothing and the spars spike up through the threadbare thatch. In the byre, two cows stand ankle-deep in shite, lowing madly. I wonder if those two head of cattle are all are that are left. Beyond the house I glimpse a fraction of our land and see how the foliage has grown thick and wild with briars. The whole six hundred and twenty-seven acres will surely be as bad. I knock on the door. No answer. I open the latch. It's dark and damp and cold inside. A gust of wind hisses past as I enter. Everything here speaks of abandonment.

'Pius. Pius. It's Victor. Are you here?' I light a match and search in the back rooms. They're so quiet. I've only ever known them noisy. We used to sleep four to a bed but the beds are empty and they haven't been slept in for a long time. It's like the end of the world. I go back to the parlour and call out once more. The

71

windows are shuttered but there's enough light to reveal the grimy mustiness of the place. Bottles are strewn across the table, the chairs, the dresser, the floor. Some are empty, some half-empty. The hearth is an unmaintained mound of ash. Shotgun cartridges are scattered about the floor. The smell of the damp wracking the walls is nauseating and there's a profound cold in the room, like the walls themselves have forgotten they were ever warm. I open the curtains. Light splashes in and illuminates the horror. An empty poteen bottle and tumbler lie sideways on the floor behind the couch, and beside them is an apparently lifeless old man.

'Pius! Pius, wake up!'

I lift his limp body by the oxters, drag him onto the couch and slap him in the face. Nothing. I run outside and lower the bucket into the well. Back in the house, I fill the empty whiskey tumbler and pour the water over his lips. 'Come on now, Pius.' He splutters and coughs and jolts. At last he blinks, opens his eyes, blinks again like he doesn't trust what his eyes are seeing, and holds his hand over his face. He groans. He takes the water and gulps it voraciously.

'More.'

I refill the glass. He drinks quickly. 'That's lovely,' he says. Colour returns to his cheeks and he opens his eyes fully. This isn't the man I remember watching in the fields, thinking he was the strongest man in the whole world. Sixty-two is old in anyone's book but he looks much older.

I'm cold and tired and hungry and I want heat and comfort and a cup of tea so I pick up the brush and shovel by the hearth and set to work sweeping it out. I can feel him watching me from the sofa but I say nothing. I wouldn't know what to say. Better to work than to talk. He refills the glass and glugs it thirstily. When the hearth is cleaned out, I go outside to the woodpile and I'm surprised and pleased to find there's a bit of firewood and turf there. It looks like it's been here for quite some time, but it's chopped and seems dry. I fill my arms and go back inside. As I'm building the fire, Pius sits up.

'Did you get the train up from Dublin?' he says. I nod and grunt an affirmative. 'Many on it?'

'Not really.'

Do you have nothing else to say to me, old man? Shouldn't you be slaughtering a fatted calf, instead of asking about the traffic in Jerusalem?

'Sorry I wasn't at the dance. Was there many turned up?'

'Hundreds. They had bunting and red flags out for me and everything.'

'That bunting is for the footballers. They're playing Derrynoose in the final in a couple of weeks.'

Charlie said something about that all right, about how the Madden footballers are in the county final. Of course. Red gansies. 'I mean they had a big banner up for me in the Parochial Hall.' The wood is burning well and slowly catching with the turf. I'll get this fire going soon enough. 'Will they win the final?'

'Not at all. They're useless.'

The fire is starting to catch, the first bits of real heat are emanating from it. I leave it alone and hunt for the kettle to make a cup of tea. I find it, bizarrely, lying in a dark corner, beside a shotgun that's snapped in the middle with shells strewn around. I pocket the bullets, make sure the gun's empty, click it together and stand it in the corner. I fill the kettle and hang it above the fire, bring in the pail of milk, rinse two dusty cups and a teapot I find in the dresser, and make the tea. Pius takes the cup from me.

'What time did you come in last night?'

'Late enough.'

'I must've fell asleep in the chair here.' He drinks his tea and sets down the cup. Without a further word he gets up and walks out the door. I wait a moment to see will he come back in but when he doesn't, I follow. I reach the bottom of the lane and see him up ahead. He's almost at the village. I walk more quickly than him and close the gap, but I'm just passing the Parochial House as he's clambering clumsily over the wall into the Poor Ground. His eyes are trained on the ground, where the stones burst through the shallow soil. I stand atop the Poor Ground wall for a moment and watch as Pius stops at a little pile of stones and manoeuvres himself gingerly onto his knees. He clasps his hands together and bows his head. I hop down with a squelch and draw closer, past a few other little piles of stones scattered around. Pius's lips move silently. A hard and bitter wind whips in from the east.

'He wouldn't even let you put in a gravestone,' I say.

'I know the right spot.' Pius mumbles through the words he has come to say. He opens his eyes. 'Would you not say a prayer for your mother?'

'Ma's dead.'

He makes a sign of the cross, rises to his feet and takes a couple of steps back. He reaches inside his coat pocket, pulls out a tin hipflask and takes a swig. He offers it to me.

'I don't think you should be starting ...'

'God damn you, I said take a drink.'

I take the flask, unscrew the lid and, looking him in the eye, pour it out onto the stony ground. He lunges desperately to try and save the last few drops but he's a sozzled old man and he's too slow. He looks down at the little poteen puddle, more crest-fallen than a man with his own distillery at home need be. 'Why did you do that?' he hisses. He has hateful vengeance in his eyes, but I'm not a child any more and I'm not afraid of him.

'I'm home to save you.'

His expression shifts. Anger. Scorn. Mirth. Shame. He tries to speak but whatever is going on inside him, the words won't come. A long and violent exhalation is all he can manage. He looks broken-down, confused, bitter, old. He can't contend with the world swirling around him.

'We're going to fix up the house and get the land back to the way it should be. And there'll be no more drinking.'

Again his face shows a kaleidoscope of passion but again he settles on shame. 'I need it. It's for my condition. I have a terrible affliction without it. My hands shake something terrible and nothing else will stop them.' He turns his eyes to the ground. He looks so pathetic that, despite everything, I relent.

'I'll make you a deal. You can drink after dark, but by day, we work. No matter how bad you have the horrors.'

'All right, son.'

*   *   *

*It's drizzling and dark clouds hang overhead. You hop over the rickety wall of the Poor Ground and look for a relatively soft part among the stones. You pick a spot and thrust the spade into the soil, hoping it's virgin territory. Everyone knows the awful tales of accidental exhumations. Ordinarily the neighbours help in digging graves but not for a burial such as this. It's just you and your brothers. No-one even stops to offer condolences while you work. Best not to talk about such things. This is for family alone. Pius isn't here. He's been drinking poteen all night and he's lying unconscious at home. But Charlie comes. 'She was like a mother to me too,' he says. With nine men at work, the hole is soon finished.*

*Charlie waits with you by the graveside while your brothers go and get Pius from home and your mother from the wake house. She's wrapped in a brown blanket and they carry her on their shoulders. You go into the grave and they pass her down to you. You lay her gently on the earth and kiss her forehead before you get out of the hole. Then Maggie arrives, a black shawl draped over her head. She could be family too. You could make her a Lennon today if you wanted to. Your brothers heap soil on Deirdre while Pius watches silently, swaying in the breeze. He doesn't look at you, not at any stage. The clouds begin to spit, turning the fresh-dug earth to mud, and your brothers work quickly to get finished. There are no prayers over the grave. Pius won't allow it. Afterwards you stay until only you and Maggie are left.*

*'I'm getting the train this afternoon,' you tell her. 'Come with me. It doesn't matter where we go, let's just go.'*

*'I have a family, I can't just leave them. I have to stay here, Victor,' she says.*

*'You can't leave and I can't stay.'*

*'You could stay. You could stay if you wanted to.'*

\*   \*   \*

People would have seen the newspaper report. Stanislaus held it in his hand as he waited by the downstairs window of the Parochial House while Father Daly cranked the starting motor on his buggy. All but a few would have been shocked by it. Stanislaus had planned to devote his homily to the article, and to the disgraceful behaviour at the dance, but when he spotted Pius Lennon sitting alone in the pew, with no sign of his son in attendance, he decided to hold his peace. People would have noticed Victor's absence. If Victor thought he could inject atheism into the spiritual bloodstream of the parish, like he was some travesty of an evangelist, he misjudged the people of Madden. Stanislaus believed the best strategy was to allow Victor enough rope to hang himself.

The automobile coughed into life and as he hopped gleefully behind the steering column, Father Daly signalled to Stanislaus that they were ready to depart. Father Daly seemed to spend half his life poking around the engine trying to fix the latest malfunction in his disgustingly dirty and unreliable vehicle, and he had a devil of a time washing off the grime and oil from his hands – hands that were supposed to be worthy of handling the Blessed Eucharist! Stanislaus climbed into the vehicle. It was a crisp and clear spring day, it didn't look like rain, but still, it was a relief that the vehicle had a retractable canvas awning. Most of the ones Stanislaus had seen before didn't. He accepted Father Daly's offer of a blanket for his knees, to keep the cold off, but rejected a pair of goggles. Stanislaus had spoken to the curate before about the need for men with spiritual responsibilities to present themselves to the outside world appropriately, yet here was the young man wearing not only goggles but a leather jacket fastened with one of those hookless interlocking-teeth fasteners. Pearls before swine.

Every bump in the road felt like a kick up the backside. Stanislaus changed his mind about the goggles when he realised that the front window merely reduced the amount of flies and dirt rushing into his face, it did not prevent them entirely. He lurched violently in his seat as the uneven road delivered another kick, and told Father Daly to slow down. Stanislaus disliked automobiles as he disliked the general mania for the new. War always had the effect of speeding up the new. Automobiles. Moving pictures. Aeroplanes. Even telephones were becoming more common. He had read a report from America that they planned to read out news 'bulletins' in the future via radio waves, and they were working on mass-producing wireless sets small enough and cheap enough for people to have in their homes. This theme of mass access and participation seemed to be every-where, and Stanislaus was sure it had something to do with the Marxians. He did not look forward to the world the war would leave in its wake.

'At this speed we would cover almost thirty miles every hour. Every hour, mind you, road permitting,' Father Daly roared in triumph above the engine and the onrushing wind. Stanislaus had to admit these automobiles moved quickly. They were prob-ably about halfway to Armagh already. It was extraordinary that this could be achieved without the use of rail. Still, he felt sure the discomfort involved would ensure it stayed confined to a minority of enthusiasts.

He still had the *Armagh Guardian* in his hand. He looked at it again, for the same reason he couldn't help poking at mouth ulcers with his tongue, and flicked inside to the main news story, set between the ads for Boys' Whitby Suits, Beecham's Pills, and below GW Megahey of Scotch Street's promise of an 'Extraordinary Cheap Sale, with Bargains For All and Boots, Shoes and Slippers at Ridiculously Low Prices'.

# COMMUNIST SOWS DISCORD

## Took Part in Sinn Fein Rebellion

### RETURN OF VICTOR LENNON DIVIDES MADDEN

#### Controversial Opinions on Church and War Effort

##### CELEBRATION ENJOYED BY ALL, OTHERWISE

OPINION is divided in the village of Madden on the homecoming of Mr Victor Lennon, who was recently released from the camp for Irish prisoners at Frongoch in Wales. During a dance held in his honour at Madden Parochial Hall, Lennon was heard to criticise the Roman Church and Cardinal Logue, as well as make seditious and wholly unpatriotic remarks.

#### KNOWN FELON

Mr Lennon has been domiciled in Dublin for several years past and was associated with the Communist wing of the outbreak of anarchy last April. His return to Madden was attended with great ceremony but his speech, made while clearly under the influence of intoxicants, caused great consternation. The following is an extract.

#### MISREPRESENTS CONDITION OF WORKERS

'Workers in Armagh face the same humiliating, inhuman conditions as everywhere else, and we will not have justice until that exploitation is at an end. A foreign nation denies us control of our destiny. Empires are rapacious and capitalistic, so neither socialism nor the justice manifest in socialism can be achieved as a colony of empire. That is why we proclaimed the Republic on Easter Monday, but the Republic is not an end in itself. Irish capitalists are no different than English ones. The lockout taught us that.

#### ARGUMENT WITH ECONOMICS, NOT EMPIRE

'The Republic is a necessary first step. We must overthrow the institutions of empire and build institutions of the people. Unions. Co-operatives. Pearse said Ireland unfree would never be at peace, but an Ireland ruled by capital shall always be unfree, no matter where the parliament sits. It is firstly capital that enslaves us. Peace will come when Ireland is sovereign and socialist, and when the people have ownership of the means of production.

#### SEES ALMOST EVERYONE AS ENEMY

'We must defeat the empire, but the empire has no monopoly on tyranny. We must overcome the reactionaries and counter-revolutionaries, the so-called reformers and crypto-capitalists who claim to want change but in fact buttress the status quo. Our political process is the property of spineless collaborators like Redmond. Our economy is run by and for slavers like William Martin *(expletive)* Murphy. Our society is dominated by churches more insidious and corrupting than any empire. Comrade Connolly died to ensure a dynamic social programme at the core of our revolution and Comrade Lenin is continuing that work in Petersburg *(sic)* as we speak. Without that social programme, so-called Irish freedom isn't worth a Dublin-minted farthing.'

#### CONSTERNATION WIDESPREAD

Reaction to Mr Lennon's speech was mixed. There were cries of disgust but also shouts of 'Hear Hear!' from the large crowd in attendance. Mr Lennon, 27, is a former docker and tram driver. He was sacked for his part in the failed Larkinite strike of four years ago, and is believed to have made his living as a trade union organiser and journalist since then. He attended Madden National School before leaving for Dublin, where he is not known to have furthered his studies. He was the only speaker at the event in Madden, which was a social gathering rather than a political meeting, despite Mr Lennon's unfortunate outburst. Otherwise the event was a great success and enjoyed by all. Mr Ignatius Harney, 35, won a week's supply of mincemeat from Sweeney's Butchers of Ballymacnab in the raffle, organised in aid of Madden GAA.

'Apparently Victor said far worse things that they couldn't print,' said Father Daly.

'What they did print is quite bad enough.'

'Victor must have been very drunk, to say some of those things.'

'In vino veritas. From the looks of this article, he was eloquent as a serpent.'

'I think TP may have tidied it up a bit.'

'Some of the people applauded him,' Stanislaus scolded. He was perturbed by Father Daly's sanguinity.

The car hit a bump in the road and Stanislaus cursed the pain to his poor back. Cars like this cost a hundred pounds or more, a sum that could be gathered from a priest's salary only after years of sacrifice and prudence. For Tim Daly, though, the car had been, like his youthful handsomeness, easygoing manner and seminary education, a gift from his parents. The Dalys were well-connected businesspeople who rejoiced in their son's entrance to the priesthood. Tim's academic ability too had been a gift. Success for him had required little of the character-building labour that leads to excellence. Stanislaus had known many fellows like him; fellows who had never known sacrifice or hunger or failure. Life was easy for them, and this ease led to complacent liberalism. They could no more grasp the danger of a Victor Lennon than lemmings grasp the oblivion beyond the cliff. 'This is no time to play devil's advocate, this is not a seminary game. We must find out who supports him. We need to know who's against us,' said Stanislaus.

'Madden people aren't communists, Your Grace,' Father Daly countered. 'If Victor waves a green flag they'll salute him. If he waves a red flag, they'll just be confused. To them he's an Irishman striking a blow against the English, that's all.'

Father Daly may have been right. Mrs Geraghty was usually a good barometer for how people were feeling – the decent people at any rate – and she had been appalled by what Victor had said. That kind of talk might find an audience in the slums of Dublin, but these left-wing fellows he admired so much spoke of collect-ivising agriculture. That meant the government taking the land off the people, and that conjured all-too-recent nightmares in Irish country people.

The two great spires of the cathedral, visible for miles around, were close now. They had covered five miles in little more than twenty-five minutes. Cold, dirty, uncomfortable though it was, the motorcar was undeniably fast. But when they left the macad-amised road and hit the cobbled streets of the city, the car bumped and rocked and jiggled so much that Stanislaus consid-ered walking the rest of the way. Riding these contraptions on cobblestones was impossibly punishing. Another reason they wouldn't catch on. At least the streets were quiet – people would have laughed their heads off at the two goggled priests bouncing around like unfastened cargo in their spluttering, juddering buggy. The motorcar chugged up Irish Street, losing speed with every yard but just making the summit without rolling back-wards. They passed the Protestant cathedral, an unassuming, ancient building that they too named for St Patrick, before free-wheeling with a merciless velocity down the hill to the Shambles yard. The car cornered like a dreadnought around the dogleg of Edward Street and Father Daly brought it to a full stop at the gates of the Catholic St Patrick's Cathedral. He put the car in reverse with a guttural clanking of the gears and manoeuvred it to point away from the gate and the cinder path that snaked up the hill to the cathedral. Navigating out the egg-shaped window sewn into the back of the canvas awning, he let go of the hand-brake and reversed uphill in a whirl of dust.

'What on earth are you doing?' asked Stanislaus.

'The fuel is in a tank at the back but the engine is in the front. The fuels flows forward to the engine by gravity, but I'm low on fuel, so gravity doesn't get the job done. If you're low on fuel, you have to reverse uphill.'

'Silly contraptions.'

Four great granite institutions bestrode the hill like a citadel: St Patrick's Cathedral; St Patrick's College and Junior Seminary; the Synod Hall; and Ara Coeli, official residence of the Cardinal. Stanislaus was surprised to see motorcars parked everywhere, most of them, like Father Daly's, the black, Henry Ford variety they made in Cork. Good thing he'd arrived in one after all. He saw an elderly infirm-looking man being helped from a car by two young curates. It was Johnny Mangan, an old friend. He was four years younger than Stanislaus and had always been the picture of health, but the years did terrible things. Stanislaus hopped out and moved across the yard with sprightly steps. He put his hand on Johnny's shoulder, as much to help him as to greet him.

'Ah, Stanislaus, 'tis great to see you, boy. It must be twenty years.'

'Neither of us was in purple, at any rate. You haven't come all the way from Killarney in the motorcar, have you?'

'God Almighty no, that would have killed me. We were met at the station by that contraption.'

'Long old journey.'

'To tell you the truth, Stanislaus, the doctor said I was mad to come at all. But when the boss calls, you have to come running, don't you? What's it all about anyway? I felt sure you'd be the man would know.'

'I haven't been in the know for a long time now, Johnny.'

'Oh, of course.' He paused. 'It's fine and well you're looking now though. You're well off out of it. Heading up a Diocese, it's all politics.'

'It is nice to have time to spend with my books.'

'That last paper of yours was something else. You always know how to stick it into the liberals.'

They went in the massive mahogany doors of the Synod Hall. The insistent rumble of talk and chatter tumbled from the Synod chamber down the vast, sweeping staircase, and Stanislaus and Johnny started up the mountain of stairs towards it. 'Take my arm, Your Grace,' said Johnny's young curate. Stanislaus informed Father Daly with a scowl that he needed no help in ascending this staircase that he had ascended a thousand times before, and started to move up, passing beneath the portraits of the archbishops. St Patrick himself. St Malachy half a millennium later. The Penal-era martyrs another half-millennium after that. They stopped on the landing halfway up for a breather, Johnny needed to sit down on the stairs a moment, beneath the bust of Blessed Oliver Plunkett. Stanislaus recalled once tearing strips off a young priest who had joked that it was a funny thing to commemorate someone who had been beheaded with a bust. Below, two men deep in conversation were starting up the stairs. Though he had not met either personally, Stanislaus recognised them as the new Bishop of Clogher, Patrick McKenna, and Edward Mulhern, recently installed as Bishop of Dromore. They were impossibly young-looking, neither man looked fifty, and they bounded up the stairs. Johnny greeted them as they arrived on the landing. 'You know Ned and Pat, don't you, Stanislaus?' he said.

'Bishop Benedict, isn't it? Pleasure to meet you,' said Mulhern, offering his hand.

'Congratulations on your elevation. If you do half as well as Henry O'Neill, Dromore will be in good hands,' Stanislaus said.

Dromore was a proper Diocese, not a titular, semi-mythical one. Not like Stanislaus's well-known Episcopal See of Parthenia. Parthenia. A fifth-century outpost in pre-Islamic Algeria from which Christendom had been driven, not by the Mohammedans but the sands of the Sahara. Mick Logue had recommended it to Stanislaus, and Stanislaus had often wondered if it had been his intention to mock. He wondered if young Mulhern – Ned, apparently – knew that Henry O'Neill had been a surprise appointment to Dromore, that everyone had said Stanislaus's name was carved on it. He probably did. Stanislaus had a mortifying memory of taking a day trip to Newry Cathedral, just to acquaint himself with his new surroundings. But Henry O'Neill had been given the nod because Henry O'Neill was younger. That was the Cardinal's explanation. Now young Henry O'Neill was dead.

'You've come a long way, Bishop Mangan,' said McKenna.

'Two days. Seven changes, sixty-one stops, and I still don't know what this is all about,' Johnny replied.

'I heard that it might be something to do with …' Ned began, but stopped when he saw Pat O'Donnell and Charlie McHugh, Bishops of Raphoe and Derry respectively, coming up the stairs behind them.

'Lads, you can't block the landing like this. Let's get a move on here. You're the last to arrive and the Cardinal will be here in a minute,' said O'Donnell. O'Donnell was Logue's favourite, it was no secret he was being groomed for the big job. Everyone ascended in silence like scolded schoolboys. At the top of the stairs Stanislaus noticed Johnny Mangan was looking unwell. He put his hand on Johnny's shoulder. 'Are you feeling all right there, Johnny?'

'A hundred per cent, boy,' he said, but his creaking and wheezing gave the lie to the brave face.

'Hurry up there, we can't keep the Cardinal waiting,' said O'Donnell.

'You know, there was a time in this country when priests were expected to show a bit of courtesy and compassion,' Stanislaus snapped. O'Donnell's first reaction seemed to be irritation, but he buttoned his lip and relented. Stanislaus and Johnny went inside when they were good and ready.

The wide spaces, stained-glass windows and high, baroque ceiling of the great Synod Hall reverberated with the sound of important men used to hearing their own voices and unused to being challenged for attention. Perhaps a hundred old acquaintances, friends and colleagues greeted one another with excitement and curiosity. Chairs were set out in neat rows but no-one was sitting down yet. Deans, canons and monsignors were present, but only bishops wore purple sashes around their waists and Stanislaus had worn his for the occasion. Ireland had forty-nine bishops, from archbishops to ordinaries, auxiliaries, co-adjutors, titulars and bishops emeritus, and it seemed a great many of them were present. Stanislaus was disturbed to see several men in purple that he didn't know.

Once, it had been his business to know men such as these inside-out.

Everyone sat as the Cardinal entered. He wore full scarlet regalia, even his galero, and nodded here and there to familiar faces as he made his way forward. He did not see Stanislaus as he passed. The Cathedra had been removed from the sanctuary to the Synod Hall, and he sat in it now, facing towards the assembly. The ranks of black and purple sat in hushed deference for the only man in Ireland entitled to wear red.

'I thank God to see so many old friends and brothers in Christ. I thank you all for gathering here today,' he began. 'Recently I joined with the other cardinals and the Holy Father in Rome to discuss the crisis in Russia, of which you will all be aware. Bolshevist victory there now seems certain, and therefore Russian withdrawal from the war is inevitable. But worse: the Bolshevists propose to make Russia atheist. They aim to wreak holocaust on the Faith, and they would seek to spread this evil message world-wide. It is the view of the Holy Father that this represents a threat to mankind's very spiritual essence. This evil ideology is the most grave threat the Faith has faced since Luther. Furthermore, it is the opinion of the Holy Father and the College of Cardinals that this country, Ireland, is the most likely to be next.'

Around the room a hubbub grew up and took a moment or two to die down. Mick could play an audience like a fiddle, and he knew it. Even in the Conclave Mick Logue probably regarded himself as the smartest man in the room. He might even have been right. He continued in a sonorous register spiced with the right amount of piquancy.

'The Holy Father wants to know what is going on in Ireland. The country is overrun with subversive groups. Some are openly revolutionist, others like the so-called trade unions or the Gaelic Athletic Association operate under more benign guises. Men like Lenin, Trotsky and Zinoviev are merely the Russian answer to James Larkin and James Connolly – of whom people speak blasphemously as a martyr. Everywhere in our country, dangerous men meet in shadows and plan our destruction. We are the front line in a war for the souls of man.'

The Cardinal signalled to O'Donnell, who handed him a newspaper which he held up for all to see. The blood drained from Stanislaus's face. It was the *Armagh Guardian*.

'Here is a story about a parish very near here. A criminal using Church property to deliver a blasphemous oration. This is a self-confessed communist and atheist, yet the people of his parish revere him because he took up arms against the English. Now, our day of reckoning with England will come soon, and whether it brings Home Rule or something else, men of the worst calibre are readying themselves to seize the spoils. In every parish of every Diocese lurk men as dangerous as this fellow, men who will attempt to cause ferment, to corrupt the people and turn Ireland into a colony of Moscow. They will prey on weak opponents such as lazy or careless priests.'

The Cardinal was staring straight at Stanislaus, and he felt the stares of others bore holes in him. He wanted to run away as fast as his aged legs would carry him, but he held up his head and tried not to flinch from the Cardinal's stare. If Mick was going to knife him in the guts, Stanislaus would make him look him in the eye as he did so.

'This shabby episode,' the Cardinal said, slapping his hand disgustedly against the newspaper, 'shows that even the finest can fail in his duty.'

As soon as the Cardinal had finished his oration, Stanislaus fled, speaking to no-one as he left. He was glad Father Daly had the wit not to speak throughout the entire journey home. Peers and colleagues throughout the country would swap stories of this humiliation. He cursed Father Daly's softness in allowing the use of the Parochial Hall in the first place. But the ultimate responsibility was his. Who had allowed the event to go ahead? Stanislaus Benedict. Because people would have been annoyed if he hadn't. Because it would have been unpopular. Weakness borne of vanity. He wouldn't make a mistake like that again. What people wanted, their daily, petty desires, their transient emotions, would not be his concern ever again.

\* \* \*

*You have a pocket full of money when you arrive. Your brothers' guilt in pounds, shillings and pence. It's enough to pay for digs at a nice south-side boarding house for a few weeks. You only cross to the north side on Sunday mornings to attend mass at Marlborough Street. That's the mass the respectable Dublin Catholics go to. The businessmen, the professionals, the Irish Party fellows. You try to fall in with some of them. Maybe someone will offer you a nice office job or something like that.*

*Soon the money runs out. You take a tiny room in a tenement in Monto and get a job shovelling coal off the boat for three measly shillings a day. You step over men lying dead drunk in the street while youngsters with no shoes steal from their pockets. Women hang out of windows with their bosoms hanging out of their blouses. Soldiers liquored up and looking for something to rut or to kill or both run amok every night. You didn't know Christian people could live like this. You still go to mass at Marlborough Street and hold off as long as you can before you pawn the good suit. Your last hope of a ticket out of here. But eventually it goes too. Hunger will make a man forgo even pride.*

*What's so special about these hateful rich bastards anyway? They talk about working people like a sub-species in need of extermination. One fat, obnoxious fellow says the Monto prostitutes should be flogged on a weekly basis. 'That'll keep them off their backs.' They all laugh. In Monto they'll knife you in the guts for a shilling, but only because they want the shilling. They're not like these people with their tailored suits and their fancy ways. These people* hate *like you've never seen.*

\* \* \*

Pius always did have an aptitude for business. He's distilling poteen by the drum-load because, he says, it's as easy to make a gallon as a pint, so why not make a gallon? He sells it because people want to buy it and it'd be unneighbourly to say no. He's not interested in making money, since this is not a business but a long-drawn-out suicide, and his prices reflect that fact. Now it's not economic for anyone else in Madden to even bother distilling their own, so they don't. Without even trying, he has built up a poteen trust, and though he only wants to drink himself to oblivion, he has made a stack of money. Some people just have the knack, I suppose. And because he spends virtually nothing, he has a bag full of cash under his bed, not so much saved as taken out of circulation. All this on top of the fact that he was a rich man to begin with.

The work starts with him. Get him shaved and bathed, get his clothes washed and his boots repaired, so he's looking something like a human being again. We give the house a rudimentary clean-up, and after I've been home a few days, we take a fistful of cash down to Quinn's General Stores in the village. Charlie is leaning across the counter studying a ledger with pencil in hand. He greets us with a cheerful shop face. His hair is centred and slicked with a severity that attests to the seriousness of the man. Crisp shirt, starched white collar, middling-expensive watch hanging from his waistcoat pocket. Every inch the prosperous businessman. He could be a Presbyterian. It's strange to think that the shop is Charlie's, though apparently he's owned it a few years now, since his old man, always a corpulent ball of stuffed arteries, keeled over and died of an exhausted heart. Charlie was left with the handsome property, the well-stocked shop, the thriving business. A handy, bourgeois living for the rest of his days. I explain that Pius and I are trying to get our property back to the way it was before. He takes a ring-bound notebook from the counter and the pencil from behind his ear, licks the lead and tells us we'll need scythes, yard brushes, paint brushes, paint, tar, hammers, hatchets, tin for the new byre roof, mops, saws, nails, sanders, planks and beams, turpentine and soap and bleach and whitewash and a lot more besides. 'That should be enough to get you started anyway. Don't worry, I'll do you a deal.'

Pius and I push two new wheelbarrows full of items we've bought, up the road home, and I think about the article in the paper about me. Not a bad article. The compelling political arguments shone through, despite TP McGahan's best efforts to stitch me up. I wonder has Maggie read it yet. I wonder what she thinks. I'm not ready to face Maggie yet, not after what I did. And God forbid I should see Ida.

Over the next while Pius and I fall into the habit of rising with the sun and working long days. There's a lot of work to be done and there's nothing else for it but to get stuck in. We start indoors, scrubbing the walls and repairing beds, chairs, dressers and tables. Room by room, the old place starts to look halfway presentable. Pius mostly sticks to our agreement to wait for nightfall before starting to drink, or at least makes an effort to hide his daylight drinking from me. Some days he's violently distressed by the thirst and asks the time incessantly, as if willing the sun to go down. On those days I turn a blind eye though I can see the hipflask in his trousers and the redness in his eyes. Other days he's fine and needs only to be kept busy. You can't stop a man from drinking, you can only help him to function regardless. So we only talk about the jobs in hand, nothing else. Certainly not the past, thank God. I think we're both relieved about that.

We hire Turlough and Sean to help out, and they're glad of the work. They whitewash the walls of the house and the outbuildings while we weed and sweep out the yard. We trim the laneway while they mend the fences, or replace the ones that can't be mended. They take some of Pius's cash into Armagh on market day and buy two dozen head of cattle while we nurse the few remaining cattle back to health with regular milking, feeding and grazing. The herd lows curiously from the field as they watch us transform their dingy dungeon into a proper cowshed. Sean and Turlough repair the trap, rescuing it from rust and ruin, and negotiate the purchase of a horse for us. They hire in lots of lads from across the parish to work on the outlying acres of our land. I don't know how they're out of work. They're strong and doughty as horses and are able to do any job that needs doing. It's a treat to watch them work. There's plenty of money in farming. With all the young, able-bodied men in trenches or graves, the farmers of Ireland are feeding the Empire. That's why the British haven't imposed conscription here yet. But Sean just says: 'We're no farmers.'

'What about the factories across the water then? They're full of women. They're crying out for men. Would you go over to England?'

'They'd conscript us if we went across, and we're not going to France to fight for that syphilitic fucking king and his butcher's apron,' says Turlough. 'Not after what you lads did in Easter Week. Faugh-a-Ballagh my arse.' He hawks up and spits.

'Somewhere else?'

'They won't let men of military age emigrate for the duration so we're stuck here, us and thousands like us, scrabbling around for the same few jobs.'

'The slim pickings of the rural proletariat,' I say.

'But as soon as the war's over, America here we come.'

'There's still the land, though. There's work to be had in Ireland on the land,' I persist.

'Like he says …'

'We're no farmers.'

It's a pity to see two men with the muscles of Clydesdale stallions but the sense of thick-skulled mules. They'll do what they're told, and they'll do it better than anyone, but they have no independent thought beyond stubbornness. Turlough has a bit of shrewdness, I suppose, and he sometimes asks about politics, but all Sean's interested in is football, and whether I'll turn out for Madden in the county final. Still, they seem willing to do whatever I tell them. They finish the day felling a copse of small trees and helping Pius and I chop up wood for the winter.

Later, Pius sips from a large glass as we roast ourselves by the hearth. 'All the Moriartys were always great workers. Their father, God rest him, could work with anything, wood, tin, thatch, you name it,' he says.

I hold a piece of bread on the end of a toasting fork and look to the roof. There's more work there. All the whitewash in the world can't hide the dampness in the walls: the ridges, the gables and all around the chimney is decayed past the point where local repairs will suffice. There are tarry brown stains at the top of the walls, proof that our problem is that there is water in the dunnish, long-past-useful thatch. The roof rafters are sitting in pools of water atop the walls, and the whole thing will collapse if left indefinitely. Pius must know this, but I don't suppose he has cared before now. I watch his head lurch forward, asleep, and see in his slumbering face spots of scarlet ruddiness materialising there. Chopping the wood earlier reminded me of how, as a child, I used to watch him work the axe. He seemed a gigantic figure then, wreaking violence on the huge logs and splintering them with a power and technique that, to my childish eyes, was indistinguishable from the superhuman. Despite all the drinking, he's still a strong man and I think he's getting stronger every day. Our labour is doing for Pius what the roaring fire before us is doing for the house, what God's breath did for Adam in that old bedtime story.

\*   \*   \*

When I wake the next morning it's still dark but the dawn isn't far off. Maggie and I used to go up to the lake every Saturday morning, almost religiously, and I'm dying to know whether she still keeps to our old routine. This is the third Saturday since I've been home, and I can't help but wonder whether she has been up there for the past two Saturdays, waiting in hope that I might appear. I dress and wash and comb my hair, I pick up the only reading material I can find – the *Picturegoer* from Phil Shanahan's – and head out into the direction of the rising sun. All the doors in Madden are still closed, which suits me fine as I don't want to see anyone. I reach the top of the street, I'm passing the Harte household, I've almost made it … The door opens. Ida appears in the doorway in her nightdress and untied dressing gown. She's holding a broom, as if she's just out to sweep her front step, but her eyes, sparkling crazily like diamonds rough in the mine, give her away. She has caught me. 'You've been keeping a low profile,' she says, 'I wasn't sure you were still about. Or maybe you're just avoiding me.'

'Busy, that's all,' I say, not stopping.

'Don't worry, I didn't tell anybody,' she calls after me. I glance around surreptitiously, in case anyone has overheard. Ida pulls her dressing gown tight around herself and steals up to me, conspiratorially close. 'There's a lantern in the window of my shed. If ever you feel lonely, you light that lantern and I'll keep you company,' she says.

I turn away from her. God knows I don't judge whores for the way they eke out a living, but Ida Harte is appalling. There's really no call for that kind of wantonness. Yet I can't help the fleeting images that flicker in my mind like a cinematograph, of those black-as-night eyes laughing at my foolishness. She should learn some small degree of reticence, she hasn't the slightest bit and it just isn't ladylike. As I walk, I have to put my hand into my pocket to fix myself. She really is the most distressing woman.

It's a couple of miles to the lake, which was my favourite place once. As I walk out the road, I think of the last time I walked it, all those years ago. I remember asking everyone I met along the way whether they had seen my ma. Aye, she went that way, they said, she doesn't look well, they said. She's in her dressing gown, they said, still in her slippers. Just five minutes ago. Straight up the road there. Towards the lake.

I reach my old spot, where low-hanging branches form a little canopy over the water's edge. I sit on the boulder there and listen to the waves. Someone told me one time that the sound of the water is the only thing a man can listen to forever without going insane. Testing out that theory, listening to this sound forever, is not the most unappealing idea I've ever heard. I used to spend endless hours here, skimming stones or vainly attempting to catch fish with a hazel wand, string and a bent nail. One day, I suppose we were about thirteen or so, Maggie showed me her father's copy of *Candide* (Dr Cavanagh was the sort of Catholic who reckoned any book on the Index had to be worth a look) and she was terrified of being caught with it, so I took her here, to my special place by the water. Shaded from the rain, we huddled together and read the book, our noses almost touching over the illicit pages. Maggie read faster and was forever chastising me as she waited at the end of each page. We became avid in our reading. If it was forbidden, we wanted it. We read whenever the chance arose, but always, always, we spent our Saturday mornings together up here, lying side by side, devouring the most corrupting material we could get our hands on. Why'd it have to be here my ma came? I wish I could sit here and think only of kissing Maggie's lips, but I can't. The good memories are corrupted. *What are you doing here, Ma, you shouldn't be out of the house. Victor, son, life is in the letting go. Life is in the letting go.*

I skim stones off the surface of the lake for perhaps an hour or more, all the while wondering whether she will come, until I see in the distance a figure approaching, growing larger. She's tall and willowy, quick but graceful, thrillingly Maggie, my own Maggie. I knew she would come, I just knew it. She wears a heavy black dress and a white blouse and a dark red shawl. When she gets close she looks slightly vexed, perhaps to see me. I point at the newspaper she's carrying under her arm. 'Why are you reading a paper that's two weeks old?' I say. She unfolds the broadsheet and reveals a tattered, dog-eared copy of *The Count of Monte Cristo* hidden inside. 'I haven't read that one.'

'You wouldn't like it,' she says, 'far too bourgeois for the big socialist.'

'Maybe you'll let me read along?'

'You're too slow.' She concedes a half-smile.

'Sure I saw the moving picture of it anyway.' I hold up the *Picturegoer*, the circular imprint of a whiskey glass haloing Kitty Gordon, and she reaches for it with zeal. She can't hide her interest, and she accidentally drops *The Count of Monte Cristo*. Fussily she picks it up again, but the pictures and stories of film stars have her attention. She flicks through the pages as I rise from the rock. 'Kitty Gordon isn't my favourite, to be honest. She's no Mildred Harris. No Florence La Badie.'

'Have you been to the pictures?'

'Hundreds of times.'

'What are they like?'

'Like magic.'

Her hair is rich and arranged in ringlets of the most time-consuming sort. You can see the character in a woman of such elaborate appearance. Her skin is soft caramel and I want to know if it tastes as good as it looks. The nape of her graceful neck nearly has me believing in God. When I look at her I want to kill something, but at the same time the sight of her siphons the heat from my veins. That doesn't make sense, I know, it's a contradiction, but there it is. I want to tell her that I've dreamed of her every night since I can remember.

'I haven't seen you around lately,' she says.

'I know. It's just, Pius and everything, I mean, things are bad. But I just wanted to say to you, I'm sorry. I'm sorry for everything.'

She doesn't look up from the magazine but I can tell she's not reading it. She flicks the page, flicks again.

'I hear there's a picture palace just opened up in Armagh. Maybe we could go together some night?' I say.

Something seems to snap. She stands up and throws the magazine at me. She slaps me in the chest again and again. 'Who the hell do you think you are?' she demands. She makes to walk away but I seize her arms by the elbows and hold her tightly. She's defiant, she wants to go, but I'm never letting her go. Our eyes wrestle and her lips purse, the colour of blood and consistency of granite, but in the end, her ice-hard stare is thawed by a hot, salty tear.

She yields.

I envelop her safely in my arms, protecting her from the salt wind that whips off the water. She buries her face in my chest and her shoulders jolt until eventually, sniffling, she breaks away, steps back and straightens her skirt. She lifts her hand to my eyebrow and touches the weak skin softly. She looks at me with great tenderness.

'You need to get this sorted out once and for all,' she says.

I nod.

'I'm sure you won't thank me, but I pray for you, you know. All the time, I pray for you.'

'I do thank you.'

\*   \*   \*

A priest's hold over his people was always tenuous, however it might seem from the outside. Stanislaus opened the parish ledger and copied in longhand the names of the two hundred and sixteen people of more than fourteen years of age in his pastoral care. Beside each he placed a tick for those he could definitely trust, an X for those he could not, and a question mark for those he wasn't sure about. It was a devil of a split. He banked eighty-seven as solid Christians; honest, hard-working people of faith who appreciated all the Church had done and whose loyalty and deference could be relied upon. He put fifty-four names on the rogue list. They weren't atheists – there were no atheists in Madden, everyone attended mass – but they were insubstantial people whose wont was to latch onto any fashion of radicalism that laid blame for their own failures and shortcomings else-where. People like the Moriartys. He put seventy-two names on the undecided list. They were the small-holders who filled the pews but contributed little else to the parish. People for whom newspapers were bulletin boards containing commodity prices and train timetables rather than public conversation. They would bend with the prevailing wind, seeing little distinction in which direction that wind might come from. It struck Stanislaus as unfitting that such disinterested, uninterested people should be the deciding constituency in any struggle. All politics, Johnny Mangan had said of the bishopric. Maybe it was better after all to spend the winter of his life in the calm certitude of theology than the world of men and their grasping.

Three names Stanislaus set aside. First was Pius Lennon. It seemed Pius and Victor were working hard to restore the Lennon land, and Stanislaus supposed this was a good thing, but any improvement in the father's wretchedness was overshadowed by the son, hiding out and biding his time like some rapparee. Ordinarily Pius could be assumed to be the most reliable of men, his loyalty to the Church verging on the desperate, but Victor was his son and that placed him outside any calculation Stanislaus could make.

Second was Charlie Quinn. He was Victor's friend, but the Quinns had always been solid businesspeople who donated generously to the Church. Unusually, Charlie was an only child – his young mother having died giving birth to him – and since his father's passing he had sought in the Church what others found automatically in family. He chewed his pencil before he decided to add Charlie's name to the trustworthy list. It was important to recognise friends, and Charlie would be a good ally to cultivate. Support from the substantial people was sure to beget further support.

Third was Margaret Cavanagh.

Stanislaus watched the schoolyard from his window. Girls with ribbons or ringlets in their hair, uniformed in smocks and dark dresses billowing in the wind, watched aloof and unimpressed as red-faced, knee-grazed boys in knickerbockers and jerseys ran frantically after a lump of coal doubling as a football. It was pleasing how few children were barefoot nowadays – how painful it had been, he recalled, to kick coal in bare feet! Miss Cavanagh in white blouse and long black skirt opened the school door and clanged the hand-bell. Upon hearing the bell the children lined up with impressive discipline and Miss Cavanagh shepherded them inside. Children from the better-off families handed her coins but most threw coal or turf into the pile by the door. A couple of children brought water from the well at the side of the school, while the last handful of children picked fuel from the pile and carried it inside. Stanislaus watched the empty yard till wisps of smoke slithered from the chimney, and with the lesson presumably begun, he strolled towards the schoolhouse.

It really had been too long since Stanislaus had sat in on a lesson. He was one of the commissioners appointed by the county council to govern the school. Strictly speaking, six commissioners took charge of the three National Schools in the area – three clergy and three laymen – but in practice, C of I children went to Milford, the Presbyterians had Aghavilly and Madden was for Catholics. Stanislaus, Reverend Bell and Reverend Armstrong, the three clerical commissioners, were the very best of colleagues, and never interfered in each other's business. Stanislaus's lay counterpart had been Dr Cavanagh, but even several years after his death his replacement had yet to be named. Stanislaus had appointed his daughter as schoolteacher out of pity for her then-invalid father, and she had proven an excellent teacher, but now that very excellence weighed against

her. The other schoolmaster, Leonard Mallon, was an old-fashioned, rote-heavy plodder; a nineties relic who would never have
got his start nowadays, when teachers were expected to understand what they were drilling into children. Mallon was no agent
of radicalism. He was no agent of anything. It would be safer if
all teachers were like him.

Stanislaus straightened his cassock, overcoat and hat, and
lightly lifted the latch. Miss Cavanagh was near the back of the
classroom with a textbook in her hand, far from her desk by the
fireplace. What on earth she was doing all the way back there?

'Good morning, Your Grace. Children, say Good Morning to
Bishop Benedict,' she commanded.

'Good morning, Bishop Benedict,' they incanted.

'Miss Cavanagh. I thought I might sit in on the class and see
how you're all getting on.'

'Always a pleasure to have you, Your Grace,' she said sunnily,
and with a swish of her skirt she turned to a boy at the back of
the class and instructed him to move, so as to make room. The
boy took his copybook and writing materials to the other side of
the room, leaving a tiny space between a young girl with her
wool and needles out for her knitting work, and an older boy
with copybook and pen in hand, who seemed to be trying to
look irreproachably busy. Stanislaus's knees rubbed against the
underside of the desk. The overcrowding was worse than he had
realised. People were always complaining that there were too
many pupils for such a small school. Some people had even
suggested sending some of the children to the other schools –
the Protestant schools – where they had spare capacity. He
looked up at the blackboard, decorated with Latin verbs on one
side and times tables on the other. Usually the problem of

overcrowding was alleviated by the fact that on a given day you could expect a third of pupils wouldn't turn up, but, problematically, Miss Cavanagh seemed to have a very high attendance rate. Still, it was better for them to be here than outside, meeting adulthood too early in the fields or, like those cursed to live in cities, up chimneys.

'What lesson have I interrupted, Miss Cavanagh?' Stanislaus asked.

'The younger girls are knitting, the younger boys are doing free-hand drawing,' she said, pointing to a huge green map of Ireland with the place names in Irish. Stanislaus could have sworn there had been a map of the Empire there previously. 'I'm leading the older pupils in dictation,' Miss Cavanagh went on, showing him the book she was reading from. Thucydides. Many learned and respected men sang the praises of the ancients, of course, but Stanislaus still didn't know why one would read works of paganism when one could reach for the Gospels, for St Paul, for Thomas Aquinas. Miss Cavanagh walked up and down the aisle between the desks reading aloud from the textbook.

'The greatest achievement of the former times was the Persian War; yet even this was speedily decided in two battles by sea and two by land. But the Peloponnesian War was a protracted struggle, and attended by calamities such as Hellas had never known within a like period of time. Never were so many cities captured and depopulated – some by Barbarians, others by Hellenes themselves fighting against one another; and several of them after their capture were re-peopled by strangers. Never were exile and slaughter more frequent, whether in the war or brought about by civil strife. And traditions which had often been current before, but rarely verified by fact, were now no longer doubted.

For there were earthquakes unparalleled in their extent and fury, and eclipses of the sun more numerous than are recorded to have happened in any former age; there were also in some places great droughts causing famines; and lastly the plague, which did immense harm and destroyed numbers of the people. All these calamities fell on Hellas simultaneously with the war, which began when the Athenians and Peloponnesians violated the Thirty Years' Peace concluded by them after the capture of Euboea. Why they broke it and what were the grounds of the quarrel I will first set forth, that in time to come, no man may be at a loss to know what was the cause of this great war. The real though unavowed cause I believe to have been the growth of the Athenian power, which terrified the Lacedaemonians and forced them into war.'

Something unnameable in the passage disturbed Stanislaus. Two millennia and more had passed since the Athenians and the Spartans had thrown their respective alliances into total war against each other, and Grecian civilisation had passed into history soon afterwards. Why should this be troubling now?

'Well, what do we think, class? Is Thucydides right? Is that really why the Peloponnesian War happened? What do you think, Master McCoy?' she asked, pointing to a young fellow near the front. Stanislaus shifted in his seat. This was dictation?

'Yes, Miss,' said the boy. The teacher's expression told him more was required. 'The Spartans were the main ones out of all the Greeks who beat the Persians so they thought they'd be the main men, but the Athenians were getting stronger and building up a big alliance, so eventually something was bound to happen.'

'It was bound to, you say? Why was it bound to? Geraldine Smith,' said Miss Cavanagh, pointing across the room to a girl with ringlets in her hair. The girl hesitated. 'Come on, Geraldine, think,' said Miss Cavanagh, 'what are the rules?'

The girl's face brightened. 'Everything is made up of opposing forces or opposing sides. Gradual changes lead to turning points,' she said proudly.

'Turning points. What happens at a turning point? Sarah Foy?'

'One of the opposing forces overcomes the other,' said Sarah.

'That's right,' said Miss Cavanagh. 'The Spartans had been the strongest but after thirty years of peace the Athenians gradually caught up. Sparta was militarised, Athens was civilised. The Spartans were invincible on land, the Athenians at sea. The Spartans had muscles, the Athenians had brains. Eventually the Athenians were too strong to be simply dismissed by the Spartans. You see how everything in existence is a unity of opposites?' She locked her fingers together in a double fist to demonstrate the two forces pulling against each other. 'One of the opposing forces had to overcome the other. The turning point had to come.'

Stanislaus stood up noisily from his seat, clattering his knees painfully against the desk as he rose. 'Miss Cavanagh, what on earth are you teaching these children?' he said.

The children dropped their pens and chalk. The young girls looked up from their knitting. Miss Cavanagh seemed shaken. 'It's dictation, Your Grace,' she said.

'This is not dictation. Do you think I'm unaware of what you're drip-feeding these children? Everything is a unity of opposites, gradual change leads to a turning point – you're teaching them revolution. In my own school!'

'It's dialectics,' she whispered.

Stanislaus stepped into the aisle and strode towards the teacher. 'That was Marx, what you were just telling them.'

'It's Plato.'

'I don't care who it is! Your job, Miss Cavanagh, is to teach these children skills that will help them in life. Reading, writing, arithmetic, handiwork. If you have any pupils with vocations, you will direct them to me and I will arrange for their further instruction. Otherwise, you teach them the how, not the why. This is a schoolhouse.'

Stanislaus stared at her till her eyes dropped to the floor. He walked to the door, turned and looked around the classroom, as if to make clear that he would be keeping an eye on things from now on. When he was satisfied that Miss Cavanagh seemed to understand, he left the shamefaced schoolteacher. He would put a big question mark by her name, he thought as he headed back to the Parochial House. What was it she said it was: dialectics? It had been forty years since he'd read Plato, but that did ring a bell. He would have to consult his *Republic*.

*   *   *

The blinds of Quinn's General Stores are still drawn but the lights are on inside. I bang on the door and shout for Charlie to hurry up. It's not quite opening time but I'm too close to Ida Harte's for my liking.

'*In Dublin next arrived, I thought it was a pity to be so soon deprived of a view of that fine city, 'twas then I took a stroll …*' someone sings, loudly and badly. Jerry McGrath comes around the corner: '*… all among the quality, my bundle then was stole in a neat locality, something crossed my mind …*'

105

'You're in great form this morning,' I say.

He pats the postbag hanging limply from his shoulder. 'That's my duties discharged till Monday morning. *"Says I, I'll look behind, no bundle could I find upon my stick a-wobbling, inquiring for the rogue, they said my Connaught brogue, it wasn't much in vogue on the rocky road to Dubbelin, one two three four five."'*

Charlie opens the door and ushers me inside. 'My favourite customer,' he says. I tell him about our roof and he whips out notebook and pencil. 'Spurtles, grapes, rope, wire mesh: I have everything you need,' he says, gesturing to the highest shelves behind the wooden counter.

'Spurtles?'

'Spurtles. Fletches. Thatching forks. Whatever you want to call them.' He sets a thatching fork on the counter. It's like a square hairbrush the size of a tennis racquet with nails for teeth. I scrape the sharpened points against my palm. Charlie sets a bundle of two-foot sally sticks on the counter. 'You'll need loads of these. Scallops. You remember what scallops are, city boy?'

'Shellfish.'

'You twist and bend them into a U-shape and use them like wooden bands to hold the thatch in place,' he says, demonstrating the process.

'Yes, I know what fucking scallops are. I have thatched a roof before, you know.'

He smiles as he scribbles on his notepad. 'I'll draw up a list of all the things you need and get one of the young fellas to drop everything up to you this afternoon. Have you plenty of straw?'

'I thought I'd get the tools first and then see about cutting some of them reed spires that grow over there in Granemore …'

He loops his thumbs inside his apron and leans forward on the counter. 'They're no good, them reed spires. Leave it with me. Straw is a bloody nuisance, truth be told. There's plenty of people around here mad looking rid of the stuff since the wheat was harvested.'

'Thanks, Charlie.'

'Is it just you and Pius doing the whole roof? Big job. You should take on a few men.'

'I'll get Turlough and Sean.'

'I'll come and help too if you want. But I'm not much use up a ladder any more though.'

'Shite, I don't think we have a ladder either.'

Charlie shakes his head, as if he's looking at the most pathetic sight in the world. He ushers me under the counter, through his little office and out to the yard at the back of the premises. Under a canvas tarpaulin he shows me a huge stock of perhaps twenty ladders laid out carefully: some are six or eight feet, others must be thirty, all expertly crafted in cedar, I think, with smoothly rounded rungs buttressed by metal strips. I see the price-tag on one of them and whistle. 'I'm getting a nosebleed just looking at the price of that. I didn't know they were so dear.'

Charlie puts his hand on one handsome-looking twelve-odd-footer. 'I'll loan you this one for the job, as long as you promise not to get any scratches on it.'

'Big demand for these, is there? You're carrying a lot of stock.'

'Big order in from the Fire Brigade, but keep that to yourself now.'

\*   \*   \*

The next morning the sun is still rising and the fat in the pan hissing and sputtering as Pius fries up breakfast when Charlie and the Moriarty boys arrive with straw enough to thatch the shell of the GPO. They've brought young Aidan Cavanagh, Maggie's brother, with them. We take the squelchy, gristly bacon and kidney sodas in our hands and meet the lads outside. Turlough looks to the sky and says he reckons we might have nine hours of daylight ahead. The day will be cold but dry.

'And how much am I going to have to pay you?' I say to Aidan.

'Nothing, Victor, nothing. It's my honour,' he says, and he's so earnest that it's hard not to be embarrassed.

'A working man has to be paid. Let's say five shillings for the day.'

'Honestly, I wouldn't accept it, Victor.'

'Six shillings, and you have to tell your sister I was asking for her. My last word.'

'Tell her yourself. She's bringing me up my dinner this afternoon.'

We get to work straight away, investigating the roof. The existing thatch is threadbare and soaked and brown, and worn back almost to the mud layer at the base of the roof. Hardly any scallops remain and the spars, which shouldn't even be visible, stick out like spikes. Water runs throughout the body of the thatch and the walls are stained brown with moisture. Turlough tells us gravely that if the water has penetrated beyond the surface of the walls, we'll have to replace rafters and all. He climbs up the ladder and crawls along the bottom of the roof, stopping to cut away a fistful of thatch with a knife. He puts his hand onto the wall, holds it there and thinks about it for a long moment before shunting across like a crab and repeating the process on another section. At last, he tells us we're lucky: we don't need a whole new structure. We've gotten away with it. A little longer and there would've been structural damage. He starts hacking away the rotten, spindly reeds from the ridges, the gables and around the chimney, where it's most decayed. I organise the workers. I direct Aidan to carry loose armfuls of straw from the cart to Pius and Charlie, who tie it together in bundles of fresh thatch. Then Aidan and I bring the thatch to Sean, who carries it up the ladder. Meanwhile Turlough strips the roof, and he and Sean together lay the fresh thatch onto the naked spars. 'Make those bundles extra thick, eighteen inches at least, remember they're going onto a bare roof,' I tell them.

'Whatever you say, Henry Ford,' Sean chuckles.

Cheeky comparison, but the production line is soon moving quickly and efficiently. We all work like mad and soon we're all sweating. It's good to see Pius with a bit of colour in his cheeks. Pius, Aidan, Charlie and I have a hell of a time keeping up with Turlough and Sean, who plough through their work like ten men. They end up doing half of everyone else's job too, helping tie together bundles, carrying them up on the roof, laying them in place. I get the feeling they'd almost rather the rest of us just got out of their way. As we work, Sean says there's something he wants to ask me.

'People are selfish, that's just human nature, and you can't change human nature. What do youse socialists say about that?'

All eyes turn to me. I pick up a bundle of thatch and throw it across my shoulder, so everyone knows to keep working while I explain a few things to them.

'Say you're being employed to do a job of work. Well, you're the labour end of the equation, right?' I say, handing the bundle up the ladder to Sean. 'The man paying you provides the capital. Capital and labour. One without the other is useless. So they divide the wealth created as a result. Capital's share is called profit. Labour's share is called wages. But how do you know where to make that division? What criteria do you use? It's like you said yourself: people are selfish. So capital will always want the greatest possible profit margin and labour will always wants the highest possible wages. That division is a constant source of conflict. That's the central reality of capitalism. It's a conflict that can never be reconciled.'

'I'm just checking here, but you're still going to pay us what we agreed?' Sean jokes.

'So how will socialism help us kick the Brits out of our country?' Turlough goes on, looking serious.

'Working men have no country,' I say. I can tell that they neither understand nor care for my argument. 'Lookit, the Empire exists for two reasons: one, so the Brits can access physical and labour resources. Irish farmers feed Britain's industrial cities and Irish labour builds their railways and canals. It would be contrary to British interests if Ireland ever became rich. That's partly why we've had so many famines here, and why half our people have to emigrate. And two, so the Brits have markets to buy their surpluses. Ireland is virtually made of peat and turf yet we import boatloads of coal every day. No colony can have economic justice within the Empire, since the point of the Empire is to prevent it. Everything is rigged in favour of the master. Imperialism is the enslavement of nations. Socialism is the emancipation of the people through economic justice. That's poison to empires.'

Turlough seems pleased but Sean isn't following. 'The way I see it, there's only one way to get the Brits out of our country and that's at the point of a gun. I would've thought you boys from Easter Week would understand that better than anybody,' he says.

'You think an Irish boss would be any better than an English one?'

'Bastard probably wouldn't be but at least we wouldn't have foreigners ordering us about in our own country.'

We're into the second half of the job by early afternoon. The roof looks like a flag: half thin, meagre, greasy, sickly-looking; half golden, thick, secure, new. By increments, the new is overwhelming the old all across the Lennon land. The courtyard is clean. The outbuildings are tidy-looking. We're in the ascendant in our war with the overgrowth. In the fields, cattle sidle around. One of the cows is due to calve any day. It almost feels like the place I grew up, when we were the envy of the parish and every family in Madden wanted one of theirs to marry a Lennon. That's what I'm thinking when Maggie walks gracefully into the yard, carrying a wicker basket under her arm. She wears a fancy golden brooch that ties her blouse together at the neck and she has her hair plaited elaborately. I clamber down the ladder to greet her.

'What are you doing here?' Charlie asks her. She wrinkles her nose at him.

'Come on inside to the kitchen,' I say, and lead her by the elbow away from the rest of them. I close the door behind us and take the basket from her. My fingers brush against hers and our eyes meet for a second. She snatches back the basket.

'I've brought our Aidan his lunch.'

'Why don't you stay a while and make lunch for the men?' I say. She stands between the table and the sink and I squeeze past her to get to the scullery. I come back with eggs, liver, kidneys, lard and dripping, and look at her with my most pleading eyes. She's giving me a look and honest to God I don't know what it means. I blink, as if to say give me a clue, but she has a hard stare about her. I reach into the drawer, take out an apron and offer it to her, but still she doesn't thaw out. 'What's wrong?' I say when I can think of nothing else.

'I had a visit from the bishop the other day, he sat in on class. He said he'll be watching me. He got really angry with my teaching. It was *The Peloponnesian War*, for goodness sake.'

'Him and his whole stinking class are scared to death, and so they should be.'

'Victor, would you ever just shut up? I'm a teacher in this parish and Bishop Benedict can change that any time he wants. He's out to get me, and all because of you.'

I put my hand on hers and squeeze it. 'I won't let any harm come to you, I promise.'

She turns purple and lets out a loud exhalation of frustration. Honestly, she's the most confounding person sometimes. But there's a softening in her eyes, and after a long pause she says, with only the thinnest layer of bitterness: 'You're a bloody nightmare!' She ties the apron around her waist and takes a knife from the drawer. She knows instinctively where to find it. She takes a loaf from the wicker basket and starts slicing it. 'You go on back to work, I'll call you all when the dinner's ready.'

I float into the yard singing, 'If you were the only girl in the world', ignoring Charlie's daggers and singing ever more loudly, though the others are starting to get annoyed too. Sean is still banging on about whether I'll turn out for Madden in the county final, but instead of answering I just sing the next line a little louder, and keep singing until Maggie, my beautiful Margaret Nora, calls us inside.

Maggie is at the stove, fussing and clattering around as she puts the food onto plates. Yellow cotton cloth and the cutlery laid neatly on the table. A large pot of tea sits steaming in the middle. Baskets filled with bread and boiled eggs piled high in their shells. This place looks like home. I sit at the head of the table. Sean makes to sit at my right hand but that's Maggie's seat.

'Is Maggie staying?' says Charlie.

'Look, I've already shelled an egg for you,' I say.

She pauses a moment before she sits down. At the far end of the table Pius clears his throat. 'Bless us O Lord for these, thy gifts ...'

'... which of thy bounty we are about to receive ...' Charlie chimes in. The rest of them follow, with bowed heads, closed eyes, monotonous incanting. I touch Maggie's warm, soft hands. Her eyes open with mortification but she doesn't withdraw her hand. Aidan opens his eyes and sees our hands touching.

'... we are about to receive, through Christ, Our Lord, Amen.'

Little is said as we eat, apart from tributes to Maggie. 'Hard-working men deserve to be well fed,' she says.

'Everyone is born equal and no-one should starve, ever. That's what socialism is all about,' I say.

'The poor you will always have with you. Our Lord Himself said that,' Pius grumbles.

'Our Lord knew nothing about the theory of surplus value.'

Pius slams his fist on the table and glares furiously at me. 'By God, if you're going to blaspheme you can take yourself out of this house.'

'Lookit, let me explain,' I say. I hold up a slice of bread. 'Say this bread represents the total amount of wealth Ireland produces in a year. Now, say half goes to labour – chance would be a fine thing, but anyway' – I tear the bread in half – 'that means the workers can afford to consume half of the wealth created, right?' I stuff the bread into my mouth, swallow it down, then hold up the remaining half. 'This is capital's profit.'

'Give it a rest, will you?' says Charlie, but I keep holding up the piece of bread.

'This is capital's profit. Capital can't ever consume its whole share, so there's always a huge surplus left over. Labour's wages are spent, so labour can't buy the surplus. So capital always needs access to undeveloped markets. That's why we have empires. But what happens when there are no more available markets for capital's surpluses?'

Around me, blank stares.

'The day will come when capitalists make goods, only to throw them in the sea. They'll fill lakes with wine and build mountains out of butter. That's why the ultimate collapse of capitalism is inevitable.'

'If it's inevitable, why does there need to be a revolution? Why not just get on with your life and wait for the inevitable?' Maggie asks.

'Change doesn't happen by itself.'

'So you admit it's not actually inevitable?'

'As long as it gets the Brits out of Ireland, it's all right by me,' says Sean.

After lunch I walk Maggie down the laneway. The autumnal sunshine is a dreamy haze; it makes everything look like half-remembered memory. I see a glint of ruby red in Maggie's hair.

She tells me I should play in Sean's football match. 'Our Aidan is on the team. He thinks you're God's gift. He'd be so excited if you played with them.'

'Are you going to watch it?'

She nods. 'The whole parish is going.'

'I will if you come to the cinema with me next week.'

But I've already made up my mind to play. No way I'm going to miss a chance to impress her. She doesn't answer, save for an enigmatic smile, and as I watch her leave, all I can think is what a fool I am.

We race against the encroaching darkness to get the roof finished in a single day. Pius has slowed considerably as the day has gone on; Charlie is a soft shopkeeper and will never be anything else; Aidan is game but he's still just a boy; I have performed reasonably; but Sean and Turlough possess the kind of muscle on which revolutions are built. They are keen to do whatever I tell them, and I know why too. They grew up hearing about their granda the Fenian and they wish to God they had been at the GPO, so they're in awe of me, since I was. Good to know. The proletariat is a leviathan, and the power of any leviathan is in its muscle. Of course a leviathan requires direction from its brain, and of course the revolution will inevitably be led by an intellectual elite, but the likes of Turlough and Sean have a crucial role to play.

We're getting near the end, no more than a few batches of straw are left to be tied down and the daylight is failing, when I see someone coming up the laneway. Ida Harte.

'Hello, Ida,' says Aidan.

She gives him a cursory glance. 'I'm selling fresh salmon here, straight from the Blackwater,' she says.

'Go on, Mata Hari, take yourself away, there's nobody here wants your wares,' Sean says.

'And who are you to speak for the man of this house?' says Ida, eyeing me up with malevolent glee. 'It's Pius I'm here to see.'

I clamber down to her, grab her by the elbow and yank her across the yard. I throw open the door and fling her inside. I shut the door after us and look hatefully at her, standing by my kitchen table where my Maggie made my dinner. She opens her bag. A couple of fish flop out.

'What do you think you're doing, coming to my house?'

'I always come here for poteen.'

I get a couple of large bottles from the dresser. 'Here's your fucken poteen,' I snarl, stepping up close, right in her face, and I stare into her gaping black eyes. They're mesmerising. I lurch forward. It's not my fault, it's beyond my control. I'm not kissing her, I'm trying to swallow her whole. Her mouth grinds remorselessly against my face. Hot breath shoots down her nostrils against me. Her sweaty palms molest my neck and face and hair. Her tongue licks and caresses the inside of my mouth. I've known Monto girls to indignantly refuse to do this, saying if I want that sort of thing I can go to France. She moves her hands down from my head to my shoulders to my chest to my waist. In a single, shocking motion she grabs my left hand and plunges it down the front of her skirt. She mauls in closer and I grope the hair and the moistness.

I pull my hand away as if from fire. Ida stands before me, panting. Her cheeks are red, her nostrils flaring, her breasts are almost hanging out of her half-buttoned blouse. The crockery Maggie washed lies dripping by the sink. I watch dumbly as she buttons her blouse and ties up her hair. She snatches up the bottles of poteen from the table and says as she leaves:

'Remember, all you have to do is leave the lantern on,' and I can't help but feel she's mocking me just a little bit.

I wait a few minutes before I go back outside, where I find Sean holding a lantern as Turlough finishes the last section of the roof, just as the last of the daylight is about to depart. Pius and Charlie are sitting on the cart smoking. 'You're all flushed,' says Charlie, eyeing me shrewdly.

'She'd turn you to stone with a look, that one,' says Sean up on the roof, 'but you'd ride her all the same.'

I'm studying Aidan closely but can see nothing in him to suggest he suspects anything. Thank God Maggie isn't here. She would know. Women have a sixth sense about these things. I call up to Sean. 'I'll play in your match,' I say.

*   *   *

*Even for a Saturday afternoon, Sackville Street is buzzing. A wild-looking old drunk with wiry grey hair and bloodshot eyes presses a handbill into your hand.*

## SUPPORT THE BELFAST DOCK STRIKE!

### WHAT IS TO BE DONE?

## BUILDING SYNDICALISM IN IRELAND AND BEYOND

### KEYNOTE SPEAKER: ALEXANDER BLANE (ex MP)

**Outside the Customs House, 3pm**

*Alexander Blane. You know the name. Now you look closer at the old fellow, you see he isn't drunk at all, not at this moment anyway. You recognise him, though he looks very different from the photos you've seen of the respectable Parnellite who was Armagh's MP once upon a time. He's the first person from home you've met since you arrived in Dublin. He invites you to a political meeting, so you can talk more.*

*Alec has a thousand great stories about home. The fortress capital of a pagan empire. The only place in Ireland that Ptolemy put in his Atlas. The place Patrick chose as the new citadel of Christendom in Ireland. He knew your father. 'Always a great man for contributing to the Party.'*

*And he tells you about class struggle. How it's the only alternative to the oppression of the workers. What they call class warfare is actually working class self-defence. The warfare by the rich against the poor is ceaseless. The rich have a great advantage: their hatred and vengefulness towards the poor is bottomless. The wickedness of the rich is staggering, and the poor are staggered by it. The established order is not satisfied with the world and its riches. Their vanity requires a narrative that ennobles their base, selfish, heartless, gutless, gluttonous existence. They have armies of statesmen and journalists and artists and teachers and rhetoricians and yes, preachers, to provide it. Priests are part of the power structure, with which the working class has nothing in common. Their hands are soft, their stomachs round and their minds filled with the doctrines, not of Christ but of the established order. Remember what they did to Christ. If the preachers preached the message of Christ, they too would be crucified.*

*You're sitting in his crumbling tenement room on Burgh Quay, as you have many times before, wondering how Alexander Blane, who has dined with Prime Ministers, has fallen so low. It's simple. He stood against Cardinal Logue. Over Parnell. Now, like you, he is living in exile.*

# THREE

Stanislaus stood in the deserted street and looked up at the red bunting. When they'd first festooned the street, he'd supposed it would be for a few days, but it had been several weeks now. At least, he thought, the day of the confounded football match had finally come, so all this foolishness would be over soon. The Cardinal took a firm line that Gaelic games were awash with nefarious characters and dangerous, extremist politics, and Stanislaus believed he was right. Others disagreed, even openly. William Croke and John MacHale, God rest them. Archbishops, unimpeachable churchmen, red-clawed nationalists and perhaps the only churchmen in the country who could oppose the boss and get away with it. They had given the GAA the legitimacy it needed to sweep across the country. Boisterous crowds would return later in the afternoon with news of victory or defeat, but for now the parish was deserted except for a few women with children to mind. It was a big occasion for many, but since Stanislaus's disapproval of Gaelic games was well known, people tended not to talk to him about it. It was a poor priest who knew nothing of his parishioners' passions, so it was no harm that in Father Daly, Stanislaus had a Crokeite for a curate. Especially since Victor Lennon had shown a worrying ability to insinuate himself into it.

It was absurd that he could be challenged by a spoiled rich boy like Victor Lennon on the question of the poor. Stanislaus hadn't been born to wealth. He was born, he believed he remembered being told as a child, just as the great Pentecostal storm tore the roof off the shack he was born in. The Night of the Big Wind. The old folk always said the end would come at Pentecost, so Stanislaus entered the world to people who thought it was ending around them. Oídhche na Gaoithe Móire they called it in the old language, the language that spoke of an ignorant and hungry past, of people who wore a thin film of Christianity over hearts still essentially pagan. Whatever primitive name she had given him he had long forgotten, just as he had forgotten all but a few phrases and grammatical constructions of the old language. Stanislaus came later, after her. He felt no sorrow for the loss of that past. He felt no nostalgia for standing outside the locked gates of the grain stores. He did not miss hunger. Absurd that he could be challenged on the poor by Victor Lennon. Absurd also, that he should be challenged politically. Stanislaus thought back, as he sometimes did, to his time as a curate in Mayo. He still sometimes saw the captain, tall and doggedly proud of bearing but unable to mask a frightened, hunted look.

'When I walk into a shop or an inn I can get no service. The postman will not come to my door. The servants have quit my house. No-one will conduct business with me. I salute people on the road but they look past me as though I am a ghost.' Cut-glass accent, whiskers twitching. 'Apparently there aren't any laws against this sort of thing.'

'My parishioners have asked me to enter into negotiations with you regarding their rents.'

The captain shifts in his chair. 'So you're one of those priests, are you? I know some other landlords have allowed themselves to be held hostage, but I will not. I have legal contracts. I have the law on my side.'

'Last winter in this parish alone your men evicted fifty-nine families and burned their houses to the ground. They brutalised men, women and children. This winter we face possible famine in this area. During the Great Famine, your father refused to waive the rents. You know what happened in this area as a result.'

'My father is not the issue!' He pauses. Catches his breath. Exhales coolly. 'Perhaps there is something, some project perhaps, that I could assist your church with? Something that needs funding. I'm always happy to help friends. If you would speak for me in a sermon …'

'The plain fact, sir, is that Michael Davitt is in this county every other week, and he gives better sermons than I do. My parishioners want land reform and the Church wants it too. The people have a right to withdraw from you, sir, and withdrawn they have.'

'I will not negotiate.'

'Then your ostracisation will continue.'

Had Victor Lennon even heard of the land war, or did he understand that very great victory? He doubted it. As he walked up and down the pavement, far from the echoing of his foot-steps, Stanislaus fancied he could make out the roar of a crowd. Impossible, of course, the game was being played five miles away, but the sound of a crowd cheering was in his ears, in his head. He wondered how the game was going. He knew little of the rules, but that didn't stop images forming, images of merest savagery. Victor Lennon and ultra-nationalist nihilists in ominous red colours. Young men slogging through a muddy field. Hard not to think of the Somme. Men doing violence with baying mobs looking on. He thought of the coliseum. No doubt his imaginings were lurid, he had nothing to go on but his prejudices, but he went with them. God forbid Victor Lennon should give people further reason to fancy him a hero. His parishioners admired their patriots, but they loved their footballers.

As he walked back to the Parochial House he looked up at the bunting ruefully. One day he would wean the people off their savage pastimes and all the dangerous extremism that went with them; but he admitted to himself that it would not be this day.

\* \* \*

Everyone's telling me what a fantastic game I played. Pius puts his hand on my shoulder.

'That second point you got, that was a horse of a score,' he says, and I think there's a tear in his eye. There might be one in mine too. I did have a mighty game. There are no Dick Fitzgeralds in Derrynoose, that's for sure. Plenty of tough fellows but not a footballer among them. As the game wore on everyone around me flagged with fatigue but my fitness stood to me; by the end I was running rings around a bunch of fat farmers. Not bad for a blow-in, people keep saying as they slap me on the back. Half a dozen jokers at least say it. Madden to the backbone, I reply to them all, cut me and I bleed red. There must be three hundred cheering Madden folk gathered in the middle of the field to see the man from the county board present Sean Moriarty with the trophy. I'm hiding among them from Ida Harte, who spent the entire game screaming, absolutely *screaming* encouragement. It seemed like she ranted all the more loudly, madly, oh God, lustily, when I had the ball. She keeps trying to get close, like she's trying to hug me or something, but I take a step back from her and shout to Sean to stop hogging the cup, it must be nearly my turn to raise it up.

I spot Maggie though the crowd. She's slinking away. Soon the crowd will move for home in an armada of bicycles, but Maggie seems to want to get away before the rest. If I move quickly, we can travel the five miles home together, and I won't have to share her with the rest of them. I sidle away from the crowd as quickly as I can, though it takes a few minutes to negotiate the handshakes and back-slapping and questions, and hop onto the ancient bicycle Charlie has leant me. Maggie's fast on her feet, she has put a bit of distance behind her already by the time I see her up ahead. She turns as she hears me coming and smiles sardonically in the direction of my mud-spattered knees.

'Have you not even a wet sponge, or a pair of trousers?' she says as I pull up alongside her. Red jersey, white knickers, black stockings and studded boots. Wouldn't have been my first choice of outfit, in fairness.

'Is that how you greet a victorious gladiator?'

'More like a Christian with the lions,' she says, and I'm a bit stung, to be honest. I pat the crossbar and nod for her to sit down. 'Are you sure you'll be able to manage it?' she says, but sits herself down. She wraps her right arm around my shoulder and our faces are inches apart.

'I think you have an admirer in Ida Harte,' she says. I almost slide off the road.

'Was she there? I didn't see her.'

'She really does draw attention to herself.'

God knows I don't want to talk about Ida bloody Harte. Enough of this.

'Did you think any more about going to the picture house with me?' Maggie doesn't answer but her eyes flash like those of a child unwrapping a present on Christmas morning.

A long, steep hill rises ahead of us and I steel myself for the incline. I pump hard on the pedals, up, up, up, gritting my teeth so she won't see how the hill makes my leg muscles burn, how it makes my lungs expand and contract like bellows in a furnace. Strong, sturdy, tireless as a shire, that's what I want her to see. I'm not sure if my face will appear purple from the exertion or purest white, since I feel close to fainting. You'd think she would offer to walk up the hill. At least capitalists break your back for tangible reward; women expect you to expire in service to their vanity. I'm relieved to reach the brow of the hill, even more so to see the road stretch ahead in a long, gentle decline. I won't have to touch the pedals for half a mile. We freewheel, and it's gentle at first but we gather momentum and soon we're hurtling. Maggie clings more tightly. We're dangerously fast now. Maggie's nose almost touches mine. She doesn't shriek, she doesn't cry out in alarm, she doesn't look afraid. I take my eyes from the road and look at her. The road seems far away. She whispers something, but I can't make her out as the wind rushes by. Our noses touch. She whispers again, unconvincingly: 'Slow down.'

'I have no brakes.'

Our lips almost touch. She clings tightly. I cherish the clinging. Our noses touch again. The long downward slope ends and a little knoll puts the brakes on our momentum. We're back at a safe speed before we know it and I have to start pedalling again. Maggie loosens her grip and her nose and her lips are far away as ever. She's looking over my shoulder. 'The priest is coming. Let me off.' A motorcar splutters toward us.

'The Church pays well if the bishop can afford a motorcar,' I say.

'It's Father Daly's car. His family has money.' She extricates herself from me and straightens up, as if she hopes it'll look like she isn't with me at all. The priest honks his klaxon. 'There's someone with him,' Maggie says, steeliness in her tone now. She looks distressed. 'Victor, listen to me. I love my job. The things you say, they matter. Please don't make trouble for me.'

The automobile announces its approach with an ever louder, more dissonant din, and it's soon upon us. Charlie is sitting beside Father Daly in the pillion seat, looking ashen. 'When are we going to the pictures together? Monday?' I demand of Maggie just as the car comes to a stop in front of us. She shakes her head. 'Tuesday then?'

'Hello there, you two, you're making great time,' says Father Daly. 'You played very well today, Victor, congratulations.'

'I'm surprised to see a man of the cloth at a Gaelic match.'

'There are a lot of different opinions within the Church. Ah, Victor, you're a desperate man for the controversy.'

'Maggie, come on and get in the car,' says Charlie abruptly.

'There's a lift here if you want it,' the priest says to Maggie more emolliently. 'I'm sorry we can't offer you a lift as well, Victor, but there really isn't anywhere to put the bicycle.'

'Thank you very much,' says Maggie.

The priest gets out and moves his seat so she can climb into the back. I look past him to her, imprisoned in the back seat. I'm sure my misery is palpable, but I don't care. 'I'll see you back in Madden,' I say, my eyes on Maggie, and she nods as the car starts to pull off. There's something in the way she nods that fills me with hope, fervent hope. I mouth the word 'When?' to her, and pedal hard after the car as it starts off down the road. The shape my hope takes is, I suppose, something like a prayer. I see Maggie's silhouette in the oval window in the back of the canopy, and, just before the car moves too far ahead, Maggie's finger traces three letters in the condensation on the window:

## W E D

The whole team and a good few others – but all men – are in Turlough and Sean's house passing around our newly won trophy, drinking as deeply as we dare of the poteen it's filled with. Pius donated plenty of booze and he's sitting quietly in the corner drinking his portion. It's getting late and there won't be a hand's-turn done tomorrow, but everyone's happy. Winning a football match hardly seems significant enough to have men shedding tears, but there have been a few tears this evening. You'd think they were the Petersburg proletariat, finally free. Jerry McGrath starts into singing a rebel. I don't know the song but everyone else seems to. They jibe me for my ignorance. 'If all the patriots of Ireland are like yourself then our poor country stands in an hour of great need indeed,' Jerry says. He's flaming. It'll be afternoon deliveries tomorrow. In order to prove my credentials I give them a couple of verses of 'Skibbereen'. I learned it in Fron Goch from some of the West Cork lads. They were always scrupulous about that, I tell Pius. They weren't from Cork, they were from West Cork.

'The South Armagh ones are the same,' Pius replies. A bit of company is good for him. Everyone keeps saying it's good to see him, that he has been locking himself away too long. Plenty of lads hopeful of a bit of work. He's sitting quietly and drinking a lot but he seems contented. I pat his shoulder and tell him I'm going outside for a breath of air, it's like a smokehouse in here. I sit on the doorstep and rest my forehead on my knees for a few minutes, until Aidan Cavanagh comes out and sits with me. I ask if his sister is coming. I must be drunk, to ask so unsubtly.

'It's not really the sort of thing a lady would be at,' he says. 'But thank God for Sean and Turlough, eh? Otherwise we'd be out in the cold.'

'We deserve better than this. We won the county champion- ship, we deserve a big do that everyone in the whole parish can join in with, not just a fucken bottle of poteen in a bachelor house, and nothing but men to look at.'

Aidan nods as he lights a cigarette, his fingers clumsy. He agrees that a celebration is not the same when there's only men present. He looks like he has something to say. I wait. Eventually he says: 'Victor, what do you think about Ida Harte?'

'What? Why do you ask?'

'She treats me like I'm only a wee boy but I'm seventeen now.'

'What, you mean you and Ida …?'

'Well, there's a sort of an understanding there, if you see what I mean. But she's six years older than me.'

God knows what I'm supposed to say. 'Well,' I begin, falter- ingly, 'lookit, if she's for you she won't pass you.'

He brightens. Sweet Jesus, the lad looks almost happy. 'Our Maggie,' he says, 'she does be free most Wednesday nights, in case you were interested in a bit of information like that.'

131

We both go back inside the house. They're finishing a chorus of 'The Bard of Armagh' as we crush into the living room. I sit beside Turlough, who is talking to TP McGahan. 'Mind what you say to this boy, Turlough, he'll stitch you up in the paper,' I say.

'Och, Victor, it's the sub-editors, they rewrite everything. I read them the riot act over that article, but they do the exact same thing every week.' I hold up my palms to call a truce and he seems pacified. 'So are you staying home for good then, Victor?' I shrug. 'Any plans?' I shrug again. 'Turlough was saying you were teaching them about socialism while you were thatching the roof.'

'I wasn't teaching nothing. What are you driving at, McGahan?'

Turlough puts a placating hand on my shoulder. 'I was just telling TP what you were saying the other day about surplus value.'

'I think it's interesting that you're teaching workers here in Madden about Marxism, what with everything going on in Russia,' says TP.

'Are we on the record here or what? I don't mind being stitched up as long as you have the sand to tell me you're going to stitch me up,' I say. My raised voice attracts attention.

Aidan Cavanagh sits down beside us. 'You should've heard Victor talking about surplus value there the other day, it was amazing.' Aidan takes the tumbler from my hand and pours the poteen into his own. He holds it up. 'This glass of poteen is Ireland, right? And it has to be divided.' He pours half the poteen back into my glass. 'So this here half goes to labour, but of course labour never gets anywhere near half, but anyway ... So labour drinks it all.' He nods to me, and I down it. My cheeks burn. Half the room is watching us now. 'And this here is capital, but capital always has a surplus, so it has to go somewhere else, and that's why we have empires. You see?'

'Aye, sort of, I think,' TP says.

'I'm telling you, they'll be filling in Lough Neagh with mint imperials some day,' says Aidan.

'You talk some shite,' laughs Charlie Quinn from across the room. He lobs a bottle of drink to us. 'I see you're running a bit low there.' Aidan is about to rise angrily but I put a hand on his shoulder. He calms down.

'Don't worry about him,' I tell Aidan. 'When Marx talked about the idiocy of rural life, it was Charlie he was thinking of.' I toast the shopkeeper. He raises his glass and smiles viciously. Jesus, this is tiresome. TP starts into 'The Green Glens of Antrim' and some men sing along, but I had ten months of internment surrounded by nothing but men and that was enough. At least in Fron Goch they were serious men you could have a serious political debate with. Time for more air. I stand outside the door and peer across the street. I wonder which window is the room Ida sleeps in. Poor Aidan, to be a confused young lad in love with a slut like that. I suppose in a place like this, there's only drink and women to keep a man from the noose. I don't need any more drink. That last shot, labour's wages, hit me hard. I'm drunk as the night Ida took me by the hand and led me into the barn, and the memories make me hard. The wetness of her mouth. Her skin, like goose-flesh in the night air. Her legs wrapped around me, grinding her hips like a boa constrictor. I wonder if I went over to the barn now and lit the lantern, would she see it, or would she be asleep. Maybe I'll go over and try it

133

out. I'd be interested to know if she's asleep yet. I'm crossing the street when Charlie calls out: 'Where were you going?' He's clenching his crutch tightly and wearing that big, earnest head of his.

'What's that got to do with you?'

'Aiming for another go at Ida, were you?' he says, malevolence in his eye. The wee weasel has hidden depths. This isn't about Ida Harte, it's about Maggie, it has always been about Maggie. All the years I've been away, he's been too spineless to do anything about it. Now I'm home, I'm a damned hero and he's a cripple and a dupe, at best, if not an outright traitor. I come home and lord the midfield and kick three points to win the championship and he hobbles about on the one leg the king of England let him keep. And I'm the one Maggie loves, not him, she loves me because I'm a man and he's less than that.

'Why would I be going anywhere near Ida? I'm going to see the bishop. Me and Aidan were just talking about it. The team deserves better than a drinking session in Sean and Turlough's front room. There should be a formal celebration for the whole parish. I'm going to see Benedict now, to tell him we're using the Parochial Hall.'

'The Parochial House is the other way,' says Charlie. 'And I'm sure the bishop is in bed. You know what time it is?'

'No time like the present. Come on, Charlie, you yellow bastard. You're not afraid of an oul fella in a frock, are you?'

\*　　\*　　\*

Rap Rap Rap Rap Rap!

Stanislaus jolted. A moment ago it was early evening, now it was late at night. The candle he had lit instead of the desktop lamp had gone out and the study was in darkness. Saliva drooped down in a long thread from his mouth to the pages of the book in his lap. He looked out the window and frowned at the Moriarty shebeen, still in session. He lifted the brandy tumbler from the windowsill and threw back the finger still in it.

Rap Rap Rap Rap Rap!

'We're here to see Benedict,' he heard the Victor fellow cry out from below the window at the front door.

'Caesar had less gall,' Stanislaus mumbled, an ancient joke from his seminary days. He turned the valve on the desktop lamp letting light into the room, and turned his chair away from the window. Less charitable minds might see something peculiar in his sitting in the dark, staring out the window. As he put the decanter away, he felt a little woozy. Perhaps he got up too quickly. Downstairs he heard Father Daly open the door. He sat down and opened the Bible that had been in his lap all evening. Does He not leave the ninety-nine in the open country and go after the lost sheep until He finds it? And when He finds it, He joyfully puts it on His shoulders and goes home. The knock on the study door arrived, and Father Daly put his head around the door sheepishly.

'I'm sorry, Your Grace, but there are two men here to see you. I told them the time but …'

'Send them in.'

The Victor fellow came first, all shamelessness and barely controlled rage. Charlie Quinn hobbled awkwardly after him, looking as though he owed the whole world an apology. 'We want the keys to the Parochial Hall,' Victor snarled, staring at Stanislaus as if he hoped to burn a hole in the old man. Stanislaus sat up in his chair.

'Excuse me?' he said calmly. He was not afraid of Victor Lennon.

'The footballers won today and we deserve a celebration. We want to hold it in the Parochial Hall next Saturday night,' said Victor.

'And what do you say, Mr Quinn?' said Stanislaus, shooting a look at Charlie, causing him to turn his eyes to the ground with maximum mortification.

'Well, I don't know, Father, I just followed Victor and …'

'The workers of this village built that hall and we are entitled to use it. Now, the keys,' Victor demanded.

'You listen to me, son. There will be no revolution in this parish,' said Stanislaus.

'Come on, Victor, let's go,' said Charlie. Victor shrugged him off.

'If your objection is to me, I'll stay away, but don't deny the people,' he countered, watching hawkishly. 'You don't trust me? Get out your Communist Manifesto and I'll swear on it.'

'You're not the first thug hiding behind some political cause I've come across. I will protect my flock from you,' Stanislaus snapped.

'You're a liar, Benedict. You and your whole stinking class.'

'Please, Victor, let's just go.'

'Go ahead and lock out the people. It's what the Church did during the Famine.'

'Out! Get out of my house, both of you!' Stanislaus cried.

'The workers built this house, so you could sit in the dark behind a locked door, watching everyone and condemning everything. But these aren't ignorant, defenceless peasants you're locking out and we'll have our céilí whether you like it or not,' said Victor, singing the syllables like a preacher and slamming his palm on the table as he finished. Father Daly grabbed Victor and tugged him out the door. They descended the stairs noisily, and Stanislaus saw the curate throw Victor out the door below.

'Sober up and get your act together,' Stanislaus heard Father Daly say. He watched Charlie and Victor walk separately up the street, Charlie going home and Victor returning to the Moriarty shebeen. He would boast to them all of how he had bested the bishop once more, no doubt. Stanislaus went to bed feeling old and weary and spent, leaving the air thick with smoke and brandy. Tomorrow would be another day, he told himself.

\*   \*   \*

When we reach Moriarty's Charlie keeps walking. I call after him but he limps off, pretending not to hear me. He hasn't even said what he thinks of my idea. Maybe I went a bit far with the bishop, some of that stuff was a bit much. He leaves me without so much as a good night. To hell with him. There's too much to be excited about to be worrying about Charlie. Back inside the house I tell everyone what has happened. They all groan. Who told you to be organising anything? they ask. Sure you're the last man in Madden should be asking the bishop for anything. It was madness for you to go, Victor. And at this time of night! But all I was talking about was a bit of a céilí so we could have a few women to dance with, and was met with a ruthless demonstration of power. There is something more important at stake now than the use of a dance hall. Refusing me, Benedict refuses us all. Good. Most people spend their lives fighting straw men, rarely does true power reveal itself so nakedly. Everyone can see the battle lines now.

'I said I'd have nothing to do with it, I'd stay away. If the price of the rights of the people is the exclusion of myself, I'll gladly pay it. But he still said no.'

'He's the greatest killjoy that ever walked,' cries Sean Moriarty.

'Don't talk like that about the bishop,' says John McGrath, Jerry's son, our cussed cornerback. I can see Sean is surprised to be challenged like this by the young lad. 'It's not right, you insulting the priest like that,' John says. They're all set to disappear up a blind alley of an argument.

I intervene. 'Listen, lads, listen, my point is, it was the working people of Madden parish built that Parochial Hall. We that built that church and that mansion Benedict is sitting in. They belong to us.'

'Is right! Whose hall is it anyway, if not them that built it?' cries Turlough.

'Victor is right. He's an ould misery guts and would begrudge us a bit of a hooley,' says Aidan Cavanagh.

'You fuck up, Aidy,' says John McGrath, and everyone's surprised because they're best friends. 'Take it easy now, John,' says Jerry McGrath to his son. 'John is right, there's no call to be irreverent, but Victor has a point. It's a terrible thing that the bishop would lock us out of our own Parochial Hall. I remember laying some of the brickwork on it myself. Do you remember that, Pius?'

Pius nods gently. 'Every man in the parish would try and finish up his work early so we could do an hour or two on the new hall. We weren't long married men back then,' he says with an elegiac sigh.

'Divil the penny we asked for it,' says Jerry.

'Or got,' says Pius.

The older heads around the room nod. What I'm saying is sinking in. The people of Madden built that hall, the people of Madden own it. They're starting to think like socialists. 'Workers have a right to ownership over the fruits of their labours. Bishop Benedict is denying us access to a hall that is rightfully ours,' I say.

'We should go and talk to Father Daly. He's a lot easier talked to than the bishop,' says Turlough.

'Aye, Father Daly is a decent skin,' says Aidan.

But we can't solve the problem by running to Father Daly. The Parochial Hall is no longer the issue, it's merely the site of struggle. Benedict's authority is the issue. He has laid down a diktat, and the question now is whether he is obeyed.

'I'm sure Father Daly is a lovely man but the fact is, if we want to do something as simple as hold a dance, we have to beg and scrape to the priest for it. You can't change that by pleading with another priest to take our part,' I say.

'So how are we going to get use of the hall?' says Turlough.

'What are you saying, Victor, that we should break down the doors?' says TP McGahan, his little weasel nose sniffing.

'Forget the Parochial Hall. I wouldn't use it if he gave it to us. We should be able to have a céilí every night if we want, without a by-your-leave from anybody.'

'We could have it outdoors, I suppose. If the weather holds,' says Aidan.

'We need to build a new hall. A place of our own. A People's Hall. And by God, next Saturday night we'll dance till daylight in it.'

The idea percolates through the room. Practicalities arise quickly, and Sean and Turlough are the men for the practical questions. The hall can be made quickly and relatively cheaply with a solid timber frame covered in corrugated iron, and it just so happens they know a man in Emyvale who can sell them all the materials at keen prices. If they had five men with carts to volunteer, they could be back in Madden by lunchtime ready to start building. Jerry McGrath says there's no way it can be done within a week.

'It's not impossible,' Turlough retorts. 'We're talking about an earth floor, no foundations. Just timber stanchions driven into the ground. It'll be more of a shed than a hall. Basic, basic, basic. But it can be done.'

I reckon Turlough and Sean could almost do it by themselves.

'If it doesn't fall down first,' says Pius gruffly.

'Nothing that me and Turlough have built has ever fell down,' Sean says proudly. 'We can worry about strengthening it and making it more durable after next Saturday.'

I could kiss the Moriarty boys.

Turlough scribbles some calculations on the back of a cigarette packet. 'The Parochial Hall is about eighty foot by thirty, and our hall would need to be nearly as big. It doesn't have to be as tall but it'd need to be fifteen foot anyway. For a building that size, you'd be looking at something like twenty pound for the lumber and metal.'

'How are we ever going to pay that sort of money?' says Aidan.

'The man in Emyvale will give us a week's grace. We could raise it,' Turlough says.

'Even if we got two hundred people all to give us a shilling, that's still only half of what we need,' says Aidan. 'And not everyone can afford a shilling. I know I can't.'

'Everyone should pay what they can afford, some should give more than others,' I say.

'I thought socialism was about equality?' TP sneers.

'From each according to ability, to each according to need, that's what it's about.' That shuts him up rightly, but silence descends across the room. Even if we raise half the money we need, a tenner, it'll hurt every family in the parish. Even with labour costs at nought, capital, as ever, is the problem. Twenty pounds is the best part of a year's wages for these men. Murder Murphy would spend that on a damned dinner party, but for the want of it these workers will be separated from their rights. I'm surrounded by faces looking to me. They see I have no answer. 'Maybe we could all come up with two or three shillings?' I say, but I know it's weak.

'I'm sure every man here will gladly give every spare farthing they have, but if you add every spare farthing in the parish together, you're still ten pound short. We have to eat, Victor,' says Turlough ruefully.

Pius grunts. 'I'll put up the money,' he says.

I sit down beside my father and put a hand on his arm. 'Thank you,' I say. There's a lot more I'd like to say to him, but I can't find the words. Soon after, he falls asleep.

Turlough and Sean deserve something extra for all the work that they're going to do this week. I tell them I'll give them a pound in the morning and another pound when the job's done.

It's generous, but only a fool doubts the link between loyalty and payment. They're worth it for their muscle and loyalty. Their say-so will bring two dozen men with them. They are my vanguard. Turlough protests that if they help it won't be for the money, and if no-one else is being paid it doesn't seem right that … I tell him not to go mentioning it to anybody else. 'This is just for you and Sean. You are my main men. I'm depending on you,' I say. He's dubious but he accepts. The first thing he does is help me carry my father home.

Sleep doesn't come easily and I wake frequently throughout the night, but neither my fitfulness nor my hangover prevents me from springing from the bed excitedly as morning breaks. Pius and I have tea and fried bread together, and when I thank him for putting up the cash, it seems to take him a moment to recall what I'm talking about. After breakfast he goes into his bedroom and comes back with a stack of notes, and we wait till Turlough, Sean and their convoy of carts stop by for the cash, as arranged. He gets up and goes out of the room, leaving me with the money. I count out twenty one-pound notes for the materials and a few more for Turlough and Sean's wages and sundry expenses. He'll never miss them. After the Moriartys have been and gone, Pius and I walk down to the village together. It's a beautiful autumn morning; copper leaves still cling to the trees even this late in the year, and the very light is bronzed and dream-like. When we get to the Poor Ground wall Aidan Cavanagh salutes us from across the street. 'One o'clock,' he cries, naming the appointed time everyone is to meet up, provided Turlough, Sean and their convoy of corrugated iron and timber are back in time.

'One o'clock.'

Pius and I hop over the wall and make for the little pile of stones under which Ma is buried. Most of the graves are in this part of the Poor Ground, where the soil is slightly softer, a marshy oasis amid unwanted acres of stony, grey terrain. We'll build our People's Hall on this barren land. Spading down through it will be like digging through iron but there'll be no subsidence, and we don't have to ask anyone's permission because nobody owns it. Pius manoeuvres himself onto his knees, blesses himself, bows his head and, I suppose, begins to pray. Obligation drags at me like cargo straps, so I drop to one knee and clasp my hands together. I don't bless myself, hypocrisy must have some boundaries, but I do bow my head and close my eyes. Not for religion or priests or some imaginary friend called God, but for my da. It'll mean a lot to him to think I'm praying for Ma, and for the money he's given me, he deserves that much.

'Da, why are you helping me?' I say.

'We've done a lot of work here, got the old place back to what it should be.'

'You don't owe me nothing for that.'

'I know. But I suppose, you know, you might think you've done what you came to do, and you might be thinking of leaving again. But maybe you'll stay a bit longer now.' He pauses. 'Sure I have nothing only money now anyway.'

'That's not true. Not entirely.'

\*   \*   \*

*The clock strikes the eleven. You pull up the handbrake and leave the tram. 'Excuse me, my good man, this simply won't do. I must get to the horse show before half past,' says some button-down bluenose over from England with a rose in his lapel. Top hat and silver-tipped cane. The tram is full of them. The RDS set. You don't even answer. You get up and walk off the job. The Nelson Pillar is the meeting point and you're not twenty yards from it. You rest up against the Pillar and enjoy the sunny July afternoon while you wait for the other lads to arrive. Your passengers stay on the tram for ages, gawping across the street at you as if it's all a game and you'll soon come back and drive their tram. By half-twelve, a hundred and twenty-five of your comrades are there, almost every tram driver in the city. You're giddy as a blethering fool. Mr William Martin Murphy, your boss, is everything you hate about the country and the world. Conservative. Catholic. Capitalist. But he's met his mutch in Big Jim Larkin. Big Jim has him terrified. That's why Murphy has put together a vicious band of four hundred bosses and issued the ultimatum: quit Larkin's union or be locked out of our jobs. But Larkin's men have the courage, the dignity and the numbers to tell the bastard Murphy to go to hell. Murphy has his four hundred thieves but we have thirty thousand men with us. It's the Belfast Dock Strike all over again. We reject his ultimatum. We strike. If there's a lockout, we'll bring the city to a standstill. We are going to crush him. This is it. Armageddon.*

*   *   *

Forty-six men, I count. Not a bad turn-out considering the short notice. I stand on the Poor Ground wall looking down at them while Turlough and Sean sit behind the crowd on their carts, loaded with timber and corrugated iron. The crowd looks at me dubiously.

'I'm not building nothing on top of any graves,' says Jerry McGrath.

'There's plenty of room, we're not going to build anywhere near the graves.'

'That ground is like iron, you can't dig that up,' says Colm McDermott.

'The hard ground will make for a great natural floor. I have the plans all here,' I tell them. Turlough hadn't idled away his time on the road to Emyvale. He had sketched out plans and presented me with several sheaves of paper. I pass them round. Turlough reckons that with a bit of precise pick work we can erect a skeleton of load-bearing stanchions thick as mooring lines and build the hall around that skeleton, rather than dig foundations. His sketches are of a simple structure, a barn really, measuring about forty by twenty – far too small for the two hundred people we're hoping will turn up, but he says if we make it any bigger we'll need proper foundations. We will complete the basic structure with the standard timber two-by-four and dress it in corrugated iron. It'll be draughty as hell but it'll serve. Frank Vallely, who played full forward for the team, puts up his hand like some schoolboy. I nod to him.

'Victor, I'm glad to help, you know yourself, but, well, a man has to make his own living. I've a lot of work on this week …' He's only saying what a lot of the men are thinking. Frank has three babies in the house and livestock in the fields depending on him, and of course every man's first duty is to put food on his own table.

'This is important work, Frank,' I say.

'I know, Victor, but like, you know, there's only so many hours in the day …'

145

'Damnit, Frank, your fucken sheep has had your full attention all their lives, they can do without you for a week. Victor Lennon fought at the GPO for the Irish Republic, so if he says it's important work then the only question coming out of you should be how you can contribute,' snaps Turlough with a surprising vehemence.

'I know, Turlough, I'm only saying that ...'

'Let there be no more talk about it. We have a lot of work to do,' says Sean.

Turlough jumps down from his cart and strides through the crowd, leading them over the Poor Ground wall past where I'm standing like a rock in a stream. Sean stays back and shepherds the stragglers over the wall. When they're all over, I turn to them and they hush down.

'No man should see his livelihood suffer because of our efforts here. Any man who needs help in any aspect of his business should come to me. Help will be provided. Socialism is not about asking working men to sacrifice their material needs, quite the opposite. However, sometimes we must enter into struggle in order to secure our rights. Together, as a united class of workers, we can achieve exponentially more than we can as individuals. I ask just one week of you, one week in which you offer your services to the struggle.'

Turlough and Sean direct the unloading of the carts and pile the timber and corrugated iron sheets neatly. No-one questions their assumption of authority, and I stand by, taking more of an overseeing role. Turlough gathers together all the tools that people have brought with them: tape measures, plumb lines, string, sticks, picks, loys, hammers, nails, spirit levels, saws, hatchets, plywood boards for mixing cement. He sorts them into

146

distinct piles: hammers with hammers, picks with picks and so on. Frank Vallely grumbles that he'd better get his tape measure and spirit level back. I assure him that none of his comrades would steal from him, any more than he would steal from one of his comrades. We mark out dimensions, drive little stakes into the ground and tie string between them until the large rectangular shape is clearly laid out, running parallel with the street about five yards inside the Poor Ground wall. Sean marks out intervals in which the stanchions will stand and sets the men to work preparing the ground. Turlough organises twenty-five or more men in groups working on pre-fabricating large rectangular timber frames buttressed by vertical, diagonal and horizontal beams. 'They'll slot in between the stanchions and they'll be solid as brick,' Turlough says.

'They look like Union Jacks,' I say.

I stand back and watch my community, my people. You can deliver lectures till kingdom come about the emancipating power of work, about the intimate relationship between the worker and the fruits of labour, but revolutionary consciousness is not an intellectual exercise. The irony of revolutionary consciousness is that there's nothing conscious about it. Any socialist worth a damn is a socialist firstly in his marrow, not his mind. Nevertheless it's important to provide the intellectual framework. Heads, as well as guts, have to be politically sound. I go over to a group of lads making a timber frame under Sean's watchful eye. 'I want to teach you lads a song,' I say. Arise you workers from your slumbers. Arise you prisoners of want. I'm not much of a singer but they soon pick up the tune and after a while they're singing along as they hammer nails into wood. They're intrigued when I tell them it's the new anthem they're singing in Russia. Aidan Cavanagh has a question. I tell him he needn't put up his hand. He asks if Russia is going to pull out of the war.

'Without a doubt.'

'But President Wilson said he was going to keep America out of the war and then after he was re-elected, within a few months …'

'The Bolsheviki are different. Look, the American banks have lent billions of dollars to England and France. Not millions, mind you. Do you know what a billion is? It's a thousand times a thousand times a thousand. If Germany wins, the American banks won't get that money back, and if they don't get their money, the banks will fail and the American economy will fail with them. So American workers have to die to protect the profits of American bankers.'

'Jesus, that's very cynical,' says Jerry McGrath, hammering hard at a nail to punctuate his point.

'It's the warmongers are the cynical ones, sending working men and boys to their deaths to protect profits. They didn't foresee how bloody this war would be, I grant you, but they won't mind seeing the working class thinned out a bit. Imagine the trouble all those young men could cause if they were back home and unemployed. Better to have them fighting other working men than realise who their real enemies are.'

'But if the Russians pull out there'll be no eastern front. The kaiser will be in Paris by Easter and we'll all be Huns this time next year,' says Aidan.

'You think the war is between England and Germany? The kaiser, the king, the tsar are all on the same side. But the Russian comrades are giving example to the rest of us. They're seizing their own destiny. They think people should come before profit. Germany will be next, and if it can happen in Germany it will happen all over the world.'

'The Germans killed my son,' says Jerry McGrath sadly, 'I won't be looking to them for any example.'

'I didn't know that, Jerry. I'm sorry.'

Turlough puts his hand on Jerry's shoulder. 'Brendan was my best friend and I loved him very dear, but he should never have been there in the first place. He died not for his country but his country's enemy,' he says. Jerry's head drops.

Poor Brendy McGrath. He never had much by way of brains. I can see how the army would appeal to a lad like that. A living, a pension. Those things matter to working-class lads with few other options. That's the awful genius of the status quo. It offers short-term relief to those in need, but in doing so, it enlists into its frontline defences those with most to gain from change. 'If we have revolution, real revolution, then the war will be over.'

'Who'll have won?' says Aidan.

'Us.'

'Us?'

'The workers.'

TP McGahan approaches, well turned out in a decent brown suit and probably the only boater hat in Madden parish. He's even sporting a white rose in his lapel, like he's a real gentleman of the press, not the errand boy of a provincial unionist yellow-sheet. He whips a notebook and pen from his jacket pocket before he even reaches me and smiles a smile so patently insincere, he looks even more runtish than usual.

'I must admit, I didn't think you'd go through with it. Thought that was just the drink talking last night,' he says.

I don't exactly ignore him but I keep watching the men working on the stanchions and timber frames, and mixing the cement. They don't know it themselves, but with every swing of the pick and every nail driven in, these people, my people, are making a choice. I'll be able to rely on them when the time comes. I light a cigarette.

'What do you hope to achieve, Victor?'

'Is it not obvious?' I meet his eye with the greatest seriousness. 'Comrade Lenin reckons this parish is the key to worldwide revolution. He sent me to organise Madden Soviet.'

I leave TP standing with his pencil in his hand and a stupid look on his stupid face. He's scribbling down what I said. 'Madden Soviet? Victor, tell me more,' he says. What an eejit. I go over to Turlough as he swings a pick mightily at a large rock bursting up through the surface of the soil. I ask him how we're going. He says we've made a good start but we need ladders. As many as we can get our hands on. Erecting the stanchions will be five times harder without them.

I cast my eyes up the street towards Charlie's shop. It's probably not fair to ask him, but fairness has nothing to do with it.

The bell above the door rings as I enter. Charlie is alone in the shop, standing leaning across the counter. He stands upright and his eyes go to my feet; I have left muddy footprints all over his floor. He sighs. 'What the hell are you all doing out there?'

'We're building a hall, a hall for all the people …'

He rolls his eyes.

'We are creating an emancipated proletariat that won't cower before superstitionists like Benedict.'

He shuffles backwards, puts his thumbs into his waistcoat pockets and looks at me blankly. 'Victor, you have to stop blaming Bishop Benedict for the mess you've made of your life,' he says.

'This isn't about me, Charlie, I'm just a messenger. This is about the people. Do you not read the papers? Do you not know what's happening in the world?'

He laughs in my face. This is a waste of time. There's no sense trying to reason with such an entrenched reactionary consciousness. Only bitter experience will teach him his wrongness. Behind me the bell above the door rings and Sean and Turlough enter. Charlie doesn't look so defiant now. 'I didn't come here to debate. I've come for the ladders,' I say. 'Madden Soviet is requisitioning the ones out in the back yard for the rest of the week.'

Madden Soviet. Madden Soviet. It doesn't sound quite as ridiculous as it did at first. Once you think about it. Madden Soviet. I am the leader of … no, I am the chairman of Madden Soviet.

Charlie turns white. All he can say is: 'No.'

I nod to the Moriarty boys and they sweep past. Charlie is too stunned to shout out as they drag him to the back room and shove him down into his chair. On the desk are piles of coins and stacks of banknotes. He stares ahead sullenly and sits with his shoulders hunched. Sean spots a large bunch of keys hanging from a hook in the wall. He shows them to Turlough, who nods and, without a word, they let themselves out the back door into the yard. We hear the lads lifting the ladders and taking them down the street. Charlie looks at the ground, he won't meet my eye.

'This is vitally important work we're doing here, Charlie. You shouldn't be so selfish,' I say, as collegially as I can.

'Thief.'

151

He doesn't understand. 'You think those ladders belong to you? What about the carters who brought them from the railway station to your shop? What about the railwaymen who brought them from the docks? The stevedores who took them off the ship? The sailors who brought them across the sea? The craftsmen who made them at the factory? The lumberjacks who chopped down the trees? The smiths who made the saw? The ironmongers who made the iron for the smiths? The miners who took the metal from the earth? Do you not see, every item in this shop that you think belongs to you, wouldn't be here at all without the labour of a thousand men? Do you not see how ridiculous it is to think these ladders are the exclusive property of such a small and insignificant link in the chain as yourself? The bloody shopkeeper? They belong to the workers, and we the workers require them for the duration of our great project.'

'You're insane.'

Charlie wants me to feel guilty, but it won't work. I'm not about to get squeamish. In life, sometimes you have to choose sides. That's what the lockout was about. Murder Murphy must have seen the children starving on the streets, he must have seen them. But he was unmoved. That's what the rising was about too. That distant, bobbing tam-o'-shanter that stopped bobbing after I fired at it; the man beneath it probably had a family, was probably a decent fellow. I'm sure they all are, at some level. But you make your choice, choose your side, and you live with it. Our People's Hall is about making people choose sides. Property rights versus human rights. Bourgeois capitalist versus the workers. I've picked my side, Charlie has picked his. I inform him that he'll have his ladders back by Saturday.

Back at the Poor Ground, work can begin on erecting the stanchions. The ladders make it much easier to join together the beams. Having the right tools is half the job. Sean tells some of the lads that Charlie was in a bad emotional state when we went to speak to him, and all around are mutters of solemn agreement that Charlie was never the same man since he came back from France. Work progresses quickly and by the time Sean calls a halt to the day's work in the fading light, all the stanchions stand erect at the correct points and wet cement is starting to harden around the bases. The comrades chatter with palpable excitement as they store away the ladders and frames neatly under a tarpaulin. We work hurriedly as the last of the light is fading and it's starting to rain. It's threatening a bit of a squall, in fact. As we finish, I spy Charlie through the dullness, standing by the Poor Ground wall and watching us.

'Thieves! Robbers! Anarchists!' he cries. Idiot obviously knows nothing about anarchism. Aidan Cavanagh looks to me with confusion. Sean taps his finger against his temple. Faces appear at windows along the street. 'Those are my ladders and I want them back. Or are you going to strong-arm me in front of everyone?' Charlie wails. He looks like he might break down in tears. Seeing a grown man lose the run of himself so completely is unedifying for everyone. He approaches, close enough to hit me with his cane, and says: 'You can't just take a man's things.' He's almost sobbing now, as the rain batters his cheeks, but as he speaks, lamentably, pathetically, he loses his balance. He tumbles forward and plants his cane into the ground too successfully: it remains upright and he almost impales his armpit on it. I move in to try and catch him but not quickly enough and he falls forward on his stump, his entire body weight pushing it down into the mud. He shrieks with pain and all around, men turn away and wince. I pick him up and hold him in my arms. He pants as though he couldn't catch his breath and his eyes are wide as two-bob bits. He looks at something behind my shoulder with naked dread. 'Oh Jesus, my heart, I can feel my heart, can you not feel my heart? It's going to jump out of my chest,' he whispers, his terror terrifying, but there's nothing behind me, nothing that should scare him so. It's pitch dark save for the dim lights of lanterns while beyond, in the miserable rain, the new stanchions stick up out of the Poor Ground like the giant legs of an upturned table. Charlie convulses. Turlough, Sean, Aidan, all the men, they all look at me as though I should know what's to be done, but I have nothing. The rain falls hard on Charlie's forehead and, looking into his manic eyes and trembling limbs, I want more than anything to tell him I'm sorry.

'Stand aside. Let me see him,' a voice commands and, feeling a hand on my shoulder, I move away without protest. Benedict kneels down and takes Charlie in his arms; gently, gingerly he cradles him and pushes the hair from his eyes and forehead. Father Daly stands with him, and, when Benedict signals, the young priest picks Charlie up and carries him towards the Parochial House. He's stronger than he looks, that Father Daly.

'What's wrong with him?' I say.

'I'll take care of him from here,' the bishop replies.

\*    \*    \*

*By the end of the month you have fifty thousand men from all trades with you. Sister unions in England send essentials on supply ships and help with the strike pay. Each man on strike gets ten shillings a week. Not much, but enough to survive the duration. You know the bosses are rattled when a police contact reveals there's a bench warrant out for Big Jim; if he comes to Dublin he'll be arrested. But he's already in Dublin, holed up in a secret location only you and a few others know. You hit the streets and make sure all of Dublin knows that Big Jim Larkin will address a monster meeting on the street they call Sackville and you call O'Connell the next Saturday, warrant or no warrant.*

*O'Connell Street is black with strikers and supporters. Murphy has handed over his Metropole Hotel to the peelers for the day, and there's hundreds of them there. They're supposed to be keeping their eyes peeled but they're too busy stuffing their faces with cucumber sandwiches, the fat, corrupt bastards, to notice when a very tall, broad, angular lady in a peacock hat walks into the foyer. A uniformed 'porter' follows with her luggage. The peelers step aside for the 'lady' and they don't look at you at all. You're just the bag-carrier, not worth noticing. Big Jim walks quickly and, it must be said, gracefully up the stairs to a room on the first floor. Below on the street they must be bemused to see a lady in a peacock hat appear at the balcony, until the lady throws off the disguise and growls, in that familiar voice, for workers of all nations to unite. The crowd goes half demented. Big Jim's voice rises and falls like a trumpet. He is a great soloist, his register the melody, the roar of the workers the chord. The workers respond. Finally they're hearing something worth listening to. They cheer when cheering is right and listen silently when silent listening is needed. They raise up their heads, perhaps for the first time in their lives. His words will stay with all who hear them.*

155

'This great fight of ours is not simply a question of shorter hours or better wages. It is a great fight for human liberty, liberty to live as human beings should live, exercising their God-given faculties and powers over nature; always aiming to reach out for a higher betterment and development, trying to achieve in our own time the dreams of great thinkers and poets of this nation – not as some men do, working for their own individual betterment and aggrandisement.'

*Humiliated peelers with axes make splinters of the barricaded door. You signal to Big Jim that it's time; a comrade throws up a rope from beneath the balcony and he shins down to the safety of ten thousand comrades. They have the Dublin Metropolitan Police but you have the Irish Citizen Army. The peelers are too late to catch him. They give you an awful hiding in the cells of Store Street that night, but it's worth it.*

\*    \*    \*

Father Daly laid Charlie on the sofa in the kitchen while Stanislaus poured him a glass of water. Wide eyes and shallow breathing testified to Charlie's terror but there was none of the violent writhing Stanislaus had seen in lunatics he had given Last Rites to. As Stanislaus poured water onto his audibly dry lips he fancied he could hear Charlie's heart beating in his chest. The water was pacifying; Charlie's breathing slowed and his eyes ceased their darting. Father Daly put a cushion under Charlie's head and draped his overcoat across him like a blanket. Charlie shivered and pulled the collar of the coat up to his chin. Stanislaus told Father Daly to go and find Margaret Cavanagh.

'It was so cold, the rain went through you. I couldn't get a breath. My mouth was so dry, like I couldn't even swallow,' said Charlie, the poor lad babbling.

Thirty-one out of a hundred and seventeen Madden boys of military age had joined the British army in 1914; a large percentage if you excluded those who would have chosen the gallows first. John Redmond said Irishmen should fight for little Catholic Belgium and the rights of small nations, and Charlie's late father had been a great admirer of Redmond. Charlie asked for advice, and Stanislaus told him of Cardinal Logue's wise non-opposition to the war – true, in 1914 only a few dozen of Ireland's three thousand Catholic clergy actively supported the war and got involved in recruitment, but even fewer openly opposed it. So like the others, Charlie joined up, believing he had the bishop's blessing. Now, fourteen of the thirty-one Madden boys were dead. Sixteen remained in the field, but in the saddest recess of his heart Stanislaus knew the ratio had not finished shifting. Only Charlie had returned home so far, and to an Ireland changed by Easter Week. There would be no new recruits from Madden, Victor and his comrades had ensured that. The imperial dead would lie silently disavowed.

'What were you and Victor arguing about?' asked Stanislaus, and when the boy seemed unable to answer, Stanislaus put a hand on his shoulder and squeezed reassuringly. He went out to the kitchen and made a cup of tea with five spoonfuls of sugar. 'For the shock.' Charlie held the cup between his hands as though warming himself, and though the sweetness seemed to sicken him, drank every drop obediently.

'Victor's gone mad,' he said at last. 'People need to know the truth about him.'

'All right, Charlie, don't upset yourself now. Everything is going to be all right.' Stanislaus paused. 'But you're right, people *do* need to know the truth about him. Otherwise, how will they know which side they should be on?'

Charlie nodded. 'I'm on your side, Father.'

Margaret Cavanagh arrived brandishing her father's medical bag. She brushed past Stanislaus and started fussing over Charlie. 'Did you feel a tingling in your lips and fingers?' she asked.

'I don't have shell shock. I've seen them that has it. I'm nothing like that.'

'Did you find your vision getting blurry around the edges?'

'I thought I was going blind.'

'And the leg?'

'It's fine. It only hurt for a few minutes.'

'I'd better have a look.'

She stroked his cheek before she lifted the overcoat from his legs. The bandage was spattered in mud but there was no sign of blood seeping through. 'This dressing is filthy,' she scolded as she rolled it away. 'Tell me if it gets too painful.' She removed the last of the bandage to reveal a hairless, featureless mound of flesh stretching a few inches below his knee. 'You're lucky, the skin hasn't broken,' she said, which Stanislaus thought astonishing, so fragile was the flesh drawn across the stump of the absent limb. It was like the skin of a drum stretched so tightly it would surely puncture with the first beat. Stanislaus had seen a broken-down stump once. It was all boils and sores, and it bled and wept and cracked. Charlie was lucky. He pulled the coat further up over his face to hide his tears, and Stanislaus felt for the pale, skin-and-bones boy. Father Daly brought a basin of soapy water and a sponge, and Miss Cavanagh washed Charlie's stump.

When it was clean and smelling of Lifebuoy, she took a fresh bandage from her medical bag and, holding the stump with one hand, unrolled the bandage in a criss-cross pattern with the other, starting at the bottom and working up to a point a few inches above the knee. Stanislaus lifted the dirty bandages and stuffed them in the range door to the fire. 'These are only fit for one place,' he said. 'Miss Cavanagh, will you look in on him from time to time, to see to his bandages?'

'I will,' she said.

'He really shouldn't be living alone. He needs someone to look after him.'

Stanislaus led Father Daly out of the room, leaving Miss Cavanagh and Charlie Quinn alone together.

\* \* \*

Mercifully, the rain hasn't penetrated the tarpaulins around the feet of the stanchions, so the cement has set and they stand steady as stone pillars now. Sean gets half the men to keep making the timber frames while Turlough gets the other half up ladders, affixing the completed frames to the stanchions. By noon, a discernible shape is beginning to emerge. However, I count only thirty-five men on site this morning, eleven down on yesterday. If we keep losing men, we'll have no chance of completing work by Saturday. I ask around, to see if anyone knows where the missing men are, but no-one seems to know. I stand by the wall of the Poor Ground and watch as the clanging of the bell at the National School presages an out-flowing of schoolboys and schoolgirls onto the street. Four young fellows of about eleven with satchels on their backs walk past. Turlough calls over a skinny, gangly lad with a mess of red hair. 'Come here, young Knipe, till I talk to you. Where's your da today? Why's he not here?'

'He said he wasn't coming today.'

'And why was that now?'

'My ma says the priest is against the whole thing and he said he isn't going to go against the priest.'

'We haven't heard a word from the priest about anything. If he was against it, wouldn't he come down here and say so?' I say.

'You know who this is, don't you?' says Turlough to the young lads.

Young Knipe's face lights up and his mates nod their heads excitedly. 'Victor Lennon.'

'Why don't you lads come in and help us? All the men are doing it,' I say.

'You hear that, lads? This man stood up for his country and stuck his finger in John Bull's eye. Now he's asking you, will you do your duty for your country or will you not?' cries Turlough, and the lads clamber excitedly over the wall. Turlough stops young Knipe. 'You go to the schoolyard and round up as many of your mates as you can. Tell them there's work to be done, far more important than oul schooling.'

Soon enough we have twenty-five boys holding ladders, carrying timber and hammering nails. Sons hold ladders and pass tools up to fathers who, under the enthralled inspection of their heirs, work all the harder. I'm not thrilled about taking them out of school, but the virtue of the goal mandates imperfections in execution. The whole thing runs smoothly and we make spectacular progress. I owe everything to Turlough and

Sean; without them everything would fall apart, and I tell Turlough as much.

'Well now, I was meaning to mention this,' he says. 'We got a telegram this morning. There's a man in Darkley, a man I've done work for before. He wants us to build him a new cattle shed, but he needs it immediately. Needs us to start tomorrow. I haven't replied yet but he's offering four pounds. God knows that's a lot of money to us, Victor. There's so little work in the country at the minute.'

'I gave youse two pound.'

'Very generous it was too, Victor. And you know, myself and Sean believe in what we're doing here, really we do. We believe in you. You're a great man, Victor. So I'll tell him to keep his four pound, we're staying here and finishing this hall. If you can match it.'

There is no telegram, no man in Darkley offering ridiculously generous wages. They know their value, like the capitalists they are. Turlough smiles at me and I want to smash his fucking face in. I nod in acquiescence but I have to walk away and go and stand by the wall, holding on like a passenger gripping the rails of the deck and trying not to be seasick. I'm not sure how long I'm standing there before I hear a commotion. Maggie climbs over the wall into the Poor Ground and, safely on her feet, storms over to the work site and grabs young Knipe by the ear.

'Why aren't you in my classroom?' she demands, dragging him by his lughole away from the ladder he was holding for John McDermott, who cries out in protest. Maggie pays him no heed. She leaves young Knipe standing by the wall nursing his ear, and moves quickly towards another young fellow. 'Peter McWilliams, do you think you're going to improve your atrocious grammar

161

with a hammer in your hand?' she says as she slaps the lad hard across the face. The crack rings loudly.

'I'm sorry, Miss Cavanagh, I told the boy he could come with me for the day,' says the boy's father but Maggie shakes her head sternly and he turns away, shamefaced.

'Every single one of you who should be in school, if you're not lined up against that wall in ten seconds flat, I'll turn your hands to leather,' she cries, and as I move gingerly towards her, she gives me a withering stare. 'One. Two. Three. Four ...' The schoolboy volunteers are lined up against the wall in considerably less than ten seconds, and Maggie leads the hangdog phalanx back up the street. I hop over the wall and follow them. She stands by the door of the National School and ushers them all inside, keeping a furious eye on me as I approach. 'You stole half my class,' she says.

'There's an education to be had outside these walls, you know. They can learn a lot in a few days working with me.'

She shakes her head. 'Jesus Christ,' is all she says as she slams the schoolhouse door in my face.

As I trudge back down the street, I see Charlie watching from his window. Smirking bastard. Who is he to judge me? How many has he widowed and orphaned? Every day the headlines say the war is being won but the small print carries the names of the dead, and the lists are long. Workers killed by workers. People like Charlie killing people like himself. And he *volunteered*. Volunteered to kill fellow workers for king and empire and capital. What if they'd sent him to Dublin for Easter Week? What if he'd seen me in his crosshairs: would he have hesitated? Would I? Comrade Lenin must have friends who disagree with him, or even abhor him. And surely he has some allies who are scoundrels he'd otherwise cross the street to avoid. Politics is not about friendship, it is about alliances of interest. This is only truer of revolution. Revolution is often incompatible with human concerns like friendship or love. Let Charlie abhor me if he must. But I wish it was Charlie standing by my side now, not the Moriartys. Not those parasites.

\* \* \*

At dusk on Wednesday the pentagonal, timber-framed skeleton of the building is complete. We're ahead of schedule. I'd thought it would've been Thursday or even Friday before we got to this point. As we're knocking off for the day Aidan Cavanagh comes up to me and shows me an inside page from the *Armagh Guardian*. There's a Charlie Chaplin show at the Cosy Corner picture house, the new place on Russell Street. He says Maggie mentioned in passing how much she wanted to see the show. I doubt she wants to see me at all, but it is Wednesday. Better to assume the invitation in the condensation of the car window still stands, than risk standing her up.

When I call to the house, Aidan answers the door with a conspiratorial nod. I show him the bunch of daisies. 'Very nice, she'll like them,' he says. 'Maggie! Door!'

I lick my palm, pat down my carefully combed hair, finger my tie nervously. I never wear a tie but Pius talked me into it. No woman of calibre will take seriously a man who doesn't wear a tie, he reckons. Better to have one and need it than need one and not have it, I suppose. I'm fidgeting as she appears at the door. She gives me a look that demands I state my business quickly.

'It's Wednesday.'

She folds her arms.

'I have the cart waiting. I have money for two tickets to the pictures, two hot water bottles and two dinners at the Rainbow Café.' I jut out my arm, inviting her to take it.

'You can't be serious.'

'I made sure none of your pupils were working on the site today. I even chased a couple of young ones I found mitching off up the road there.' She eyes the daisies sceptically as I hand them to her, but she does take them. She holds them to her nose.

'I have far too much to do here to be gallivanting to the pictures,' she says sternly.

'No you don't, we're mad to get rid of you for one night,' says Aidan, sticking his head around the parlour door, and the giggles of all Maggie's eavesdropping siblings explode from inside the house. She turns vengefully but Aidan shuts the parlour door before she reaches it. She's flustered.

'It's Charlie Chaplin. You'll love him. He has the funniest walk,' I say, and taking a step back I do the little waddle I've seen in the pictures. Maggie tries not to, but she lets a little titter escape her. She tries to reassert her poker face but she can't help it. I do the little waddle again and she laughs. I jut out my arm again.

'But I haven't a stitch to wear,' she says.

'I'll wait here, you go and get yourself ready.'

She reasserts her serious face once more, and raises her eyebrow. 'Why should I go with you, Victor?' she says.

'Because you love me.'

The words hang in the air like gun smoke after a volley of muskets.

'You love me,' I say again, and her lip trembles.

'You love me.' A tear materialises like a jewel in her eye and escapes down her cheek.

'You love me.'

*   *   *

She takes a little while to get ready but when she reappears at the door, I see she was lying about not having anything to wear. She wears a blouse, coat, stockings, shin-length dress showing off a bit of ankle; all black, save the occasional white trimming here and there. All pristine, classy, conservative even, except for angular, vivid red shoes. I help her climb onto the trap, and she remarks that she hasn't seen it for years. We've done well to salvage it, she says. I admire her hat; it's one of those ones shaped like a bell that I've only seen the most up-to-date girls in Dublin wear. Maggie keeps up, it seems.

'It's called a cloche,' she says.

'Clash?'

'Cloche.'

'Claw-she.'

'It's French.'

'Well, you look beautiful,' I say, and she *does* look beautiful. As we head out of Madden and onto the main Armagh road I steal glances at her and catch her stealing an odd glance back in my direction. My eyes are drawn especially to her shoes. They do strange things to me. Narrow heels and dainty uppers. I swear it's as exciting as if she's not wearing any clothes at all.

'What was the name of that picture I read about, did you see it, the one about the negroes?'

165

'*Birth of a Nation*?'

'That's it. Did you see that one? Was it good?'

'I wouldn't shy away from calling it a work of art.'

'Really? I thought the moving pictures were just little entertainments? Like this Charlie Chaplin; he was in the music halls before he went to America, wasn't he?'

I shake my head. I don't know.

'I read that somewhere. He's actually from England. You'd hardly call a music hall comedian an artist, would you? Falling down and hitting your head doesn't make you Sir Henry Irving.'

If I ever see her without her clothes, I'll ask her to keep on those shoes. I can see it clearly in my head: Maggie, naked as a statue save for the red shoes. Maybe in stockings too. No. Too much like a Monto girl. Or Ida. Maggie's better than that. Though maybe it'd heighten the effect? I'll give it some thought. I look at her, demure in black save red shoes and caramel skin, and in my mind's eye see her on her back, panting desperately, her skin flushed and pink now, the red shoes still on her feet, up behind my ears somewhere, and then she turns into Ida and I can't shake the image from my mind even as we arrive in Armagh, even as we sit down in the Rainbow Café, even as Maggie pokes at her salmon and I devour my bloody beef.

'Penny for them,' she says.

'More than they're worth.'

She places a forkful delicately into her mouth and I try to put the vexing thoughts from my head. I'm conscious that I've said little.

'In ten or twenty years there'll be no more plays and all the theatres will replace their stages with screens. Who wants to watch somebody prancing around a stage when you can watch red Indians or moving trains or whole battlefields on a screen?' I say.

'Will we still have books?'

'People won't need them when they can go and look at reels of film. You take *Birth of a Nation*. In three hours you learn more than you would in a dozen books. Of course there'll still be books in libraries, for academics and historians and such.'

She drops her knife and fork and they clank loudly on the plate. She looks annoyed, emotional even. 'You were always so zealous about everything,' she says. 'I don't want reels of film to replace books.'

I put my hand on hers and squeeze it. 'We will always have books.'

\* \* \*

The doorman stands before the heavy, iron-clasped Tuppenny Door of the Cosy Corner Picture Palace. He surveys the long queue stretching down Russell Street and glances impatiently at his watch, as if willing the second hand to move more quickly. 'If you don't stop pushing and fuck away off from my door, youse aren't getting in,' he snaps to some young fellows near the front. Maggie is worried the seats will sell out, since the line is so long, but I wink and crook my arm and we skip past the crowd to the queueless splendour of the Shilling Entrance, enjoying the jealous glances as we go. An elderly doorman with silver hair and gentle eyes touches his cap and opens the varnished mahogany and glass panelled door.

'Good evening, Madam. Good evening, Sir,' he says as we step into a marble foyer. Maggie looks like she's going to laugh. I point her to the glass cabinet of the refreshment stand.

'But I just ate.'

'This is what people do at the pictures. They get little treats. Apparently in America they have a confection made of corn, and you can eat it for hours without ever getting full.'

'I suppose they would have something like that in America.'

She looks up and down at the mint imperials, the chocolate raisins and the Yellowman, and in the flicker of her eyelashes I see the fearless and guileless girl I once knew, for whom experience was the purpose of life. I don't know anyone else I'd say that about.

'That's a florin,' says the man behind the box-office glass brusquely. His impatience is downright impertinent. It's not like there's a mad rush of people queuing behind me, and I don't look out of place among the well-dressed people here. I drop the coins noisily and take our tickets with a humph. Maggie orders chocolate raisins and two cups of hot chocolate, and I get her a hot water bottle. She says she doesn't need it, but women always get cold in the picture house, even in the summer. The usher takes us in and points his torch to the cushioned seats inside the red rope. Behind the rope are rows of hard benches filled with Tuppenny Door folk, and it's strange not to be among them, fighting for elbow space or for standing room at the back. It's strange to be sitting among the enemy in the cushioned seats, but it strikes me that maybe sitting on this side of the red rope mightn't necessarily prove you are the class enemy. For every bourgeois seeking distance from the unwashed, there's probably a working man just trying to impress a girl. Girls *are* impressed by such things. Maybe if they get the vote they'll become less trivial. I stretch out my legs. It is nice in here, it must be said.

The lights dim and the piano player tinkles his first notes of accompaniment. The whirr of the projector replaces the hubbub of the crowd. Charlie Chaplin appears on the screen, and people in the crowd who've seen one of his pictures before whisper *that's him* to those who haven't. Maggie picks at her raisins. The pianist tries to keep up with the action on the screen as the little tramp with a funny walk spills a bottle of milk on himself while he's holding a baby. The tuppenny-seat people roar, the better-dressed folk smile. The tramp passes a police station and, in a fit of good-living zeal, goes in and volunteers to clean up Easy Street, the nastiest place imaginable. The pianist plays a snatch of something from *HMS Pinafore* and Maggie sits forward in her seat. She's wasting the arms and cushions I've paid a shilling for but I don't mind. When we were children preparing for Confirmation the priest told us how a Catholic child needed the gift of 'wonder and awe in the presence of God', and the concept had escaped me but as I look at Maggie in the flickering silver light of the screen, watching with eyes round as saucers, I think I get it. Inside twenty minutes the tramp-turned-constable has turned Easy Street into a God-fearing neighbourhood. The monstrous villain becomes a respectable bourgeois who takes the outside of the pavement in deference to his wife, herself transformed from a sluttish harpy, as they walk to church. Chaplin and his good-living girl walk arm-in-arm after them. It's reactionary nonsense, but to me, Maggie is the real show. She giggles girlishly and squeezes my hand as the screen goes black. I nod to Maggie to tell her that means the film is over. Mad applause explodes. They show two more Chaplin reels before the intermission, Maggie enjoys each one more than the last. She asks if I can explain the contraption in the third film, the moving staircase that goes up and down, and I tell her it's called an escalator.

'There's a shop in Dublin where they have one. In America they have them in their houses.'

'Oh, I wouldn't want one of those in my house. They'd be very dangerous. But it was so funny, the way he would fall down the stairs and then the stairs would carry him back up to the top, and he'd try to walk down, but the stairs would be rising up against him, and ...'

After the intermission they show a romance with Florence La Badie. I tell Maggie she looks like Florence. She tuts dismissively but she loves it. The film is quite salacious. When Florence's parents get divorced you can spot the Catholics in the audience fidgeting uncomfortably. The audience fidgeting becomes general when Florence ditches her irreproachable fiancé, a doctor type, and takes up with an obvious scoundrel who is later revealed as a free-loving type. Maggie is riveted with revulsion. I'm almost painfully aroused. The audience is mollified when, upon learning of her new suitor's proclivities, Florence brains him with a statuette, and goes back to the doctor type as the film ends.

Afterwards we walk down Russell Street towards the vast, open common of the Mall. They say it's exactly a mile around its perimeter; we walk the ash-canopied cinder path twice, and I take care to allow my lady the inside. We meet an RIC man on his rounds and he tips his helmet. Maggie stifles a giggle. 'I don't think I'll ever be able to look at a policeman again and not see

Charlie Chaplin,' she says. 'I can see why you like him. Look at how the rich people are presented in his films. They're all vain and greedy and violent.'

'What other way is there to present them?'

Maggie chats excitedly and unguardedly about the films and I cherish each step we take, arm-in-arm, in the flickering, gas-lit prettiness. The Mall is ringed with churches and Georgian terraces, courthouse and bank, gaol, museums and war memorials, but once, horses raced here by day and whores whored by night. This was the centrepiece of some long-dead archbishop's resurrection of Armagh, Patrick's gone-to-seed citadel. I ask Maggie if she knows cock-fighting and knuckle-fighting and gambling and carousing and all sorts went on here, once upon a time.

'If you're going to reform a place, you start in the most rotten part,' she says.

We walk the path bisecting the middle of the Mall and sit down on the bench by the Crimean cannon. She says her favourite bit was when Florence gave the scoundrel his comeuppance with the statuette. My favourite bit was when Charlie boots the policeman up the arse at Ellis Island.

'I'm not surprised you liked that bit. That big statue of the woman holding the torch; was that the Statue of Liberty?'

'Did you never see the Statue of Liberty before?'

'Of course. I mean, I think so. I think maybe I saw an etching. It's beautiful.'

'You're beautiful.'

She frowns. 'I've had a lot of fellows knocking on my door,' she says proudly. 'Yes indeed. Some were quite ardent.'

'And did you entertain any of them?'

171

'It would have been queer if I hadn't entertained any.' Her brow furrows. She looks so melancholy. 'A couple of them I tried very hard to love.' She pauses. 'There are fewer interested parties lately,' she says, just as matter-of-fact as that. 'Twenty-eight and still a virgin. I think men are suspicious of that.' She snatches her hand back and doesn't dare look me in the eye. 'I have a proposal of marriage. From Charlie. He asked me a few days ago. I told him I'd consider it.'

I laugh, but only for a second.

\*   \*   \*

We get into the trap and head for home. It's true that Maggie's most marriageable age is a few years behind her, and it's not good for a woman to have her first-born when she's looking at thirty; the window is closing and she knows it. But Maggie has the beauty, the brains and the breeding to make up for it. We stop outside Madden, looking down the gentle incline into the village. The skeletal frame of the People's Hall, partially robed in tin walls, is vaguely discernible in the dimness. We'll reach the eaves and make a start on the roof tomorrow, and with a bit of luck we'll have the whole thing finished by Friday night. I take Maggie's hand and she lets me hold it for a moment.

'Will you stay?' she asks.

'I don't know. I'd like to, but there's a fight I'm supposed to be in.'

She laughs bitterly. 'Of course, the big socialist!' She takes back her hand. 'Ask people around here about socialism and if they've heard of it at all, they'll say it means the government is going to take their land off them again.'

172

'I have forty or fifty of those people you're talking about working with me, standing up to Benedict,' I say.

'Only because Father Daly says it's all right.'

I'm nonplussed.

'Father Daly is a Sinn Féiner,' she says. She can see I didn't know. Usually the dog-collars clamp down hard against any kind of boat-rocking, especially among their own. 'Everyone thinks you're Sinn Féin too,' she says.

'Sinn Féin are a bunch of bollixes.'

'You fought in the Sinn Féin rebellion so you're a Sinn Féiner. There's only one question people care about, and you and Father Daly are on the same side of that question.' She puts her hand to my face, strokes my cheek gently. There's tremendous sadness in her eyes. 'The girl you knew had to grow up. But my Victor never grew up, did he? He'll never change. Always full of spiels and knows nothing about himself. Purest gombeen, born and raised, and everybody knows it. So why is he playing the socialist?' she says softly.

When she puts it like that, and gives me the look she's giving me, I honest to God don't know what to say.

\*　\*　\*

*Hunger is worse in winter. You have burned all the furniture for fuel, and food is scarce. First the strike pay dropped from ten shillings to five, and now it has stopped altogether. The supply ships from England have been fewer. There has always been a population of youngsters living on Dublin's streets but their numbers seem to have multiplied as the lockout has gone on. Packs of dirt-caked gurriers scavenge like jackals around the north side. The Monto girls aren't on strike. Murphy's four hundred thieves keep coming to Monto for entertainment every night, even as they wreak famine on the working families of the area by day. But some of the Monto girls donate food or money at the Liberty Hall. You have to sneak them in the back door – if your workers or their wives knew where their meal had come from, the food would turn to ash in their mouths. Every now and then, Peggy O'Hara makes you liver and onions, and by God, you're grateful for it.*

*Connolly arrives from Belfast with a plan to evacuate the children to sympathetic families in Liverpool for the duration. They can eat and live like human beings there, leaving their parents free to win their emancipation. But Cardinal Logue denounces the plan. Better that the children should starve in Catholic Ireland than be corrupted in heathen England, he says. His priests board the ship and seize the children, taking them back to the land that starves them. Their parents, the same people who have struggled like lions against the bosses, let them. The starving armies of Dublin's socialists start drifting back to work soon after. They accept whatever terms they are slapped with, no matter how degrading.*

*You have failed.*

*After this, you must never again mistake capitalists and imperialists and clerics for equally human beings. They are heels treading on the face of humanity. You should have remembered your Thucydides: the strong do as they wish, the weak endure what they must. Justice exists only between equals in power, and the strong know it. After the lockout, you know it too. You know what you have to do.*

# FOUR

By the time the light fails on Thursday, no more than a quarter of the structure of the People's Hall remains to be done. Counting myself, twenty-eight men down tools at the end of the day and the consensus is that only a few hours' work will be needed tomorrow to finish the job. I stand up on the wall of the Poor Ground to address my men.

'Comrades, it has been another fine day's work. Our great task is almost completed and it will stand for many years to come as a testament to the energy, the productiveness and the solidarity of the Madden proletariat.'

Sean Moriarty patrols the perimeter of the crowd. He slaps John McGrath hard on the back and says: 'Go on there, Comrade, sing up that song Victor taught you.' John looks uncomfortable and makes no noise until Turlough starts to sing: '*Arise you workers from your slumbers*.' I sing up, '*Arise you prisoners of want*', and by the end a good few others chime in to make a halfway decent chorus. Afterwards I dismiss them and tell them I'll see them all tomorrow morning at nine, but Aidan Cavanagh says they can't come at nine. They'll all be at mass. It's a Holy Day of Obligation, he says. I bite my tongue. They still feel the need for their opiate, so I'll let them have it for now. Better to acquiesce in the short term. Their revolutionary consciousness is developing whether they know it or not. They filter away, leaving only Sean and Turlough with me.

'Something has come up, boss. Something unforeseen. It's the bishop,' says Turlough.

'At mass tomorrow. He's going to denounce you,' says Sean.

'He's going to tell everyone you are to be excommunicated,' says Turlough.

'That everyone should shun you.'

'That anyone working on the People's Hall will be barred from the chapel.'

'Turned away from the altar.'

'Maybe even excommunicated themselves.'

'That mightn't bother you, but it'll scare the hell out of people around here.'

'Or put the fear of hell into them.'

'Nobody wants to be a heretic.'

'This is serious stuff, Victor.'

'We could be the only ones left here tomorrow.'

I don't know what to say. I look at the People's Hall and for the first time I'm afraid it might never be completed. This might be as close as I ever get. 'How do you know about this?' is all I can think to ask.

'We know everything that goes on in this town,' says Turlough.

I run home, not even stopping for a smoke despite the painful stitch that stabs at my side before I'm past the Parochial House. I want only to be home. Even if we get the hall finished, people might boycott the céilí. What a humiliation that would be for us.

Who am I fooling? The humiliation will be mine. I dash up the road, up the lane, and make it home quicker than I've managed since my school days.

'Pius! Daddy!' I cry. 'Daddy, where are you? I need to talk to you.' I open the door of the bedroom. Inside, Pius lies slumped across the bed, his feet dragging on the floor. He hasn't even managed to collapse properly. Poteen is spilled across the floor, an almost empty bottle lies on its side, telling of Pius's afternoon and his broken vow. I check in case he's dead, but of course it's a stupor, so I put him into the bed and sit in the armchair beside him. I sit there for a long time, two or three hours or more in the pitch black. I'm ready to talk to my father now, I wish to God he would wake up. Excommunication. Even the word sounds like a particularly vicious kind of amputation. Benedict is as formidable as the collar he wears, and I've seen men who fought like lions against earthly kings fall to their knees before one of those collars. I wish I could talk to my dad, but I'd settle for just anyone right now. At this hour, there's only one person I can call on, God help me.

I enter the barn as quietly as possible, God forbid anyone should see me, and light the storm lantern, which hangs exactly where she said it would. Light flickers across the dim, opaque barn. I wonder whether I ever truly intended to keep the promise I made to myself not to come here. Maybe it was always inevitable. How long before she'll see? I take the watch from my pocket. Twenty-three minutes past twelve. Almost midnight by the new imperial time that people are too spineless not to acquiesce to. Fat king George gets his extra labour and people just go along with it. If ever a revolution was needed … The barn door opens. Ida comes in and closes it noiselessly behind her. She faces me with a flamboyant flick of her tousled hair. Her eyes flash in the intermittent light of the storm-lantern. 'It's you. I knew you'd come,' she says.

I make no reply, no move, no gesture, as she comes closer. She's been asleep, or lying in bed at any rate, and hasn't even stopped to fix herself before coming to me. She opens her shawl. Her breasts heave up and almost out of her under-dress, and she looks down at her body, then up through her lashes to me, as though issuing a challenge; I should get on with taking what surely I have come for. I reach out my left hand to her right, and my right hand to her left, and slowly, gently, I pull them together, closing over the shawl. 'I'm not here for that.'

She's surprised. She tugs the shawl tightly around her shoulders and steps back. 'There's no charge, if that's what you're thinking,' she says, and my expression must convey how appalled I am at the suggestion. 'What do you want, Mr Lennon?' she demands, and I'm surprised to realise she's embarrassed.

'Benedict is going to denounce me from the pulpit in the morning. He's going to try and have me excommunicated.'

'I thought you were an atheist anyway?'

'But excommunication … I have turned away from the church, but it's just that …' I'm struggling, I don't have the words. I don't understand myself.

'You signed up to be the Prodigal Son, not Lucifer.'

'He's going to denounce anyone who stands with me.'

'What are you coming to me for?'

'I don't know. There was no-one else.' I pause a moment and take her in. She's easy to talk to. There's nothing at stake. 'Somebody asked me recently why I'm socialist. I couldn't answer her but I can answer you. I watched the bosses starve a hundred thousand families for the best part of a year. And when we had the bosses beat, it was the priests that finished us. You have never conceived of such cruelty to so many people for so long. God forgive me if I ever make peace with that.'

'I know exactly what you mean,' she says. 'Victor, you were at the GPO. The way people talked about you, I thought you'd be eight feet tall. You were a hero. They still want you to be a hero. They haven't definitely decided you're not one yet. If you stand against the bishop now, a lot of people will be torn, for a few days, at any rate.'

There's wisdom behind those black-as-coal eyes. I must force people to choose sides. They'll likely fall back in step with the Church after a few days, but those few days and that confusion are there to be used. The iron is hot. If he denounces me from the pulpit, I'll denounce him from the pews. By the time everyone calms down the People's Hall will be built and we will have triumphed, and maybe that'll mean I'm not a false prophet after all. Maybe that's what prophets are: people who keep a fiction going long enough for it to become true. I thank Ida. She opens her shawl once more, but I shake my head.

'I'm in love with the schoolteacher,' I say.

\*   \*   \*

Maggie comes to the door in her night-dress. 'Do you know what time it is?'

'I'm so sorry for destroying everything. It makes me so sad, but it's in me and I can't help it and this time tomorrow I don't know where we'll be so I want to tell you now, before whatever happens tomorrow, that I love you and I don't ever remember not being in love with you and only you.' I pull her into my arms

181

and our lips come together as though every future kiss hinges on this one. Her lips are so marvellously soft, it's like they've never been kissed before. I open my mouth French-style and she opens hers too, thrusting in her tongue like there's something in my mouth she desperately wants. Suddenly she withdraws her lips and steps back, looking dazed, but she takes my hand and leads me inside. Closing her bedroom door behind us she turns with eyes wide and dilated and throws her arms around my shoulders. I clinch her waist tightly and move her onto the bed. She pulls me down towards her as my hands fumble stupidly, throwing aside her shawl and undoing her petticoat. He skin smells warm and earthy and moist and her nostrils are splayed wide, and she kisses me angrily as I lift up her skirt and try to untie her knickers. Little beads of sweat form on her brow. I look into her eyes for a sign that what I want, she wants too. 'Let me,' she whispers. She undoes the knot, lifts her hips from the bed and slips her undergarments past her hips, her knees, her ankles, and down to the floor. I undo my belt buckle, unbutton my trousers. She opens her legs and I lower myself into her. It takes a moment but we get there. She's warm and wet, and she holds me tightly. All the time, we peer into each other's eyes. Sometimes she smiles, sometimes she moans gently, I suppose I do too, but mostly we whisper to one another, over and over, the words 'I love you, I love you, I love you.'

When it's over we hold each other for hours. It's deep in the night when she lifts her head from my chest and looks at me. 'You still have my heart, Victor. Take care with it this time,' she says. And I'm gripped with the strangest sense that I've done something terrible to her.

\* \* \*

It was late and he had to rise early, but Stanislaus wanted to read through his notes once more. He had said the Feast of St Margaret of Scotland was a Holy Day of Obligation and no voices had been raised to suggest it wasn't, so at nine o'clock the next morning the chapel would be full and they'd all be anxious to hear what he had to say. He wasn't sure whether he wanted Victor to be there: it might be best to denounce the ruffian to his face, but his reaction couldn't easily be predicted. Stanislaus hoped the sermon was enough to rescue the flock from the demagoguery of a madman. He considered making it starker but forced himself to put down the pen. The sermon had pleased him earlier, before the brandy had warmed his blood. Best to trust that judgement now.

'No compromise between the man defending his home and the arsonist,' he read aloud. Overdue fighting words. He had the pulpit, he had the authority of the Holy Church and the right-eousness of God on his side, yet he had wasted days paralysed at his window watching Godlessness wrack the parish like disease in the body of a loved one. They had almost finished their shrine; a tumour on the landscape. He sipped from his glass. Mrs Geraghty had given him a look when he'd asked her to pick up some more brandy, he had run out already. What business was it of hers? By any but Old Testament standards he'd had a long life and lived through many battles. He had one more in him, then never more. Tomorrow he would declare his parish for Christ and defy anyone to dispute it, but younger men like Tim Daly, with their softness and liberalism, would have to carry on the fight.

What did Victor Lennon know of famine? Stanislaus had seen famine. And he had seen how the Church had saved the nation from mental and moral collapse afterwards. What is there but the cloth and the bottle, after holocaust? Even yet the nation had not begun to understand its trauma: how could it, having been cleaved from its language by the rusty blade of ethnocide? Having but a mercurial relationship with the brutish new tongue? Victor Lennon and the likes of him were toying with issues deeper than they knew. They were asking too much of a bewildered amputee of a nation, the surviving sibling of a murdered twin.

Someone was at the front door. Stanislaus looked at the clock but it was a blur in the darkness. He heard Father Daly explain that it was long after a decent hour but soon, footsteps on the creaking staircase were followed by a light, apologetic tap on the study door. Father Daly stuck his head inside. 'I didn't know if you were still up. It's so dark in here, can I turn up the lamp?' He waited a moment and, hearing no objection, turned up the main lamp, bringing light where there had been a vague glow. 'Smoky too,' he said.

'Who the hell is at the door now?' Stanislaus demanded.

'Charlie Quinn wants to see you. I told him to come back tomorrow but he seems very determined.'

'That boy keeps appalling hours. Tell him to come in.'

\*   \*   \*

Maggie is gone from the bed when I wake but she's outside the bedroom door, fussing around and making sure all the Cavanaghs are ready for mass. The clock on the wall shows a quarter to nine and I'm ashamed to have slept so late but thrilled to be where I am. I pull on my trousers and shirt, and

I'm washing my face in a basin of clean water left thoughtfully on the dresser when Maggie comes in. Neither of us knows what to say so we share a nervous giggle, and drying my face quickly, I sweep her into my arms and kiss her. She pushes me away with feigned mortification. 'What if someone comes in?' she says, but I'm not fooled. I seize her again and plant my lips on her till she's well and truly kissed. Her resistance revives when she realises I'm manoeuvring her towards the bed. 'No, Victor, I have to go to mass,' she whispers, and I'm about to reply but she silences me with a finger to her lips. 'Wait till we're all gone to the chapel before you let yourself out. And please don't let anyone see you.'

We kiss again and she straightens herself. She opens the door and she's about to leave when I say: 'You can't marry Charlie. You have to marry me.'

She closes the door and stands inside with her back to me for a moment. Facing the closed door, I fancy she wears a rueful smile as she whispers, as if to herself: 'If I could talk to myself when I was ten ... Charlie and Victor ... What would I say?' She turns to face me. 'I don't think I'd be in the least bit surprised.' Her expression is that of the officious schoolmistress now, no longer the lover. 'I won't be a widow in some Dublin tenement.'

'What are you talking about, widow?'

'You said marriage. Marriage means a future and a home. I won't be mistress to a man married to a cause.'

'Och, Maggie, I've asked you to marry me. Are you saying yes or no to me?'

She opens the door. 'I'm saying yes to you. But only if we stay here. Both of us. You need to let me know if you can say yes to me.'

After she's gone I wait a short while before letting myself out of the house into the empty street. The vacated homes and suspended workplaces are eerie in their silence. All the parish is enclosed behind the granite walls and mahogany doors of the chapel, and the sound of their incantation is at once massive and distant, suggestive of great clamour without drowning the song of the sparrows. The incanting grows louder as I get nearer. No-one has ever before heard of St Margaret of Scotland and it's no Holy Day of Obligation, but Benedict has issued a summons and that's the end of it. Sucking down a lungful of air, gently and quietly I open the church door.

Young men stand solemnly inside the door. Turlough and Sean are among them. They nod as I nudge through. Aidan Cavanagh greets me with eyes that implore me to peace. There's standing room at the top of the centre aisle, staring straight down the spine of the church to the altar. The pews are packed, and on the altar Benedict mumbles the mumbo jumbo. He's facing away from the congregation so I don't know whether he knows of my entrance. Everyone else knows. Whispers ripple through the seated ranks like the thrill a prize-fighter's arrival sends through a crowd previously unsure the fight would go ahead. TP McGahan brazenly takes notes from the back pew between prayers. He'll have to explain his lateness to work on a day that is not holy anywhere outside Benedict's teetering realm, but his Protestant boss and Protestant readers will enjoy a yarn about quarrelling Catholics. Kate McDermott gives me a look that is positively hostile. Charlie turns away after the briefest second, as if he can subject himself to the sight of me no longer. Pius kneels with his forehead on clasped hands, while Maggie kneels in the same posture. I look at her auburn ringlets, her delicate shoulders, her graceful neck. She turns to look at me, something desperate in her eyes. She mouths something, but I can't make her out. She simplifies: 'Please. Victor. No.' A few seats over, Ida Harte ogles me with maniacal glee. Father Daly the Sinn Féiner fixes me with a stare. I've met a thousand green-orangeman like him, all with the same prejudices and inconsistencies of thought. Though the dog collar is novel, I will say that.

'Per evangelica dicta deleantur nostra delicta,' Benedict intones, and the congregation mumbles its part of the call-and-response routine like somnambulant parrots. He puts down the chalice, bows at the tabernacle and walks to the pulpit. I fancy he stalls for a second as he spies me, standing square on and looking straight down the aisle at him. Benedict mounts the stairs of the pulpit slowly, deliberately, and shuffles his papers below the marble lectern, taking time to compose himself. Someone breaks the silence with a hacking cough that seems loud as gunshot. Benedict looks up.

'Most of you will have read about the terrible events in Russia. Some small number of anarchists claim to have affected a revolution in that vast and benighted nation. Time will reveal whether the lawful and moral authorities will return their country to peace, and we must pray that they shall, for the revolutionists do not believe in Christ.' He pauses and looks down the aisle at me. He speaks well, the old bastard. Clear and commanding. 'They wish to destroy all forms of religion, these Bolshevists. They are not all Jews, but they would all be Christ-killers. They would give their country over firstly to the kaiser, and then to the devil. Their talk is of equality but their business is the murder of priests.'

187

The congregation shifts in the pews and Benedict affects another skilful pause. He leans forward and continues. 'In this country, we remember Blessed Oliver Plunkett. We remember how we were hunted and hanged for our fealty to the one true faith. We remember when our loyalty to the Holy Father was called treason by others. We know that freedom of faith is not a right but a hard-won and easily lost prize. I am old enough to remember the old folk speak of the Mass Rock. I remember old priests telling of their lives as fugitives. These were heroic men, criminalised for their vocation. Those hellish days, in truth, happened only a moment ago. Only our vigilance prevents their return. The faithful in Russia are confronted with that reality this very day.'

He pauses for a long time and casts his eye around a congregation planted in rapt silence. The thrust for my jugular is coming, I can feel it, but for Maggie's sake I will remain silent.

'And yet despite all this, people in our midst applaud the Bolshevists. Some people in this country and in this very parish feel quite relaxed about such an attack on the faith. The evidence of this is plain to see in the temple of wood and tin being built in the Poor Ground, just yards from this holy place.'

Unrest washes through the church. There's naked shock in the eyes of men who've worked by my side all week. They only want a bit of a dance on Saturday night to celebrate the footballers. He's telling them that hammering a nail through tin at Madden Poor Ground is like hammering one through flesh and sinew on a bloody cross at Calvary, and I don't think the congregation wants to shoulder it. Unless I miss my guess, Benedict is over-playing his hand.

'Many of you have helped build that monstrosity with the most honest motives, and have no truck with any wicked Russian creed. My good news to you this morning is that it's not too late to turn away from those who would mislead you. I say to you, in the name of the Lord, I will not stand idly by and watch an agent of evil lead my flock as lambs to damnation. Victor Lennon, you are the corrupter. You are the serpent. You choose to rule in the Poor Ground rather than serve in heaven,' Benedict says, the scorn oozing like slime from the pulpit. He's staring at me, daring me to the struggle. I do not avert my eyes from him, but for Maggie's sake, neither do I speak. 'Your empire, your *soviet*, is built on the bones of the damned, where no respectable Christian will touch it.'

Johnny Morrissey stands up and cries angrily: 'The Poor Ground was good enough for my daughter.' Everywhere, heads look up from their study of the floor. The silence is stunned. 'My Daisy only lived for an hour. How can she be damned?' Johnny says.

'I have a twin brother in the Poor Ground,' says Jim O'Hagan, full-back from the football team. 'He died when we were born and but for the grace of God it would've been me. I don't believe I won't meet him some day. I won't believe it.'

And one person after another stands up and shouts about the person they love who's lying in the Poor Ground. The chapel is noisy with the anger of those confronting the bishop and those defending him. Benedict grips the side of the lectern, as if he's afraid he'll be swept away. He has turned white. Maggie's head is buried in her hands.

'My Daisy is in heaven,' Johnny Morrissey cries.

'Get out of this church, Victor Lennon. I cast you out, and all those who would stand with you,' Benedict shouts, recovering

189

sufficiently to muster some ferocity. There seems no point in staying silent now.

'My mother is in heaven,' I say. 'Yes, my mother, Deirdre Lennon, stands acquitted anywhere there is justice. And by God there is none in this place. She is damned only by you and your dogma.'

TP McGahan can't write quickly enough. Pius's head is bowed. Maybe he's praying. Maggie is crying. Charlie struggles to his feet. 'Get out of this parish, Victor, get out and don't come back, you fucken lunatic,' he cries, his oath prompting gasps.

Turlough brushes past me and storms towards Charlie. 'Sit down and shut your mouth, Quinn, you're not in your regiment now. Victor Lennon has done more for this parish and this country than ten generations of youse leeching gombeen bastards,' he snarls. Charlie shrinks. Turlough would take Charlie out and shoot him like a dog if I ordered it.

'Out! Out of this chapel, Lennon, Moriarty and all your fellow-travellers. I cast you all out,' Benedict roars, trying to take back control of the situation.

I summon the attention of the congregation. 'Let me say this to you all: go to any village in Ireland and the priest will have the biggest house while working people struggle to live. Bishop Benedict talks of the Penal Days but he forgets the Famine, when the priests locked their doors and let the people starve. I have seen priests collude to keep Irishmen out of work and out of food. I have seen priests bring starvation to children and claim it as Christ's will. I have seen priests lock people out of their very graves. And the Bishop has locked us out of our Parochial Hall. As always, when the people are in need, the Church locks us out.'

'The Parochial Hall is Church property,' Benedict replies, but I'm surprised at how weakly the words slither out.

'It is built by the sweat and muscle of the men of Madden. All the Jesuitical capitalist dogma in the world can't dilute our rights!'

'It belongs to the Church,' he says again, still more weakly.

'These people are not the poor, illiterate peasants of the Famine days. These are proletarians and they have built their own People's Hall. The People's Hall is our Mass Rock.' I turn away from Benedict, I am finished with him. I speak to my people. 'Comrades, our work is not yet finished. Let every able-bodied man, woman and child come with me now to the Poor Ground to complete our great project.'

Maggie is still crying.

Turlough whoops and Sean press-gangs some of the young lads around him towards the door. I stride through the throng and out the door, not stopping till I'm on the other side of the street. Turlough comes first, Sean last, and between them a crowd of fellows emerge blinking into the daylight, shocked and scared and angry but most importantly, there. They remind me of some of the Volunteers who turned out on Easter Monday expecting to do the usual drills and manoeuvres and be home by dinnertime. Sorry, lads, today's the day you do the thing you've talked about doing for so long.

I count the men. Aidan Cavanagh's there. Jerry McGrath. Johnny Morrissey. Jim O'Hagan. Plenty more. Maybe twenty men. That means twenty families, which means a hundred or more people we can rely on. Not bad at all.

Maggie probably hasn't stopped crying yet.

You had to do it, Victor. You just had to, didn't you?

* * *

191

Stanislaus closed the vestry door behind him, tugged the stole from his neck and threw off his vestments with a roughness that was almost irreverent. He exhaled, long and loud. Father Daly came in, picked up the vestments and folded them. 'Almost everyone is with you, Your Grace. Lennon hasn't twenty followers,' he said gingerly. 'It is shocking to see scenes like that inside a church.'

'Where do you stand now, on this fellow, and the threat he poses?' Stanislaus demanded.

'I think his stay in this parish should be concluded very soon. I thought that even before this morning's ... unpleasantness.' He paused. 'You decided against telling them what Charlie Quinn told you?'

'You were right. It would have been wicked, to condemn Ida Harte. Particularly since the rumour may not even be true.'

'Our Lord often reserved his greatest compassion for fallen women.'

'Yes, thank you, Father.'

On leaving the vestry they found Pius Lennon alone in the empty chapel, looking like he had barely moved since the mass ended. Stanislaus glanced over to make sure Pius was well. The man was deep in prayer. Outside they found a crowd milling on the street. The mood was ugly. As long as they'd been inside the church walls they had mostly kept their heads bowed but now, unbounded, they were angry and unstable.

'We're with you, Father, we don't want the like of that there here,' said Kate McDermott. 'What you said about the Penal Days was right, these youngsters nowadays don't know how we had to fight.'

Charlie Quinn had a fearful zeal in his eye. 'Why are we standing here talking when the communists are building their hall as we speak? Why aren't we over there burning the place to the ground?' he cried, and the emboldened crowd cheered. 'Let's drive Victor out of Madden on the end of a rail!'

Charlie looked over his shoulder and saw Pius Lennon behind him. He blanched. Stanislaus was slightly glad. There had been a sight too much speechifying lately. Charlie seemed to steel himself.

'Go on about your business, every one of you,' said Pius, and the crowd dissipated quickly.

* * *

Stanislaus was relieved to get back to the sanctuary of his study. He poured himself a large brandy and noticed Father Daly looking askance. 'If every morning was as eventful as this, society would look very differently on an early-morning stiffener,' he said defensively as he slumped into his chair.

Charlie Quinn bounded in suddenly, uninvited and un-announced. 'Why didn't you tell them?' he demanded, sounding quite deranged.

'Charlie, sit down before you fall down,' Stanislaus commanded.

'I will not sit down. Victor's in there every night fornicating with thon hoor and you are saying nothing.'

'I am not prepared to destroy Ida Harte's life.'

'Last night you said you would. Last night you told me to say nothing because it would carry more weight coming from you.'

'I know what I said,' Stanislaus snapped, though he remembered only hazily, 'but I have to believe this parish can be saved without denouncing one of our own.'

'She's not one of us and she never will be.' Charlie paused. 'Are you going to tell the people about Victor and his whoring?'

'I am not.'

'What if I did?'

'I must do what I believe to be right. So must you.'

Mollification spread across his face. Father Daly and Stanislaus exchanged grave glances as they heard Charlie's crutch negotiating the creaking stairs.

\*   \*   \*

Later, in the early afternoon, Stanislaus was alone in his study when Mrs Geraghty poked her head around the door. 'There's a girl to see you, Father. She says you sent for her but I hardly think …'

'Send her in.'

Mrs Geraghty did nothing to mask her distaste as she showed Ida Harte into the study. Stanislaus signalled for her to sit down. 'Thank you for coming. Can Mrs Geraghty get you anything?'

'Cup of tea would be great. And I'd take a sandwich if there was one going. Or a biscuit or whatever you have handy. I didn't get a chance to eat anything yet. I'm starving.'

Mrs Geraghty's lip almost curled in on itself as she sloped out with the petulance of a Frenchman. She will boil-wash the cushions Ida's sitting on, he thought.

'Do you know why I asked you to come here?'

Ida shrugged.

'Victor Lennon.'

He hoped she would betray herself with a panicked comment or look, but he saw no recognition, no admission that she had even heard the name before, in her wide-open, black eyes.

'Ida, you know it's a sin to lie to a priest?'

'Is that all the time, or just in confession?'

'All the time.'

She grinned mischievously, as if she didn't believe him. Stanislaus hoped his own expression betrayed no doubt. 'I never lie, Father,' she said.

'Do you know what Victor has been up to at the Poor Ground?'

'I know the same as everybody else.'

'I thought you might have knowledge of a more intimate nature.'

Again Ida's expression gave away nothing. Mrs Geraghty came in and set a tray on the desk. She poured two cups of tea while Ida grabbed a ham sandwich and bit off a chunk. Mrs Geraghty tutted as she retreated from the study, as if the sight of this feral creature in her pristine Parochial House was more than her good manners could tolerate. Ida seemed not to notice as she devoured the sandwich, and when she finished it, she reached for another. Finally she met Stanislaus's gaze. She gulped.

'Have you anything to say?' said Stanislaus.

She swallowed and shrugged. 'You seem like you have something you want me to say, Father. Why don't you tell me what it is, and I'll tell you if you're right.'

Stanislaus slammed his fist down on the desk, at last seizing her full attention. 'Who do you think you are, to speak to me with such presumption? But for me, you would be run out of this parish with your head shaved. I alone vindicate you. I alone do not take you for a whore.' He paused and took a breath.

'Rumours are circulating. You have been carrying on with Victor Lennon. So far, I have suppressed the rumours, but Ida, you must tell me the truth. Ida, you must confess.'

This time, every wrinkle and crevice in her face bore witness against her. But it wasn't guilt Stanislaus discerned. It was more like some diabolical pride.

'Who has been talking about me? I want to know who has been talking about me,' she demanded.

'You deny it?'

Ida stood up, picked up a sandwich, and turned to leave. 'I'll find out myself if you won't tell me who has been casting aspersions. Good day to you, Father,' she said.

'I can't protect you any longer,' Stanislaus replied as she walked out the door.

\*    \*    \*

Sean comes over to where I'm sitting on the Poor Ground wall, my thoughts miles away, and tells me we're finished. 'One more nail and it's done. Come on, get up the ladder. You should be the man to do it,' he says.

I look at it: the People's Hall. It's rudimentary and ugly and it'll be draughty as hell – it's a glorified hayshed, truth be told – but it's *there*. It's a tangible statement in wood and iron, and for all my talk, I realise now that I had never really believed we'd finish. My twenty men, my last remaining stalwarts, look to me now. They are proud men, discovering for the first time in their lives what it's like to be in the saddle instead of under the lash. From the looks of it, they like it. Aidan Cavanagh beams as he hands me a hammer and Johnny Morrissey hands me a six-inch masonry nail. My men whoop and holler as I ascend the ladder and drive home the final nail. From atop the ladder I wave down to them. This must be what victory feels like. I descend and shake hands with every man there. Aidan Cavanagh prises off the lid of a bucket of paint. 'Just the right shade of red,' he says, and dunks the paintbrush bristles into the scarlet goop. He hands it to me and nods. I take it and daub a long diagonal line on the wall of the People's Hall, and top it so it looks like an elongated capital T tilted to the side.

'What's that?' says Turlough.

'It's a hammer,' say Aidan.

From the corner of my eye I spot Ida Harte coming out of the Parochial House. My heart falters. Benedict is sitting at his window, watching. What the hell is Ida doing at the Parochial House? Be calm, Victor. Calm now. The vultures are circling, but don't panic. Panic burdens good comrades. Panic is selfish and childish. Panic is moral incompetence. Bad comrades panic. Don't panic, Victor. Calm now. I plunge the bristles once more, and I make a question mark, tilted on its side and crossing the elongated T.

'And what in God's name is that?' says Sean.

'A sickle,' says Aidan, pleased with himself. 'The hammer represents the proletariat. The factories and the cities and such. The sickle represents the peasants.'

'And that's us, is it?' says Johnny Morrissey.

'The workers in the fields,' I say. 'The hammer and sickle together represents the alliance of workers in all countries. It'll be on the Irish flag after the revolution.'

'After we kick out the English fuckers!' cries Sean, to a great cheer.

197

'*Arise ye workers from your slumbers, arise ye prisoners of want,*' I sing. 'Come on, lads, you know it by now.'

'*For reason in revolt now thunders, and at last ends the age of cant,*' Aidan joins in, and Johnny Morrissey starts in as well. Soon enough, they're all at least trying.

'*Away with all your superstitions, servile masses arise, arise.*'

Ida stops near Kate McDermott's doorway across the street and regards our ceremony with amusement. People start coming out of the houses along the street to see what's going on. At first they come slowly but soon there's ten, fifteen, thirty and more people in the street, facing we twenty singing workers with only the Poor Ground wall standing between us.

*We'll change henceforth the old tradition and spurn the dust to win the prize.*

They look with morbid fascination at the strange symbol daubed on the wall of the People's Hall. And grimly they look at we who built it.

*So comrades, come rally and the last fight let us face. The Internationale unites the human race.*

I stride up and down our line exhorting the comrades who look like they might falter before the undisguised hostility that faces us from the other side of the wall. Kate McDermott. TP McGahan. The Murphys. The other Murphys. They look at us like they hate us.

*So comrades, come rally and the last fight let us face.*

Charlie hobbles into their midst.

*The Internationale unites the human race.*

'That's the symbol the communists use to signal to start killing priests,' says Charlie, pointing to the hammer and sickle.

'That's bullshit,' I say.

'Listen to him, with his fancy Dublin sayings,' Charlie replies with a scorn that seems popular on his side of the wall.

'Aye, it's bullshit and you're nothing but a dirty fucken crippled Tommy fucken liar, you and your fucken king.'

'Calm down now, Victor,' says Turlough.

'Don't tell me to calm down. What was he doing when I was fighting for Ireland? He was bayoneting fellow workers and singing about how the sun never sets on the British fucking Empire. Hoping to get himself an OB fucken E.'

'There's no call for that now, Victor,' says Jerry McGrath at my shoulder.

'Charlie Quinn is a traitor to his country,' I say. 'He joined up because he's loyal to the king of England and he thanks God the surgeon saved his knee because that's where he lives, on his knees.'

Father Daly appears at the back of the crowd and calls on everyone to break up the scene. The mob parts and I see Ida, still standing in the doorway across the street, watching. 'Stand aside there, let me through,' Father Daly commands. 'What's going on here?' he demands when he reaches the front.

'Look at what they've painted, Father,' Kate McDermott shrieks, pointing to the hammer and sickle.

'That's just a squiggle. Ignore it,' says Father Daly.

'Are you siding with him?' Charlie snaps dementedly.

'I'm siding with no-one, now all of you go home,' barks the priest.

'You're siding with this dirty fucker who has been in and out to Ida Harte every night since he got home?'

'Shut up now, Charlie,' said Father Daly.

'Every night he's in to see that little kitty. Sure half the street hears her moaning like a banshee.'

Aidan Cavanagh turns to me. 'Victor, it's not true. Is it?'

Every night, indeed. Charlie's a liar. I don't suppose people will appreciate the distinction if I tell them it was only once, though. But they aren't even looking at me. They're turning to Kate McDermott's doorway, where Ida stands. The crowd is satisfied of her guilt. A stone the size of a chestnut thuds savagely on her breastplate. She puts her hand to her throat and her impish face screams but no sound comes out. A smaller stone hits her shoulder and she makes a pathetic appeal for mercy, but a rock the size of a whiskey tumbler cracks sickeningly against her temple, and a jet of blood flashes across the street as she falls to the ground. Aidan Cavanagh leaps over the wall into the crowd and throws punches left and right, his face contorted with hate. No more stones are thrown but cries of whore and slut and jezebel rain down on Ida with as much ferocity, if less injurious an impact. Father Daly is unable to rein in the mob as they shout for Ida's hair to be hacked off and for her skin to be tarred. Ida is a ball curled in Kate McDermott's doorway, her head and face covered. They might kill her and I won't be able to stop them. Thank God Benedict sweeps into view, cassock swishing and cane clicking with menace. He stands over the visibly trembling girl and faces her tormentors. The mob shrinks from him.

'All of you. Home,' he hisses. No-one moves until Benedict slaps his cane against the ground. 'Now!' he roars, and on both sides of the Poor Ground wall the crowd thins in an instant. Through the dissipating mass I watch Benedict crouch over Ida. She clings to his garments. Aidan Cavanagh comes up and tells me I'm a filthy whoring I-don't-know-what, but I'm looking past him, watching Benedict wrap his cloak round Ida and help her up, like a bird protecting its young. Kate McDermott shamefacedly bows and waits for the bishop and the jezebel to vacate her doorstep. Benedict looks at her with contempt. Aidan spits in my face but I can't take my eyes off Stanislaus Benedict as he leads Ida away. So *that's* how you do it.

Maggie exchanges glances with Charlie as he walks away, and soon everyone is gone but she and I, face to face across the Poor Ground wall. Her eyes sparkle like dew. I'm about to speak when her nose wrinkles and I feel her palm crack across my left cheek. It's loud and it burns. Her shoulders shudder as she hurries away. 'I'm sorry,' I call after her with the half-heartedness of one who knows the insufficiency of the words. 'I'm so sorry.'

I am alone in the Poor Ground now. Every house has its curtains pulled, as if a funeral is passing. I look at the People's Hall. It was supposed to make a proletariat of these peasants. The hammer and sickle paint is the same colour as Ida's blood. All revolutions are baptised in blood.

'Jaysus, Victor, I've seen shooting, I've even seen a hanging, but never till I came to Armagh did I ever see a stoning. Youse are worse than Mohammedans in these parts,' says a voice behind me, an accent exotic in its broadness. Arthur Fox and Bat McClatchey are standing across the street dressed in long tan coats with trilbies pulled low over their faces. 'They should never have let you out of Fron Goch,' Arthur adds, smirking.

'We need to talk,' says Bat.

# FIVE

When we get to the house Pius is suspicious. Bat demands to know who this man is. 'Who am I? This is my house! Who are you?' roars Pius, so incensed that he spills a drop from his cup. Bat looks at the spillage and shakes his head. I tell them Pius is my da.

'We're sorry to intrude, Mr Lennon. My associate and I have business with Victor here. I'm afraid I can't elaborate. I'm sure you'll understand, sir, that it's better for everyone if you don't know any more than that,' says Bat, with a conspiratorial wink, and Pius seems mollified; Bat and Arthur carry with them a seriousness that demands respect. I give him a little nod, and he withdraws to the next room.

Bat sits down at the table but Arthur waits till I take a seat before he does. Arthur's eyes dart left and right, up and down, taking in every detail of the place. I don't like having him here, in the house I grew up in. It looks good, now that we have tidied it up, and we're sitting on furniture that would have been expensive in its day. We're in a big, bourgeois house, my comrade and I, one that testifies to money, and I just know he's sitting there, contrasting it to the purity of the squalor he comes from.

'The Big Fellow wants to see you,' Arthur says.

The Big Fellow? That's what the Volunteers call Mick Collins. We don't. Arthur's one of us, Citizen Army to the backbone. We weren't fooled by that hallucinating poet Pearse and we aren't about to be fooled by some bourgeois bogger with gombeen pretensions. Not Mick Collins and not that strutting Spanish peacock DeValera either. Connolly was a big fellow. Collins doesn't measure up. Not to us.

'You never showed at Shanahan's,' says Bat.

'I was there. Phil threw me out.'

'All right then. But a few weeks pass and still no word. A man starts to wonder,' says Arthur. 'And then we get wind of this.' He reaches inside his coat and takes out a newspaper. It's this week's *Armagh Guardian*. I haven't seen it yet. He sets it on the table so I can see the headline.

## SINN FEIN COMMUNIST DECLARES 'MADDEN SOVIET'

'TP, you bastard,' I mutter under my breath.

'This confuses the issue, Victor,' says Bat.

'Am I in trouble?'

Arthur holds up his hands and Bat shakes his head, as though the very thought is ridiculous. 'I told the Big Fellow you probably just needed some time at home, back on the home patch. Back on home soil,' says Bat.

'Back to see the family,' says Arthur.

'It's understandable. Perfectly understandable.'

'See some old friends. Maybe a sweetheart?'

'Everyone understands. You'd need a heart of stone not to.'

'The Big Fellow doesn't blame you.'

'Nobody blames you.'

'You're not in trouble.'

'We all have families.'

'But it's time to come back.'

'Back into the fold.'

'The work is only getting started.'

'He wants to see you. We need good men.'

'You've proved your worth. Everyone respects you.'

'But this,' says Bat, pointing at the newspaper headline, 'this sort of shite only confuses the issue.' He sits back in the chair. Arthur leans forward and fixes me with a stare that, I suppose, is meant to convey a guarantee. I meet his stare.

'I never heard one of us call Mick Collins the Big Fellow before,' I say to him.

'Fool around with me and I'll fucking bury you, Lennon,' Arthur replies.

'Cool down, both of you,' says Bat. 'Victor, it's going to be different this time. No more fighting on their terms. We have a new strategy, like what Zapata's doing.'

'And if we succeed, what kind of Republic will it be? Good and Catholic.'

'There's Protestants with us,' Bat says.

'Not from around these parts there's not.'

'They'll fucken learn.'

Arthur seems anxious to avoid this particular blind alley. 'It's not about religion, Victor, it's about escaping from the empire so we can build socialism.'

'A revolution without a social programme is no revolution at all, it's just a sleazy wee coup. Tell me about Mick Collins's social programme, comrade.'

'First the political revolution. Then the economic and social revolution.'

'Fucken Menshevik.'

Arthur reaches across the table for me in a rage but Bat stands up and holds him off. He gives us a moment to cool down before he turns to me. 'Lookit, Victor, fuck the social programme. This isn't some high-stool debate, this is war with the British Empire. We are tearing down the butcher's apron and kicking king George out of our country, that's our social programme. Support around the country is growing every day. We have the numbers now. What's needed is leadership. And anyone who was out for Easter Week qualifies. A thousand lads will die for you, just because you were there. You're an Easter veteran, Victor. People see magic in that.'

'So we're all Volunteers now, are we?'

'Sinn Féin is the new vehicle,' says Bat.

'Those Austro-Hungarian fruitcakes aren't even republicans.'

'They are since we took them over. The press all over the world called our rising the Sinn Féin rebellion.'

'Sinn Féin had nothing to do with the Rising.'

'There'll never be another one without somebody calling themselves that. It might as well be us. Right or wrong, the name has currency now,' says Bat.

So a tone-deaf, know-nothing sub-editor in London, knowing little of politics and less of Ireland, makes a stupid mistake, and now we're all Sinn Féiners. I suppose that's mostly what history is: morons messing up the details.

'Is Peadar O'Donnell with us?' I ask.

Arthur nods. 'And he's ten times the socialist you are,' he says, looking round the room with feigned admiration, really making a show of it, like he has never before seen such opulence. I suppose to a man from the tenements it seems big, but he's acting like he's in the Palace of fucken Versailles or somewhere. 'Some of us didn't get to choose our class enemy. You don't know what it is to watch your child go hungry for the sake of your principles, Victor.' He stops glancing around and looks me dead in the eye. 'The lockout was easy for you.'

I dive across the table and before I am able to remind myself that he'll make mincemeat of me, I smack his rotten mouth. He falls back off the chair and I move towards him, but Bat steps between us and pulls a revolver out of his coat pocket. I stop dead. The barrel of the gun points me a few steps back. 'I told you to stay calm,' he says. Behind him Arthur gets up and wipes a tiny sliver of blood from his lip. The look he gives me is terrifying. He grabs my lapel and I try to shrug him off but he's strong as a piston. I await the blow but it doesn't come. He thrusts an envelope inside my jacket. 'That's your train ticket,' says Bat. 'Now start walking.'

Behind me the door swings open and Pius steps in slowly with the shotgun cradled in the crook of his arm and pointed straight at Bat's chest. 'Stand aside, Victor,' he says, directing Bat and Arthur to the door with the gun.

'Please, Da, you don't know who these men are,' I say.

'You: you set that gun down,' Pius says to Bat, ignoring me.

'I'd do what he says,' Arthur mutters tersely to Bat. They both seem respectful of the violence they imagine Pius to be capable of.

209

Bat sets the revolver on the ground and steps away. 'Just so you know, and just so you can't say you don't know, that weapon is the property of the Irish Republican Brotherhood. Someone will be back for it,' Bat says.

'You know the OC in this area?' says Pius.

Bat and Arthur exchange glances. 'Maybe,' says Arthur.

'Well, maybe you can tell him I'll meet him tonight. Tell him to watch for me at the Poor Ground. I'll return it to the ranking officer. That's the way you're supposed to do it, isn't it?'

'All right.'

'You two had better not be anywhere near.'

'Fair enough, Mr Lennon. But if the OC doesn't have the gun by tonight, well, we'll be back soon enough. That fair?' says Bat.

Pius nods. 'And if ever I see you again, I won't ask your business, I'll just start shooting. That fair?'

\*   \*   \*

Stanislaus laid Ida on the couch in the kitchen and cleaned out the nasty cut to her left temple. She braved the icy sponge and the sting of the vinegar with the stoicism of a nun. When the wound was cleaned and dressed with a sticking plaster he pressed a large cut of rump steak into her hand and guided it to her eye. 'To prevent the swelling,' he said. After a while he lifted the steak and examined the eye. 'I've seen a lot worse,' he told her. Mrs Geraghty gave Ida a cup of tea, and Ida scrunched up her face as she sipped it.

'Sugar for the shock,' said Mrs Geraghty.

Ida fell asleep, and Stanislaus followed the housekeeper into the hall. 'Thank you, Mrs Geraghty,' he said.

'She didn't deserve that. But it was bound to happen. She has every married woman in this parish driven to distraction, Father.'

\*   \*   \*

Father Daly spent the afternoon walking the parish and gauging the mood. He came back and told Stanislaus that some thought Victor Lennon was a living prophet, that it was all lies about himself and Ida and by God they'd be at the dance; others, a majority, thought he should be run out of the parish and Ida Harte too, and anybody going near the Poor Ground Hall should be excommunicated or shot, or both. The second group included some who had helped build the hall, and had walked out of the chapel with Victor. Stanislaus went to the couch and woke Ida. He told her it would be safer if she waited for darkness before he brought her home. She insisted she wasn't afraid of anyone, but he told her to hush. 'It's time I heard your confession, child,' he said.

Ida shrank and shook her head violently, her hair moving like a nest of serpents. 'I confessed the other day, Father.'

'You will not address me as Father. I am Stanislaus Benedict, Auxiliary Bishop for the Metropolitan See of Armagh, retired, Titular Bishop of Parthenia, Bishop Emeritus. You will address me as Your Grace and I will hear your confession, child.'

At length she wilted beneath the bishop's implacable stare, and slowly, she blessed herself. 'Bless me, Father, for I have sinned. It has been six days since my last confession.'

'Tell me all.'

'I used the Lord's name in vain. So that's blasphemy. I was disrespectful to my parents, so that's – what commandment is that again? And wrath. I feel wrath.'

'Against whom?'

'All of them.'

'Tell me about the fornication.'

'Not since my last confession.'

Stanislaus hadn't thought of this. If Ida had already confessed her fornication she was under no obligation to confess it a second time. He could ask Father Daly what she had confessed to him, but that would mean breaking the seal of the confessional and it would be better to let the whole world fall first. He tried another strategy.

'Ida, is fornication something that you have confessed more than once?' She stayed silent. 'I'll take that as an affirmative. You know, Ida, any absolution a priest might grant is merely provisional, and dependent on whether it's a good confession. A good confession is when you're truly sorry and resolved not to repeat the sin. I don't think your previous confessions qualify.'

Deep in her abysmal eyes Stanislaus saw a weakening. Tears formed, as if the weight of her wickedness was wringing droplets of remorse out of her. He waited patiently. 'I don't want to do it any more, but sometimes there's no food in our house and you'll do anything when you're hungry,' she said. Stanislaus put his hand on her shoulder, the rock of patience. 'I lay down and opened my legs for money,' she went on.

'Who?'

'In Monaghan, before we came here. Soldiers, mostly.'

'And here, in this parish?'

'No soldiers here,' she said, putting up her hands as though she expected to be slapped at any moment. Eventually she nodded. He could see she needed reassurance.

'We may not be in the church but we are in the confessional, Ida. Nothing you say will be repeated. No-one will know what you say.' He took a breath. 'Now tell me: who?'

Ida too took a breath. 'Jerry McGrath. Sean Moriarty. John McDermott. Thomas Murphy. Nicky the other Murphy. Aidan Cavanagh. He keeps saying he wants to marry me, so I keep telling him he's not to come any more. Pius Lennon ...'

'Enough!' Stanislaus cried in astonishment. He gathered himself. 'Tell me about Victor Lennon.'

She met Stanislaus's eye dead-on. 'No, Your Grace, not Victor.'

\* \* \*

For now, we can only wait till Pius decides to go and see the OC. Pius sits in his armchair with the rifle cradled in his lap and Bat McClatchey's revolver on the floor beside him. He has turned the armchair by a few degrees towards the door so he can warm himself by the fire while he's waiting to blow the first intruder to smithereens. The evening is creeping in and the darkness will help those who wish us harm, but we have two guns and I don't suppose Arthur and Bat have one. I know how difficult guns are to come by, and though I don't know whether Bat and Arthur can afford to go back without me, I'm betting they dare not go back without the weapon. They'll give us a chance to return it but if we don't, they'll find a way to kill us. I'm certain Pius isn't IRB himself, as the Church forbids membership of secret societies and Pius wouldn't ignore the injunction. Besides, he isn't their type. An IRB man needs to be a spy, a politician and an assassin all at once, and Pius is none of these.

'Who is the OC?'

'You're supposed to be the revolutionary. You should know better than to ask.'

I look in the fire at the sprightly flames and think of the hurt in Maggie's eyes as she slapped my face, with all my betrayal and her humiliation behind her hand. Charlie Quinn, that bastard gombeen bastard Charlie Quinn, will be with her at this very moment, comforting her and soothing her and wooing her with promises of comfort and mediocrity, tomorrow and forever. Tormenting her with a sales pitch as she watches the door and waits for me to come and explain and apologise and beg and reset the clocks; to clear all the debris so only the salient, un-assailable fact remains: that I love her and she loves me and we belong together. Yet I'm absent. Imprisoned by assassins at large, but she can't know that. All she knows is I'm not there to offer any words or deeds to salvage things. The one-legged shopkeeper is there instead, whispering in her ear that I have claimed enough years of her life already, that she's a fool for having waited so long for me.

I hope Ida's all right.

I tiptoe around and check the windows, make sure no-one's coming. Pius throws his cigarette in the fire, spits the hocked-up saliva into the grate and takes a sip of poteen. His eyes glower like blazing turf logs, and he looks more terrifying than anything that might lurk in the darkness without. 'You shouldn't drink poteen when you're holding a loaded shotgun,' I say.

'It's after dark. I'm allowed to drink all I want.'

'I know, I know, but to be honest, you're scaring me.'

'If you're afraid, so will they be,' he says with a malevolence that does nothing to reassure me, but suddenly his expression changes to the most disarming tenderness. 'I stopped drinking during the day just because you asked me,' he says.

'Most of the time,' I say.

'Out of respect for your mother.' He pauses. 'You look like her.' He pauses again. 'I stopped my drinking ways when I first met her.'

'I never knew you drank before.'

'There's a lot of things I tried to leave in the past. For your mother.'

'Tell me what Ma was like when she was young, Da.'

'She was the most beautiful girl in the county. Men would come from everywhere looking to court her. She could have married a millionaire. Nobody knew why she would take an interest in a man like me. If there's any goodness in me, she put it there. She put the drunkenness and meanness out of me. She brought me to the Church. It keeps me civilised, now she's not here. There's them would say I'm not civilised, but all I can say is I'd be worse but for the Church.'

He takes a long swig.

'I'm tired, son. I'm tired of playing the civilised man. I'm going to hell. There's no avoiding that. Sometimes a man does things and there can be no redemption. But your mother gave me twenty years of peace and it was more than I deserved. Maybe God will give me peace in the next world, but I don't suppose He'll be much inclined to.'

* * *

It's after midnight when Pius says it's time to go. The important thing is to hand the gun to the proper authority. Pius says he believes the OC can be trusted. Either way, it's the only chance we have of not seeing the gun turned straight back on us. We walk slowly into Madden. Pius keeps the rifle cocked and I hold the pistol carefully, my hand tucked inside the breast of my coat. It's pitch dark and we walk with great deliberation till we get to the wall of the Poor Ground. The night is moonless and starless without a sliver of light. Only the smouldering glow of fireplaces inside slumbering homes punctuates the still gloom. How will the OC, whoever he is, even know we're here?

'When he comes, take the bullets out and hand him the empty gun. We'll leave the bullets by the side of the road further up. We'll leave a cigarette lit beside them so he can find them.'

Something stirs. I look up the street, back the way we came, and in the darkness perceive a figure moving towards us. Pius squints. 'He's alone, isn't he?' The figure comes closer. 'Right then, take out those bullets.'

*   *   *

Stanislaus was wakened by shouts and screams and cheering and jeering. He went to the window but his bedroom faced away from the village so he could see nothing but a dim orange tint in the black night. He dressed and went down the stairs quickly, and was surprised to find Father Daly at the kitchen table sharing tea with two men he had never seen before.

'You're up late, Your Grace,' he said.

'Who are these men?'

'Motorists. They were passing through and had a bit of trouble. They've thrown themselves on our mercy.'

'There's something going on outside. Are you deaf, man?' Stanislaus hurried out the door and saw angry orange shards dancing in the night sky. Bleary-eyed families stood in the street, some looking on passively, others scurrying furiously, as the barn that Victor Lennon had built burned like a bonfire. Sean Moriarty exhorted everyone to join the relay of people slopping buckets messily from hand to hand from the well by the National School. Victor, Pius and Turlough dashed recklessly in and out of the burning building, momentarily dampening the most urgent areas until the blaze blew beyond control elsewhere. The sheer violence of the fire struck Stanislaus as odd. The building was mostly metal, the fire could only feed on the thick beams that formed its skeleton. Though hardly fireproof, the stanchions would have been a reluctant accomplice to an arsonist. Yet looking closer he saw the fire had indeed eaten deep into the wood. Some patient firestarter had nurtured it from a mere flicker to the great conflagration that now licked through the body of Victor Lennon's building.

Crowds were gathered across from the Poor Ground. Kate McDermott. Jerry McGrath. TP McGahan and his notebook out. Aidan Cavanagh looked manic. Many others were there, and in the dancing light of the flames, Stanislaus fancied he saw hate in their faces. Kate McDermott said it was like the *Titanic*: this was what happened when men poked their fingers in the eyes of God. A great crack and creak announced the imminent collapse of the far end of the building; the fire-fighters shrieked with terror while the rest looked on with grim satisfaction.

Margaret Cavanagh, the schoolteacher, ran towards the onlookers in great distress.

'Please help us. There aren't enough of us to fight the fire. Please, before someone is killed,' she begged.

'Stop running after that fucker and making a fool of yourself, Maggie. Come here to me now,' Aidan Cavanagh cried to his sister.

'Shut up, Aidan,' she replied.

Jerry McGrath turned to Stanislaus. 'What should we do, Father?'

Stanislaus marvelled dumbly at the flames as they leapt exultantly heavenwards, defying the night. So it is by fire that the parish will be cleansed, he thought. So be it. Victor threw more water, like an emperor putting down rebellions left and right, though his engulfment in revolution was already assured. The flames would have their way. Stanislaus's flock looked to him. He gripped his cane tightly and shook his head. 'You should tell them to stand back and let the fire burn itself out,' he said.

'Victor is inside there. Pius and Turlough too. If you tell people to help we can still put this fire out.'

'Miss Cavanagh, I have spoken.'

'But Your Grace …'

Stanislaus didn't wish harm on Pius or Turlough or even the Victor fellow, but that wasn't the issue. Those helping Victor fight the fire weren't necessarily choosing his way – when confronted with a fire, it was natural to try and put it out – but those who took a step back with Stanislaus now, their inaction was definitive. Their standing by was a profound statement of solidarity with Christ.

'Sometimes one must surrender to a greater opposing force.'

Charlie Quinn came hurrying up the street as quickly as his good leg would carry him, looking murderous. 'They smashed my window. They've robbed me again.'

*  *  *

We're arriving home safely when I first spot the daggers of flame shooting up in the sky, and I know it's the People's Hall. I don't need to waste time trying to discern detail, I *know*. And we aren't going to be able to save it. Even as we sprint back down the road we have just crept up so gingerly, even as we arrive in the village and see the conflagration, even as we smash into Charlie's shop and commandeer all his buckets, I know it will all be in vain. Blinking, sleep-eyed neighbours emerge from their front doors to see what's happening, and I exhort them to help. I form relay lines of the willing and, steeling every sinew, throw myself into the fight. I promise them the hall can be saved but I know it's finished. The fire will reduce the People's Hall to a burned-out shell, and each pail I throw at the flames is as forlorn a gesture as Cúchullain at the waves. At the far end of the barn, the stanchions holding up the roof look like used matches, pillars of packed carbon retaining their shape but no more now than ghosts of the wood they were. They'll fall soon. The others will follow.

No more buckets are coming in. No more water. Turlough has abandoned me, only Pius remains. He pleads with me to flee but I shake my head, I'm staying in this poisonous, crackling heat. I gulp the smoke. My lungs scream, my skin bakes and detachedly I note how the roof threatens with searing credibility to collapse. This fire must be put to good use. If I die beneath a fiery beam,

219

how might that help bring about a serious social programme? How can I use it to wrest the initiative from the likes of Arthur Fox and Bat McClatchey and Father Daly and Bishop bloody Benedict? The people need example. It's a parish of spineless fools and it needs a shock.

'Victor, son, please, please, son, take my hand,' says Pius, and his tone is so startling that I stop beating the flames with my jacket. It's as if he's going to cry. 'It's over, son,' he says.

I take his hand and he leads me outside. It's like plunging into ice and my poor crackling skin tingles with relief. The clear, clean air dives into my lungs and swirls in my belly, cleansing as the first smoke of the day. Buckets are strewn in an abject pattern across the Poor Ground where people have gathered to watch the demise of the People's Hall. Maggie is in the crowd, her relief undisguised. I suppose most people are glad I'm alive, all things being equal. I look back to the People's Hall as it creaks and groans and the fire hisses and roars. Only now does terror visit. I think I went a bit mad just now, standing under a burning roof and thinking only of how to implement a social programme: that is *mad*.

'You fucken thief, you fucken robbin' thief! You'll pay for my window and for all them buckets too,' I hear Charlie Quinn cry out, and as I turn my head his cane swings for me. I hear the crack of wood against my skull an instant before I feel the pain. It's like someone is pouring hot tar in my ear. I slump to the ground and feel the cane bang against my ribs, but it all seems somehow far away. My head lies against a large stone on the ground. Maggie runs forward to try and stop Charlie as he swings his cane but she won't make it. He's going to dash my brains out. Yet it's the strangest thing; everything seems to happen in half-speed. The red second stretches out. My head is gone before Charlie's cane reaches it, and I'm on my feet before he has regained his balance. My instincts have preserved me against stronger and faster than Charlie Quinn. I wipe the blood from my eye, that same cut as always, and ignore the pain's urgent pleadings. I plant my back foot in the turf and throw a straight left, out from the shoulder, and the shopkeeper collapses like an accordion. He's unconscious before he hits the ground. I draw my boot and aim for about nine inches behind the heart so my steel toecap will still be travelling when it connects, but Maggie throws herself in my way. I seize her in my arms so as not to send her falling back onto Charlie.

The moment is over. Thank God I didn't kick Charlie. I'd have killed him.

The bottom section of the hall collapses in a ball of fire. There's also a high-pitched, piercing bang but, in the din of the collapsing hall, no-one hears it except me. They hear the second shot, this time the low boom of a shotgun. I look around wildly. Forty yards away, around the side of the People's Hall, my father slumps down on one knee, the shotgun in the crook of his elbow pointed towards the blasted remains of Bat McClatchey.

*   *   *

The percussive noise from the crowd ceased and the whooshing violence of the fire scored the wordless scene. Stanislaus looked to the bloody, lifeless body of the dead man, and Pius Lennon, slumped to one knee, presumably drunk. A wisp of smoke came from the barrel of Pius's shotgun. He had finally done it. Stanislaus moved towards them but with a head start of thirty yards and fifty years, Victor Lennon got there well before him.

'Da! Da, are you all right?' Victor cried in panic. He took his father in his arms and howled, primal as a wolf. Stanislaus finally arrived, looked with dread to the dead man and checked whether there was a last breath in the poor fellow, that he might administer the Last Rites, but the dead man was dead as could be. His chest was a mangled shambles and he wore an open-eyed look of wonder. He would have to meet his maker as he was. A second man approached, and Stanislaus realised the dead man was one of the motorists, the men who had thrown themselves on Father Daly's mercy. Stanislaus put his hand to his mouth in horror. Two men passing through, needing only refuge for a few hours. They must have been trying to help fight the fire when, for whatever crazed, drunken reason, Pius had done murder. The other motorist brushed past Stanislaus and bent over his dead companion. Stanislaus supposed he was praying for him until he saw the other motorist wrench something from the cold fingers of his fellow. Stanislaus looked back across the distance to Pius, and saw that Pius was not all right. His shotgun had fallen to the ground and he lay in Victor's arms, holding his belly. The flickering firelight showed Pius's middle to be dark and sticky and wet, as though someone had thrown oil over him. Stanislaus looked back at the motorists. This was no mere murder. The living one stood over the dead and aimed the pistol at Victor, but by now Victor was standing over his father and pointing the shotgun back at the motorist. The pistol sent a high-pitched syllable screaming into the night. Women shrieked and panic was everywhere but Victor Lennon did not panic. His rifle contained only two shots, one of which was spent, but Victor was all decision. He dropped to one knee, no doubt as he'd been taught in his jerry-built army, and fired. The boom of the rifle was like a bass drum to the pistol's snare. Half the motorist's shoulder came away, and he spun backwards, landing five yards from his dead mate and maybe four from his pistol. Victor sprinted across the intervening ground quickly and picked up the gun. He pointed it at the motorist, who was still alert enough to feel every bit of the pain he was in.

'Victor, don't,' Stanislaus cried. Victor turned wildly and let the gun follow his eyes so it was pointed at Stanislaus's heart, but realised the danger and turned the gun to the ground. Stanislaus was terrified. An unintentional gunman was no less terrifying than an intentional one. 'He's just a motorist passing through. You don't have to kill him,' said Stanislaus in slow, regular syllables, hoping to soothe the beast.

'Motorists? Where is their car?' Victor demanded.

Stanislaus could not say he had seen their car. Nor gloves, goggles, leathers or anything else that might have corroborated their story.

'Ask your curate who these men are,' Victor said. The motorist's eyes were open but he had gone quiet and wasn't moving. His lips trembled. Perhaps he was praying.

'Your father needs you, Victor. Put down the gun and go to him,' said Stanislaus.

'You go to him. It's a priest he'll want, not me,' said Victor.

Stanislaus felt the hand of Margaret Cavanagh the schoolteacher on his shoulder. He told her to tend to Pius, as she was the nearest thing to a doctor present, but she shook her head. 'Victor's right. Please, go to him, and leave me with Victor.'

Pius Lennon lay motionless now. I must go to him, Stanislaus told himself.

\*     \*     \*

*Shards of metal and glass and stone are strewn across the copper roof of the GPO. You're flat on your belly peeking out from behind the marble toes of Hibernia when someone shouts: 'Take cover, they have snipers everywhere.' You see one of the bastards across the way, on the roof of the Metropole Hotel. You have a clear shot, and you fire. He disappears. Three or fours shots come at you in a short burst, riddling poor Hibernia as you crouch beneath her. Lumps of the statue fall off and as you look up, Hibernia's falling right hand punches you in the temple on its way to the ground. Immediately your eye starts to weep blood. That same old eye wound as always. You try to see whether the sniper at the Metropole is still there, but instead see a shell screaming up from the south. The rumour is true: they really do have a gunboat on the Liffey and they really are shelling the second city of the Empire. The shell falls short and blows half of Clery's department store to kingdom come. Clery's, the jewel in Murphy's crown, reduced to rubble. You laugh and your comrades look at you like you've lost your mind. Another shell comes from the direction of D'Olier Street, sailing over you and blowing a chunk out of Jervis Street. They're finding their range. A third shell spins gracelessly towards you, and while your comrades flee, you stay to watch the huge tin barrel's progress with fascination, whispering to yourself that life is in the letting go, life is in the letting go, life is in the letting go. The shell whistles past and lands twenty yards away, splattering Wicklow granite and Dublin guts all to hell. You bawl at the young fella crouched beside you, one*

*of the last comrades there: 'Damnit, Smart, you've pissed yourself.
Let's get the hell off this roof.' You grab him by the shirt front and
throw him back inside the shell of the GPO; you both trip over a
crowd of Volunteers huddled together mumbling a Rosary. Usually
they at least have the wit to save their mumbo jumbo for quieter
moments.*

*'Get up to fuck and get to your posts, d'ye not know we're under
attack?' you roar, and though you're not their OC they jump up
and run. Fucken schoolteachers and altar boys and poets, here to
fight for 'Ireland', whatever that is. Not against oppression as such,
just the indignity of being oppressed by foreigners. What the hell
sort of a country is it that the likes of them and the likes of us are
on the same side?*

*Later you're huddled in the cell among the cold and wet and
blood and piss and morphine, with the screws poking through the
doors with bayonets and screaming that you're next for the firing
squad, and you whisper the mantra to your comrades. Life is in the
letting go, lifeisinthelettinggo, lifeisinthelettinggraciouslygo. They
don't know what you're talking about but they repeat it like good
apostles anyway, and they keep repeating it till the words become
strange in your ears, and all meaning is lost. The meaninglessness
is like balm.*

\*   \*   \*

'Victor, please, no,' says Maggie softly. I don't look at her. I'll lose
my nerve if I do, and I can't afford to lose my nerve. I look at
Pius instead. I've seen men wounded less devastatingly and not
lasted as long. Benedict is talking to him. Getting him ready for
whatever he believes is coming next. He is pleading like a debtor

with bailiffs at the door, sobbing into Benedict's ear like it's a telephone to heaven. We won't speak again, my father and I. Time won't allow. Arthur's eyes are closed and his lips are mumbling. For all his talk, here he is, praying. A pathetic death-bed convert.

'Open your eyes, Arthur,' I say. In them I see more resignation than fear.

'You're going to kill me.'

'What would you do in my shoes, comrade?'

Barely perceptibly he nods, closes his eyes and goes back to his praying. I look around the dumbstruck Madden mob. I see Charlie, groggily returning to consciousness. The People's Hall teeters, and the fire must conjure in Pius's last conscious moments a vision of hell. There is nothing left to do but finish the scene. I will go to Mick Collins and beg for absolution, but I know that two graves demand a third. Things are serious now. Even the rising was innocent compared to now. All I signed up for was socialism, but the revolution has become something else, evolved into something darker and altogether more real. I don't know when this happened.

'Victor, please put down the gun,' Maggie keeps repeating, 'put down the gun and come away with me and we can get married, we can go straight to the priest and he can marry us tonight, he can marry us right now.'

'It's not in my hands, Maggie, the world doesn't work that way.'

She stamps her foot on the ground. '*This* is the world, right here,' she cries, and slaps her hand hard against her chest. '*This* is where you make your mark. *I* am the one you have to fight for.'

A support stanchion falls, taking another stanchion with it in a howitzer-like cacophony, enough to make me fear for my hearing. The last few stanchions endure, but they too will be smouldering wreckage soon. I look at Maggie. Her glistening eyes are bulbous with tears that stain her beautiful face. 'Maggie, you are perfect. I'd have to be perfect to be worthy of you. Well, I'm not perfect. I'm not even good. I'm so sorry.'

The last, flimsy pillars of my creation burn away under the heat and I can hardly hear the gunshot over the terrible noise of things falling apart.

\* \* \*

There wasn't any hope, he had lost too much blood. He was babbling, could say nothing coherent. His pain was terrible but his release would come soon. 'You don't have to speak out loud, Pius, God knows your sins. You need only ask His forgiveness. God is merciful. You have nothing to fear, my son,' Stanislaus told him, but he looked terrified as the end came. Stanislaus heard his last breath. It was always the same sound, like a door being sucked shut in the wind. Stanislaus closed over his eyelids. No-one needed to see the terror in his eyes. He looked much more at peace this way.

After the last of the barn collapsed Victor stalked towards Stanislaus and Pius with gun in his hand and murder in his eyes. Women screamed. The second motorist was motionless now.

'Did you give him his Last Rites?'

'Yes.'

'He would have wanted that.' Victor looked at his father, and it seemed he might weep. He looked away, as though the sight was too terrible.

'Let me say some prayers over those other men,' said Stanislaus.

'They're not men, they're dead,' said Victor, his finger twitching on the pistol by his side, latent and terrifying. Victor looked at Margaret Cavanagh, who knelt sobbing and wailing, then looked back to Stanislaus.

'Get her out of here. Get all of these people out of here. Get them all back to their homes. I don't want to see anybody. I'm going to bury my father.'

*   *   *

Father Daly slammed down the telephone hurriedly when Stanislaus came in. He was shaking. 'I had to place a telephone call,' he said.

'Good man, you called the police?'

'Uh, yes, that's right. I called the police.'

'What did they say? Are they coming straight away?'

'Uh-huh. I saw it all. Is there a gun in the house? He's out there with a gun and I have no gun. I mean, I think we should have a gun.'

'Tim, calm down. What's wrong with you?'

'He's quite mad. He could come here and try to kill us. We need to be able to defend ourselves. Have you a gun or not?'

'You know very well I don't. Why would he come here? Compose yourself, Father.'

'Keep the lights off. If he comes looking for me, you haven't seen me, right?' said the curate, before dashing out the door.

Stanislaus went to his chair by the window and watched through the gloom. Every curtain in Madden twitched but

Victor was alone in the Poor Ground, save for the dead bodies lying on the barren turf and the damned souls beneath. Only the angry red glow of the smouldering wreckage lit the scene. Victor worked like a demon though he had no shovel, no implement but his hands and planks of wood that were lying around. All the spades and shovels and loys he could want lay up the street in Charlie Quinn's smashed window, but Stanislaus supposed the boy wasn't really thinking clearly as he threw himself at the soil. Victor's laboured grunting was the only sound that punctuated the silent terror sitting over the parish, until he saw Father Daly's car pull out from behind the Parochial House and hurtle recklessly down the street and out of Madden. He realised that the curate was a man with secrets, and that the dead men had been no motorists. There was a rumour that there were two curates in Tyrone and another in Limerick mixed up with the IRB, and he supposed that if there were three young fools out of three thousand clergy, there could be four or seven or twelve …

Stanislaus stopped himself from thinking about it any further. He was getting close to articulating something he was determined not to know, so he told himself that exposure to violence affected people differently; that it was a time of blood, that Victor Lennon was a man of blood and that poor Father Daly was only a youngster who had been scared out of his wits. At most, he had been naïve, but hadn't people once said the same of Stanislaus himself? The darker rumours had never been true, not really, but he had flown closer to the flame than he should have. Poor Father Daly had been taken in by unscrupulous men claiming to be motorists, and his flight proved only his terror at the killer in the Poor Ground. Yes, that was it, that was the truth and there was no other.

Stanislaus closed the front door and moved as quietly as he could down the street to Quinn's General Stores. Victor didn't even notice him pass. The shattered glass crunched under his feet on the paving outside the shop. He reached into the window and picked out a shovel, took coins from his pocket and left them on the display where the shovel had been. When he reached the Poor Ground he waited a moment at the wall for Victor to spot him. The boy stood upright from his work. Stanislaus held up the shovel. The Victor fellow stepped closer and reached out to take the shovel. Stanislaus saw that his hands were torn to shreds.

'Will you come back tomorrow and bless the grave? For my father,' Victor said.

Stanislaus nodded. Pius deserved it. As he let go of the shovel to let Victor take it, Stanislaus was struck by something, something he had not seen before. Victor was so young-looking. Hardly more than a boy.

'Thank you,' said Victor, cradling the shovel in his hands.

Stanislaus retreated to the Parochial House, to his study, to watch Victor dig deeper and deeper till he disappeared into the hole. He watched the boy gather his father with extraordinary gentleness and grace, making light of Pius's fifteen or sixteen stone, and lay him beside his mother with the care of a priest with a relic. He watched him put back the fresh-dug earth, probably believing he had reunited his parents, and a single hot tear trickled down Stanislaus's cheek. The poor boy. It was all for nothing. The commingling of remains was meaningless. This was no reunion, unless Pius Lennon too was in hell. Then Stanislaus watched Victor Lennon leave his parish for the last time.

* * *

When the job is done I throw down the shovel and stand over the grave. It's strange: I have little memory of digging it. A couple of images in my mind, like photographs snatched from a scene, but otherwise, blank. The sound of the gunshot started something. And ended something.

I have no idea of the time but I can tell it is near dawn. I still have the train ticket. It'll take me away from Madden, that's the main thing. There is only blood and pain here now. I must go to my fate, even if it means I'll be in the shallow soil of the Wicklow Mountains soon, unremembered and unmourned. There's no-one here for me to talk to, to preach at, to persuade. I'm alone. There is only prayer. So I pray. Pius would want me to. Let it be one last act of superstition for the superstitious old bastard. Our Father, who art in heaven, hallowed be thy name. Thy kingdom come, thy will be done, on earth as it is in heaven. Give us this day our daily bread, and forgive us our trespasses, as we forgive those who trespass against us. And lead us not into temptation but deliver us from evil, Amen. There. Are you happy now? An old reflex kicks in. Hail Mary, full of grace, the Lord is with thee. Blessed art thou among women and blessed is the fruit of thy womb, Jesus. Holy Mary, mother of God, pray for us sinners, now and at the hour of our death. Amen. Rest in peace, Mammy.

Benedict has courage, it has to be said. I wish he was here again to pray for my parents. I wish he would hear my confession. Not that I believe in that stuff, it's just that, well: I think I might be ready to tell the truth, if only there was someone to tell it to. I might tell him I envy Charlie, and all like him put on this earth to follow orders. I might tell him I wish I could surrender my judgement and my conscience to other men, and wade through fields full of men's brains and guts and evacuated bowels and merely feel, not think. But thoughts suck the blood from me like midges on a summer's day. I might tell him how the revolution was fun at the start. We were tweaking the lion's tail. I might tell him how I see the starving children whose fathers I recruited to Larkin's union in my sleep. Their emaciation is wildly exaggerated – eyes withdrawn into their heads, ribs sticking out from their chests, like something from an old daguerreotype taken during the Famine – but the sacrifices others endure for your sake are the hardest to take. I might tell him I had no choice but to get in deeper after the lockout.

I brandish the revolver prominently as I leave the Poor Ground, in case anyone thinks of approaching. I leave the smouldering remains of the People's Hall, pass the locked doors of the Parochial Hall, the triumphal spire of the chapel. McGrath's the post office. Kane's. Murphy's. McDermott's. The other Murphy's. The Harte house, bringing the whole tone of the place down. I reach the top of the town and stop at Cavanagh's, the only naked window in a street of twitching curtains. Inside stands Maggie, and though it's dark I can see her clearly. Her face is wet with tears, I am responsible, but she is only the more beautiful for her distress. Every microscopic detail etches itself into memory. She has always been a dream. She pulls the curtain and becomes a memory.

Behind me I hear footsteps on broken glass. Charlie stands inside the smashed window of his shop. He regards me silently, without malice. There is nothing I can say to him. I simply leave.

When I'm a quarter mile out I look back down into the hollow at Madden for the last time. My eye is drawn to the Parochial House. He'll be watching me, as he watches always. The black sheep he will watch drift away. The bishop will rejoice over the one that is lost, for the hundred that might be saved.

A mile up the road a horse and cart idles at the crossroads. I keep the gun by my side and move slowly.

'It's all right, Victor, it's me, Ida. Ida Harte. Where are you headed?'

I scan around, in case anyone lurks in the darkness. 'Dublin,' I say at last.

'Will there not be people there looking to kill you?' I don't answer her, but she perseveres. 'Have you not packed any things? You have no belongings with you.'

'I don't suppose I'll need any.'

'We can get the boat and start a new life somewhere else,' she says. She pats the seat beside her in the cart. 'Come on, climb up here. I'm coming with you.'

She must sense my bewilderment at the suggestion. Her hair is hideous. Her face is lamentable. Her eyes are so black they seem as mere voids in the darkness. 'Damnit, Ida, do you not understand? I don't want you.'

'You have to choose me, you have no other choice. You can't have the schoolteacher. You can have me,' she says with bizarre assurance.

I walk away, hoping my silence will be her answer, but for miles and miles she trundles after me. I refuse to choose her. I refuse to have the choice forced on me. I refuse to accept that which must be accepted. I refuse the world and I refuse God. Let them all kill me; I'm never letting go. Let them put me in my grave; but let it be carved on my headstone, and let the words forever be associated with my name: I refuse, I refuse, I refuse.

∗ ∗ ∗

Stanislaus woke in his chair with an empty brandy glass on the floor beside him and its former contents sticky on his clothes. He had been waiting for the police to arrive but must have fallen asleep. It was daylight now and they still hadn't come. He heard someone clear their throat, and he slowly became aware that he hadn't merely stirred. Mrs Geraghty was shaking his shoulder, and she looked nervous as a kitten. Stanislaus looked up. Cardinal Logue sat across the desk from him, leaning forward and turning his cane in his fist. Stanislaus blinked and made to rise, but the Cardinal sat him down with a wave.

'Things have gotten out of control, Stanislaus,' he said. There was no possible reply. 'Your curate has told me about the agitator,' the Cardinal continued, and Stanislaus saw Daly skulking sheepishly by the door. 'I know about the building of the hall. I know about the fire. I understand a man was killed. A parishioner. The father of the agitator.'

'What about the others?' said Stanislaus.

'What others?'

It was clear to Stanislaus that the Cardinal didn't know. The curate had told him nothing about the motorists, whoever they had been. Stanislaus glanced out the window. The bodies were gone from the Poor Ground.

'Bishop Benedict is confused, Your Eminence,' said Daly.

'Shut up, curate,' the Cardinal snapped. He paused a moment. 'Stanislaus, I have placed a telephone call to Inspector Truman of Dawson Street, he will be here soon. My information is this: there was a fire here, probably started deliberately, and a man died fighting the fire. Is my information complete and correct?'

Daly stood in the shadows shaking his head. 'Yes, Your Eminence, it happened just as you say,' Stanislaus said.

The Cardinal looked relieved. 'Where is the body?'

'Buried.'

'Already?'

'What Bishop Benedict means, Your Eminence,' Daly interrupted, 'is that the burning structure collapsed on top of poor Pius and he was buried beneath it. There are no remains.'

The Cardinal looked to Stanislaus for confirmation of Daly's damnable lies. Stanislaus knew his silence implied assent but he couldn't bring himself to speak. The Cardinal looked at Daly with unconcealed disgust and told him to leave the room. When the curate was gone, the Cardinal rose and walked to the window.

'It's not your fault, Stanislaus. Your curate has a lot to learn. Young men always do. He'll be missioning to the lepers in Matabeleland this time next month. He'll learn a lot there.' He paused. 'The world is a mess, Stanislaus. Goodness knows what the future holds. What do you think? About the future?'

'I don't know.'

'Of course you don't know. I'm asking what you think.'

'I don't think. I have no opinion on the future. It's the past that scares me.'

The Cardinal smiled scornfully. 'You were always good at saying things that sound profound but that don't actually mean anything at all.' As he looked out the window, it seemed his mind was far away. 'I wish I didn't have to worry about the future. I wish I had that luxury,' he said.

'You're seventy-seven years of age. The future is not your business.'

'The red hat makes it my business.' He peered into the distance. 'You can see the river Blackwater from here.

Where County Armagh ends and County Monaghan begins.' He paused. 'They're going to partition the country, you know.'

'That's just talk, a scare tactic.'

'It's not scaring anyone nearly enough. They're going to force each other into places neither of them wants to be. You know better than anyone how these things go.'

'Yes, I know how these things go,' Stanislaus said. After the war in Europe the British would return to what they called, with all their imperial arrogance, the 'Irish question', and simple people would see in Victor Lennon and the likes of him a Ribbonman poking the English in the eye. It was in the nature of events to spiral. The rising had flushed out the specificities, and the capacity of the existing order to offer advantage to those who would serve it was already diminishing. 'Men like Victor Lennon always emerge when Englishmen kill Irishmen in Ireland,' Stanislaus said.

'They're going to partition the country and we are going to be on the wrong side of the line. We are going to be a minority locked inside a Protestant holdout,' said the Cardinal.

'You're describing a nightmare.'

'It will be our responsibility to provide leadership to our people. Sometimes leadership is about knowing where people are going, and getting out in front of them.' He paused. 'I understand the problems started when you refused the local football team use of the Parochial Hall?'

'Gaelic football, Mick.'

'I know, I know. But it does seem to be very popular.' The Cardinal went to the door. 'If they're going to partition the country, we must make our presence felt in every institution open to us. Even the unedifying ones. Let them use the Parochial Hall. Tonight. Under your supervision.'

'Yes, Your Eminence.'

\*   \*   \*

The Parochial Hall was two-thirds full. A good turnout, considering. People danced and music played and Stanislaus moved through the room noting with approval that everyone seemed to be behaving themselves. The photographer was setting up. A young fellow from Armagh, paid for by the Cardinal. There was great excitement among the footballers that they were getting their photograph taken. The photographer organised the young men and the team officials into rows: one seated, one standing behind the seated row, and a third standing on chairs at the back. Charlie Quinn handed the trophy to Sean Moriarty and said Sean should sit in the middle and hold it, since he was the team captain. Charlie took up a spot in the middle row, where the camera wouldn't see his leg.

'Are you sure you're fit to stand?' one of the young lads jeered good-humouredly.

'Och, very funny,' Charlie said, slurring slightly. He was clearly merry but Stanislaus wasn't going to cause a scene. Better to give the lad special dispensation on the happy occasion. He might just gently remind him he had a big day ahead, and eight o'clock came early. It seemed Miss Cavanagh had decided, sensibly, to stay at home and prepare for the ceremony.

The photographer took down the names to go with the faces, and when he had finished he called them out, back row first, from left to right, to make sure there were no mistakes. Everyone was where they were supposed to be.

'Don't forget Victor Lennon,' Turlough Moriarty said.

'Victor Lennon? I thought you were, let me see …' The photographer began going through the list: '… Turlough?'

'No, I mean Victor Lennon isn't here. He's part of the team too. Don't forget to write down: Missing from the picture – Victor Lennon.'

'V-I-C-T-O-R-L-E-N …' the photographer began.

'There's no such person, not on this team,' Aidan Cavanagh shouted furiously,

'He's right. Score that name out. That fellow had nothing to do with it,' said Charlie Quinn.

'What are youse boys talking about? Victor damn near won us the final on his own,' Turlough said, but the rest of them shouted him down. His brother Sean put a hand on his knee as if to quieten him. The photographer turned to Stanislaus with bemusement. Stanislaus shrugged.

'All right then,' he said. 'Now, the rest of you men: this camera is a lot better than the old-fashioned ones but please avoid moving if you can. Remember, this is for posterity, so straighten those ties and give me a big smile.' He disappeared under the cloak, and Stanislaus stood beside him while he did whatever he did under there.

'There was a young man in this parish called Victor Lennon, but he's gone now.'

'Are you getting into the photo, Father?' said the voice from beneath the cloak.

'Come on, Father, stand in here. We have to have the new club chairman in the picture,' said Charlie, and, without hesitation,

Stanislaus sat in beside Sean Moriarty in the midst of the men of Madden.

'All right, you men, and you too, Father,' the photographer shouted. 'This is history now, so watch the birdie and say a big hello to your great-grandchildren.'

# ACKNOWLEDGEMENTS

I would like to thank:

Pat and Seamus McCann: my parents and best friends, quite simply for everything.

Jacqueline Nora McCann, *née* Fleming, my partner in life, for so often carrying me.

Glenn Patterson, a wonderful writer; a great and humane mentor.

Giles Foden, a friend to a young writer who needed one.

I would also like to thank: Emily Berry, Fran Brearton, Ciaran Carson, Gearoid Cassidy, Tom Clarke, Emily DeDakis, Jennifer Hewson, Chris McCann, Jacqueline McCann, James McCann, Mark Richards, Ian Sansom, Peter Straus and John Thompson.